DEADLY CRAZY

A SLAYING LOVE NOVEL
BOOK 3

AMANDA SIEGRIST

Consequences Novel

Dark Consequences

Cruel Consequences

Fatal Consequences

Haunting Love Novel

Third Time's the Charm

Thirteen Days Gone

Holiday Romance Novel

Merry Me

Mistletoe Magic

Christmas Wish

Snowed in Love

Snowflakes and Shots

Holiday Hope

Sleigh All the Way

Lucky Town Novel

Escaping Memories

Dangerous Memories

Stolen Memories

Deadly Memories

Forgotten Memories

A SASSY WOMAN WHO DOESN'T BELIEVE IN LOVE. A SHY
DETECTIVE WHO'LL DIE TO PROTECT HER. A KILLER WHO
PICKED THE WRONG TARGET.

PROLOGUE

HIS HAND SHOOK as he swiped another glass of champagne from the passing waiter. He should probably slow it down, but he had a feeling that wasn't going to happen. Not when every time he glanced her way she was laughing and dancing with another man.

Kind of his fault. Just call him a chicken. He couldn't ask her to dance. The words wouldn't form.

It was a simple question. Would you like to dance? It wasn't that hard. Five simple words.

Five simple words to the most beautiful woman he had ever laid eyes on. That was the problem. When it came to women, forget it. Words didn't come out sounding right. He was nothing more than an incompetent moron.

"Are you sulking? Because you look like you're sulking. And champagne? Dude, go get a beer."

Sauer stifled a groan as Newman, his best friend and partner, got on his case. "It's good champagne. Have you tried some?"

Newman chugged half his beer, then belched. "Nope. Don't plan on it."

"Why is Chrissy dating you?"

"Because I'm charming and sexy. Now that you've brought up dating, what woman are you taking home tonight? You are not leaving this reception without a woman in your arms."

Sauer couldn't help it. His eyes sought her out immediately. Nope. He sure in the hell wouldn't be going home with her. Only in his dreams.

"Please tell me you didn't just look at Dee. Anyone but her."

"I don't know what you're talking about."

"Dude, she is a man-hater. She would eat you up and rip you to shreds. Pick a different woman."

Sauer patted Newman on the shoulder and grinned. "I have no plans of bringing any woman home tonight. And next time you belch, at least say excuse me. Women appreciate manners."

"Sauer, whatever you're thinking, get it out of your head. Look elsewhere," Newman half-shouted as he walked away.

The last thing he wanted to do was hear how Dee was a bad choice. He knew that. Not because she was a so-called man-hater, but because she was too beautiful and so out of his league. She was best friends with Rina, who married his good friend Ben today. The few times he interacted with her, he barely managed a decent hello. Completely tongue-tied when it came to her. Just like when he spoke to most women. But with Dee, it was ten times worse. There was something about her. He couldn't explain it.

He finished his glass of champagne rather quickly—too quickly—and decided he should eat. Something to occupy his mind. Something other than stare at Dee wishing he had the courage to ask her to dance. It was just a dance. It wouldn't lead to anything else. Or could it?

Grow a pair. That's what he needed to do. Something Newman said to him a few times when they went out for drinks. They'd see a beautiful woman, usually in a group full of beautiful women, and Newman would say, "Just go start talking to them. If you don't practice, you're never going to get it right. Grow a pair."

He'd down his beer, think about what to say, and like the chickenshit he was, he'd order another beer and continue to figure out what to say until the entire group of women left the bar and his chance was effectively over. The story of his life.

Not that he never had a girlfriend or sex before, because, yeah, he wasn't a total scaredy-cat when it came to women. The few girlfriends he had just never went very far.

Grabbing a small plate, he started to pile different hors d'oeuvres until there wasn't any room left. This way he didn't have to come back for seconds. It was easier if he stayed in his little corner until it was polite enough to leave the wedding reception. He was having a good time. He just wasn't sure he could stand it anymore, eyeing Dee dressed in the elegant silver dress that clung to her body so delicately. Nothing usually screamed delicate about her. More like outrageous and rowdy. Like her wild red hair that he loved to see, especially when she scrunched it with her hand to make it even bushier. Although, tonight she had it pulled back into a cute little updo that framed her face so well.

He needed to leave. Seeking her out, watching her have fun with other men wasn't going to help him move on.

Newman was right. She wasn't his type. She was too outgoing. Too loud. Too in-your-face. He could barely speak to an average-looking woman. How would they make it as a couple? Simple. They wouldn't because he would never have the nerve to speak more than a quick hello to her. Which was the most he had ever said to her.

"Oh, that looks delicious as shit." A hand swiped one of the breaded shrimp from his plate. "Yummy. You're the best, Sauer."

His face flamed with heat as he stared into a pair of chocolate-brown eyes. "Um, thanks."

Dee cracked a smile as her sweet laughter surrounded them. "No, no, thank you." She cocked her head to the side. "You look very dashing in a suit."

"Um, thanks."

"I'm gonna grab one more shrimp. Do you mind?"

"Um, thanks."

She laughed as she snatched another shrimp and walked away.

What was wrong with him? *Um, thanks.* That's all he could say?

Yeah, story of his life. He wanted the most beautiful woman in the room and he couldn't even say more than two words.

1

"Not like this."

He curled the left side of his lips just a little higher.

"Like that."

Slamming his hands onto the counter, he groaned as the smile he thought he perfected crumbled into a frown. "Shit. I look like an idiot." He blew out a breath. "You can do this. Just ask her out. No big deal. Tell her she's beautiful. Then ask her out."

Nodding, he watched as his head bobbed up and down in the mirror, just confirming how much of an idiot he was. He was talking to himself in his friend's bathroom. How much dumber could he get? A lot. He knew that.

He was never good with the ladies. Never. Hell, he never made it to prom because he broke out into hives when he tried to ask Stephanie, the homecoming queen, to the dance. Only a nerd who wore braces would try to ask out the homecoming queen.

He was an adult now. A grown-ass man. Asking out a woman shouldn't be difficult. Except, she wasn't just any woman. She was the perfect woman. And totally out of his league.

He jumped as a loud round of banging occurred on the door. "Dude, what are you doing? Taking a dump?"

Sauer whipped open the door and tried to give Newman the best glare he could.

"You're all red in the face. You all right, man? Push a little too hard?" Newman chuckled. Sauer stepped out of his way. "Crack a smile. I was only kidding." His bushy eyebrows dipped. "Seriously, you okay?"

"I'm fine. It's hot in here."

Newman's eyes sparkled with humor. "Yeah, Zoe has the heat up ridiculously high. It's cold as shit outside and she's afraid that Zabrina will get cold." He frowned. "You sure you're okay? You've been acting a little funny all day."

"I'm fine. Go take a piss already." Sauer laughed to ease the tension coursing through his veins and turned around. The bathroom door shut behind him. Closing his eyes, he took a deep breath, then took a step forward, colliding into something warm and soft. He opened his eyes and cursed himself inside. "So sorry, Dee."

"No problemo. I wasn't watching where I was going either." Her sweet laughter filled his heart—and nerves—with joy. Her bright-red hair was curly as usual, little wisps of curls framing her face. He had the urge to swipe a few locks back. Not that he'd do it. But he fantasized about it way too often.

"Beautiful."

Her brow rose. "What?"

Holy shit. Did he just mutter the word beautiful and nothing else? Now she was looking at him like he was an idiot. "The hallway." God, could it get much worse?

She laughed, the sound filling up the so-called beautiful

hallway. He didn't even care how dumb he appeared. He loved hearing her laugh. "You're hilarious, Sauer."

Chuckling, he ran a hand through his hair, then across the front of his jeans. "Would dance out dinner you...me?" *Shit*. It just got worse. So much worse. His words didn't even make sense.

Her face crinkled with confusion as she scrunched her hair a little. "Did you just ask me out?"

"Uh..." How should he answer that? Because he wasn't sure how to interpret her confusion. "It kind of sounded like it." He smiled. Not to the perfection he practiced in the mirror, but close enough. And he actually spoke with words connecting in a fluid sentence. He could pat himself on the back.

"You're so adorable." She chuckled, patted his shoulder, and walked past him.

Adorable? Well, that was better than her calling him an idiot. But she never answered his question. Why did she just walk away?

He jumped as a hand touched his shoulder. Newman's face beamed with laughter. "I'm damn proud of you for trying. It's the effort that counts. Although, a little surprised. Dee's not really your type. You're generally quiet and shy. She's loud and obnoxious. I thought you got over this little crush you had."

His lips thinned into a tight line. "She's beautiful."

"She also didn't answer your question. Better go clarify, if you can manage to do that again." His partner laughed as he walked away.

Ask her out again? He didn't even ask her properly the first time. Forget it. There's no way he could ask her again and look like even more of a fool.

He followed Newman to the living room where Zeke,

Ben, and a few other guys from the precinct were crowded around the TV. He enjoyed football like any other guy, but tonight, the Super Bowl held little appeal. He felt like that even before he tried to ask out Dee. His heart just wasn't into watching the game.

Plopping down next to Zeke, he attempted to act interested in the game, while trying to figure out how he could leave and make it seem like he wasn't escaping. Newman was the only one who knew he had tried to ask out Dee and failed miserably. He still felt the need to escape. What would he say when she came out of the kitchen? That's if the women decided to join them in the living room to watch the game. If they stayed there all night, then maybe he could handle staying.

Newman, who sat in a recliner near the left side of the couch, started to speak in a low tone. "Guess who tried to ask out Dee?"

His head slowly rotated. The intense glare on his face was enough to tell Newman that he didn't appreciate him acting like a dick. What kind of friend would throw him under the bus like that?

"Davies from Narcotics did. Totally got shut down in under two seconds. I do believe her exact words were, 'Yeah, not gonna happen in a million years.' Then she walked away." Zeke shook his head as he laughed. "Davies couldn't handle Dee. She needs a man who can put her in her place. She never holds back what she's thinking."

"You're going to go back on the douche list of hers if you don't keep your voice down, man," Ben said with a snicker. "And I know how much you hate being on that list."

A man who could put her in her place? Well, shit, he wasn't that kind of guy. The few relationships he had he never acted that way with a woman. Hell, he never even argued much with a woman.

Dee shouldn't have to be put in her place. Sure, sometimes she spoke without thinking, but he liked that about her—that she didn't give a shit what other people thought. He almost wished he could be like that. He was honest. He didn't lie when asked a direct question or if someone wanted his honest opinion, but he didn't blurt things out like she tended to do.

"Na. Not Davies."

All eyes turned to Newman, waiting for him to elaborate. Except him. He refused to look at Newman. He still couldn't believe Newman was embarrassing him like this. What was the point? To have a good laugh? Newman had never treated him like this before. Why now?

Some found it odd he could handle a criminal with ease. Some even laughed at him, as if it were a strange mystery they couldn't figure out. Put a murderer in front of him, or someone who committed a terrible crime, and he showed them who was boss. Nothing about those encounters made him hesitate. Any other situation, like the current one he was in, he resorted to his usual shy, quiet, reserved self. It's just the way it was.

Maybe it had to do with bullies. All through middle and high school, he was bullied. Awkward scrawny kid. Braces. Acne. He was an easy target. Most times, the kids got away with it. He didn't tattle on them. He didn't say anything to his parents. It all stayed locked away inside. Sort of like now.

When it came time for college, he moved away. Far, far away. He wanted a fresh start. He started to work out more. He became more confident, more secure. Then, someone tried to bully him—by robbing him. It was like a light switch. Off to on in a blink of an eye. He sucker-punched the guy and then called the police. Yeah, it was probably one of the dumbest things he ever did, but it felt so empowering to finally show one bully they couldn't push him around anymore.

He became a cop soon after. Criminals became bullies. He needed to keep the world safe from these bullies. Now his partner was acting like a bully. Why was he letting Newman act this way? Screw that!

"It was me." All eyes turned to him. "Do you feel better, Newman? Are you having a good laugh making me look like an idiot?" He stood up.

"Ah, shit, Sauer. I didn't mean—"

"Then maybe next time you should keep your damn mouth shut." He started to walk around the couch to the front door.

"Yo, Sauer, where are you going, man?" Zeke asked, the concern evident in his voice. "I kinda figured it was you. I was hoping Newman would let it drop when I said Davies. It's a little obvious you like her. It's just..."

Sauer turned toward him, his fists clenching and unclenching. *It's just.* Yeah, he heard that a lot. It's just, she's not right for you. It's just, you're so shy. It's just, you're different and there's nothing wrong with that. It's just. He hated hearing that.

"It's just, what? I couldn't handle a woman like her? I don't deserve a woman like her? Tell me. Or better yet, why don't you all mind your own damn business, especially you, Newman."

He grabbed his jacket from the closet, stalked to the door in three long strides, slamming it on his way out. Maybe he was acting like a jerk, or even like a baby, but screw them. He wasn't going to be bullied by his friends.

Call him sensitive. Call him whatever. He didn't care at the moment.

———

A DOOR SLAMMED.

"Geez, please tell me those men aren't getting all pissy because the game isn't going the way they want. The Vikings didn't even make the playoffs this year. Why do they get so hot about the game?" Dee rolled her eyes, primping her hair a little.

"You know them. They do get a little heated when the game goes sour. I hope nobody got called to work." Zoe frowned. "Well, at least I know it wasn't Zeke because he'd say good-bye before slamming his way out of the house."

"Or Ben. Maybe one of the other guys had to leave," Rina added softly.

"I thought Chrissy would've been here with Newman. I kind of like her. Although, she's weird sometimes."

Zoe almost spit out the sip of wine she had taken. "What is so weird about her, Dee?"

She shrugged. "She never wears any clothes that show cleavage. Flaunt what God gave you, honey."

Rina chuckled softly. "Some people are shy."

Like Sauer. Dee always found his quietness so endearing. He always had a way of looking at her as if he could see straight to her heart. When she let it, anyway. It wouldn't do good to let those looks affect her.

Or his sweet words. He surprised the hell out of her when he attempted to ask her out. Oh, it had been the cutest thing she ever experienced. No one, not one man, had ever been as charming as Sauer trying to ask her out.

She didn't even answer him properly. There was no way

she could shut him down with a simple no. Sauer was different. He didn't deserve a quick no. And she didn't deserve to say yes. That left her in an impossible situation. She had almost floundered with her words.

"Everything okay, Zeke?" Zoe wrapped her arms around him as he walked up to her. "Who left?"

"Sauer."

"Why? Did he get suckered into working while all of you enjoy the rest of the game?" Dee cocked a brow. She wouldn't put it past all of them to make Sauer handle it while they had fun. That's just what they did to him sometimes. He was easily manipulated that way. He never argued.

Zeke refused to look at her. "No. He just left."

"He slammed the door like he was pissed. He's always a happy guy."

He still refused to look at her. "Newman might've been giving him shit about something and he didn't appreciate it."

Well, it wasn't hard to figure out what that meant. Newman must've heard Sauer ask her out.

"Now you think I'm a bitch."

Finally, his eyes whipped to her.

Rina softly gasped. "Why would you say that, Dee?"

Zeke pursed his lips into a frown. "What did you say to him?"

Zoe glanced between her and Zeke, her brows dipped in obvious confusion.

"What's it to you?"

A throat cleared. "Would you two care to clarify what you're talking about? Obviously, you're talking about Sauer." Zoe continued to glance back and forth.

She started to fiddle with the bottom of her wine glass. "I accidently bumped into him in the hallway and he—"

"Asked you out," Rina softly finished.

Dee glanced at her. "He's a sweet guy. It surprised me."

"I think you should go out with him. He's a great guy. And you'd finally have a sexy detective like we have." Rina smiled brightly.

Zeke laughed, giving her a wink. "I think he's liked you for a while, Dee. He's a little too shy for you, though."

She pierced him with a hard stare. "Hey, Zeke, mind your own damn business. Maybe you should apologize to him. Whatever was said, he didn't leave here happy."

"Okay, let's all calm down. Go watch football." Zoe started to push Zeke out of the kitchen. "Did you come in here for another beer?"

"He came in here to see what I said to Sauer." Her brow lifted again. "I can tell you I didn't say anything to make him leave like he did."

"But you turned him down?"

She cocked a brow as she threw a hand to her hip. "I repeat. None. Of. Your. Damn. Business." Shaking her head, she glanced between Rina and Zoe. "I think I'm gonna go, too."

"Dee, don't leave." Zoe lightly slapped Zeke's chest. "See what you guys did."

"I...we..." Zeke mumbled as Dee grabbed her purse from the kitchen counter.

"Don't worry about it. My feelings aren't hurt, but Sauer deserves an apology."

Rina said good-bye as Zoe protested again, but Dee had enough. She enjoyed the sweet way Sauer asked her out. And the guys, acting like a bunch of douches, were ruining it. She walked out of the kitchen, grabbed her jacket from the closet, then stopped at the front door, swiveling her gaze to the living room. All eyes turned her way.

She stared hard at all of them, producing a small smirk as they started to squirm in their seats, especially Newman. No words were necessary. They understood what she was saying just by that simple look.

Swinging open the door, she slammed it as hard as Sauer had, just because. She wanted them to know whose side she was on. Even though she didn't say yes, she was still on Sauer's side. Always. No matter what. He was a sweet guy.

Ten minutes later, she pulled into her driveway. As always, she was glad she didn't live too far from Zeke and Zoe's house. Before Zoe married Zeke, she lived much farther away. She liked not having to drive thirty minutes, especially when she was irritated. A shot of whiskey was calling her name. Numb the pain a little.

Slamming her car door, still peeved, she marched to her front door. Her steps slowed as she neared it. A red rose lay on the mat in front of the door, a white card next to it.

Really? She was so not a flower kind of girl.

Picking up the card, her brow rose.

I'm sorry.

Sauer? Did he swing by her house to say sorry for asking her out?

No. That didn't seem like his style. He was way too shy to do something like that. He also didn't know where she lived. He had never been to her house before.

Ugh, her neighbor. Mathias. He was the worst pest ever.

He had been asking her out since he moved in five months ago. She enjoyed men. A lot. But one thing she never did was date someone who lived in her neighborhood. Talk about awkward when it didn't work out. Which it wouldn't because she didn't do relationships. Not the long-term kind. Another reason she turned down Sauer. Sort of. Maybe she should've said no in a nice way. Was she leading him on right now without a clear answer? Probably.

What a bitch. Well, at least she earned the title honestly.

She crumbled the note as she swiped the flower up. Stalking to the garbage can on the side of the house, she tossed the note and flower inside. Now she had to have a conversation with Mathias. Again. The guy never stopped with his antics.

Just last week his dog came into her yard and took a shit right on her walkway that led from the door to the driveway. She nearly fell trying to avoid it. She knew the dog was well-trained and listened to Mathias without fail. Which meant Mathias purposely let him shit on her property. He was obviously a guy who didn't like to hear the word no.

She knew he let his dog do it so he'd have a reason to talk to her. What a dumb reason. All it did was piss her off even more. Now he thought a dumb rose and a simple note would make it all better. Not!

Forget it. She wouldn't say anything to him. That's probably what he wanted her to do. Not going to happen. If it got much worse, she'd have no problem siccing Zeke and Ben on him. Even though she didn't get along with them all the time—Zeke mostly—they'd still do anything for her. That's just the nice guys they were. It probably helped she was best friends with their wives as well.

She slammed her front door, still in a pissy mood, not even sure it would dwindle down any time soon. Disabling her alarm, she re-armed it and locked the door.

A loud thump echoed around the kitchen as she slammed a shot glass onto the counter. Bending low, she pulled out the bottle of whiskey she had hidden in the bottom cupboard way in the back. She hid it for a reason. If it was visible all the time, she'd down it way too fast. She didn't have a drinking problem, but when irritation hit her, which happened more and more often, she needed a shot to chase the mood away. One shot normally did the trick. Sometimes, it required two. And only if she was really, really pissed.

Two shots it would be tonight.

She'd like to say it was because the guys gave Sauer a hard time. It was more like she felt horrible for denying him. She was damaged. Unworthy of a man as sweet and good as him.

What in the world did he see in her, anyway? She never attracted the good guys. Her aim was always the slightly bad guys with sex on their mind. She might complain to Zoe and Rina she wanted what they had, but she knew she'd never have it. She wasn't dumb enough to believe she could have something as good as they did.

The warm liquid slid down her throat. She cringed from the burn, then filled up the shot glass again. Without thinking, she drank that one just as fast.

Besides slamming back shots, one other thing simmered her down.

Sex. Hot, dirty sex.

She only wanted that with one guy right now. One guy she shouldn't even think about.

Sauer.

2

SAUER RUBBED his eyes as he made his way up the walkway to the front door.

"You still pissed at me? I'm sorry, man."

"We're cool, Newman. Let's just forget about it."

He wanted to forget about it. Not be reminded of it over and over. She turned him down. She didn't give him a clear answer, but he took it as a no. What else could he think? He should've known better. They were total opposites. It would never work.

Newman slapped him on the shoulder. "You get any sleep last night? Because I sure as shit didn't. The game went late and I didn't get home until one o'clock. It's too damn early for this."

"I slept fine." *Or not.* He wasn't going to admit that he dreamt about Dee's sweet laughter or her beautiful face as she said, "You're so adorable." So she turned him down. He still made her laugh. That counted for something, right?

They walked into the house, nodded at the officer by the front door, and headed for the kitchen. Sauer stopped in his tracks. Newman bumped into him.

"Holy shit."

"That's one way to put it," Susan, the crime scene tech, said with a small chuckle to Newman. Although, her eyes held no amusement whatsoever.

Sprawled in the middle of the kitchen floor was a woman in her mid-thirties covered in blood. She wore a flimsy nightgown, her underwear still on. Maybe she wasn't raped. Or maybe the killer shoved her underwear back on. Stab wounds covered her chest. The blood soaked through the material, making it hard to determine how many times she was stabbed. Her blonde hair looked tangled, dipped in crimson. Her eyes were wide open in terror. There were faint traces of bruises on her arms as if the killer had held her down.

"Murder weapon?" His voice floated out in almost a whisper. He'd seen many disturbing crime scenes, but for some reason, this one was hitting him hard.

"None that I can see. There's a kitchen knife missing from the knife rack, so I'm guessing he used that and took it with him."

"The boyfriend called this in. Maybe he did it and stashed the knife somewhere in the house," Newman offered.

"Well, he is covered in her blood. He said he came home late, found her on the floor, and tried to revive her. I'm not sure how much I believe him because you can clearly tell there was no way you could revive her. I haven't looked everywhere yet, but maybe he did hide it somewhere around here." Susan nodded toward the evidence bag on the counter. "That note was shoved in her mouth."

Sauer stood closer to the counter. He grabbed the bag and shuddered. *I'm sorry.* Weird, and a little disturbing. He wasn't sure why it bothered him so much. Two simple words, yet they packed a powerful punch.

He passed the note to Newman.

"I'd look hard into the boyfriend. He found her around two o'clock this morning." Susan raised her brow as she said that.

"It's nearly six in the morning," Newman said as he handed the bag back to him. "Why did he wait so long to call it in?"

Sauer tossed the evidence bag back onto the counter. "Good question. Let's go ask him. Anything else, Susan?"

"Not right now. I'll update you when I can."

Newman winked at her, then followed Sauer out.

Strange. Newman could flirt like there was no tomorrow, except when he was in a relationship he never did overt things like that. While it was an innocent wink, it still wasn't like him.

"You okay?"

"I'm cool. Besides the dead woman, of course." Newman grinned, yet Sauer didn't hear the honesty. He'd press him later about it.

The boyfriend sat in the back of an ambulance sitting cockeyed in the street. Blood covered his shirt and jeans, a few smears on his face as well.

Sauer didn't know much about the victim other than her name was Vanessa Colton. Captain Ganderson might've mentioned a few other things when he called him earlier, but he barely recalled her name. He'd been thinking about one thing: Dee. He still couldn't get her out of his head.

"Oh my God, do you know who did this to Nessy? Please tell me you know who did it." The man wiped his hand across his mouth, smearing more blood.

"I'm Detective Newman, and this is my partner, Detective Sauer. Why don't you tell us what happened? Start with your name." Newman had a small notepad and pencil in his hand ready to go.

Sauer had a good memory. Not eidetic, but he remembered information from an interview until he reached his computer and wrote it down. It really didn't matter. Newman took meticulous notes and always emailed them to him. He told Newman all the time he didn't need to. Some people thought he was lazy, making Newman do all the work. It wasn't the case, and honestly, he didn't care to argue with people. He wasn't a confrontational kind of guy. People were going to believe what they wanted.

"Shawn Gross. Nessy and I have been dating for about nine months. I met her at a yoga class." Shawn blew out a deep breath as he clenched his fists. "We had a small fight. I left the house pissed and went out to watch the game with some buddies. I was gonna crash at my friend's house, but I changed my mind. I came home around two and...and..." A sob escaped.

"What did you fight about?" Sauer asked.

"She was supposed to come with to watch the game. Then she changed her mind because the party was at my friend Brian's house. She doesn't like him much. And she hates his girlfriend Darla."

"Any particular reason why?" Newman asked as he scribbled on the notepad.

"I might've dated Darla before Brian. She still kinda flirts with me. But I've never cheated. I ain't no cheater. I've told Nessy this how many times. She didn't believe me."

"Did she have any problems with anyone else?" Sauer wanted to glance away. The blood was starting to make him a little nauseated. That normally didn't happen.

"I don't know. She's been having issues with her boss. He's a jackass." Shawn's face became hard. "He's always trying to control her. Even tried to break us up."

"Who's her boss?" Newman asked.

"Tony, from the Dancing Slipper." Shawn shuffled his gaze back and forth between them. "Yeah, Nessy was a stripper."

And their suspect list just skyrocketed. Any number of men could've killed her, could've taken an unnatural liking to her. Sauer almost groaned out loud, but held himself in check. "Did she have any problems with any customers?"

"Nothing too serious that I know of."

"So, Shawn, tell us, why did you wait three hours to call this in?" Shawn flinched from the accusation in Newman's tone.

"I...well...I don't know. I think I kinda blanked out for a while and realized I should call the police." His eyes bulged. "I didn't kill Nessy."

"Can you write your name for me?" Newman handed over his notepad, giving Shawn no choice.

Shawn quickly scribbled his name. They left him after asking a few more questions about his relationship with Vanessa. They didn't get anywhere with him. He just kept repeating, "I didn't kill her."

Sometimes acting so adamant was a huge red flag. Other times, it meant they truly were innocent. Sauer wasn't too sure at the moment what he believed.

"What does his handwriting look like?"

Newman showed him the notepad and shook his head. "He didn't write the note. I don't even need a handwriting analysis to prove it. Look at that chicken scratch. I barely can read it. The note was more legible than this crap." He opened his car door and grabbed an evidence bag from the back seat and slipped the notepad inside of it. "And now I need a new notepad. He got blood all over this one."

"Did you miss the fact he had blood all over him?" He chuckled.

Newman flinched. "Of course not."

"Seriously, man, what's going on with you?"

Newman grabbed his pack of wipes he carried everywhere, because he could be a huge germaphobe at times, and wiped his hands several times over before responding. "Everything's good."

His eyes narrowed. "You don't generally lie to me."

"Chrissy and I broke up." Newman threw the wipes into the small garbage bag he carried in his car and shrugged.

Not that it made it right, but Sauer figured that's why he acted like a jackass last night. So many things made sense now.

"I'm sorry."

Newman shrugged again. "We got tons of shit to do. Worrying about Chrissy isn't one of them."

Sauer decided to drop it. When Newman wanted to drop a subject, it was dropped. He respected that. He didn't know what else to say. *I'm sorry* didn't even seem appropriate. He shivered. He never thought two words could give him the heebie-jeebies.

Work sucked. Normally, she didn't think like that. She enjoyed working at Young's Accounting. Since the death of his two partners a few years ago, he chopped off the Mills and Murphy part. With their deaths, the entire company went to him. For a while, it was a little touch and go whether or not the company would go under. Seriously, you didn't have two partners in the company, a co-worker and an office manager, die, and things not get a little dicey. Young was a determined man. Dee, herself, was just as determined. She made sure shit got done. It was her job, especially to make sure his life went uninterrupted without issues. She made a damn good secretary.

She liked having control. Some people might think a secretary didn't have much control. You followed orders like a little lapdog. Nope. Not her. She figured Young realized it as well. She made the orders around here. He didn't complain. First, well, complaining didn't get anywhere with her. Second, she saved his company from falling apart. She kept it together.

Which made it strange. Why was she falling apart now?

She hated to admit it, but it was gutting her inside she had dismissed Sauer so easily. They didn't interact much. Sure, he was there at certain get-togethers, but they didn't talk to each other. He was too shy. And the few times she tried to make small talk with him, he didn't say much.

Still. She shouldn't have dismissed him so easily. She could be a bitch. She knew this. But being one to such a sweet guy rankled her. Made her sick to her stomach. She had to make things right between them. How? That's what puzzled her.

Going on a date was a no-go. He was too adorable of a guy for a girl like her. She'd break him before they got far, and that was the last thing she wanted to do. As much as she hated to admit it, she liked being alone. It suited her. It was for the best.

Not many men could handle her. Her sharp words. Her honesty. Her loud personality. She refused to do one thing:

change for a man. No man was worth it. She learned that the hard way—through her mom.

Guy after guy after guy came and went through their lives. Each time a new one appeared, her mom changed her ways.

His favorite was country music. Oh, so was hers. This one loved rock music. Well, you know what, so did she. No, no, no, give this guy a good ol' folk band and he was happy. Damn it if her mom didn't suddenly love that as well.

She couldn't even stick to a music genre and say, "Well, this is what I love and I don't care what you say." Instead, she absorbed herself into the man and agreed with every damn thing he loved and did. They could do no wrong.

Dee refused to do that. She wouldn't change for anybody. Not even Sauer.

Although, she could never see Sauer asking her to change her ways. Hell, who was she kidding? Of course he wouldn't. He could barely say hello when they were in the same room.

He asked her out, though. He found the courage to do that.

And she acted like a bitch.

"Are you okay?"

Dee glanced up to see Rina standing by her desk, a sad look in her eyes. "I'm fine."

"I get the feeling you're really not. I'm always here if you want to talk. You know that, right?"

"I know." She shoved her hand into the crazy mess of her hair and primped it a little. "Don't worry so much about me."

"I can't help it. You're my best friend. Zoe and I were really worried about you when you left like that. Sauer—"

"Did you get those reports I left on your desk? Make sure

Donaho gets those, okay?" Dee smiled, trying to lessen the fact she cut her off without caring how rude it was. She didn't want to talk about Sauer. She didn't even want to think about him, and that's all she had been doing this morning.

One of the things she loved about Rina, though, was that she got the drift right away and didn't keep pestering you. She let it go. When she was ready to talk, she'd listen. She wouldn't be offended by the abruptness with which she acted. She was rude. She knew it. Rina should just say it.

"I already made sure he got them." Rina smiled gently. "We're still going out Friday for drinks, right?"

"Unless you two married women bail on me, yeah."

A light laughter filtered out. "We'd never bail on you. See you at lunch." Rina walked away.

Why did she feel the need to make sure she'd show on Friday? If anyone was dying for those nights, it was her. Before Zoe and Rina got married, they hung out all the time. You couldn't pry them apart. Now, the only one unattached, she waited, wondered if she'd ever get a happily ever after.

As much as she didn't want to wonder, she did. Could she fall in love? Could she find a good man like her friends?

She didn't know what real love was like. She never really had it. She'd never deny her mother loved her, because she did. Her mother just had a weird-ass way of showing it. The men in her life always came first. When they lost interest, because they always did, she'd give Dee some attention, then just as suddenly divert it all to find a new man. The vicious cycle kept repeating itself over and over and over.

Relationships were hard. Even the one with her mom, if she could even call it that, when she was alive. What was the point? Life went much smoother when she avoided it completely.

Sauer was better off without her.

She grabbed her phone from the top drawer of her desk. A little tap, tap, tap and done. She had a date lined up that would erase everything. Raul was divine in bed. That's all she needed.

SAUER LIFTED his gaze to Newman as he hung up the phone. "So?"

"Susan said Vanessa wasn't raped, so good luck on getting any DNA. We don't have the murder weapon, no witnesses, and her boyfriend has an alibi. Damn luckiest thing he did was stay at his friend's party until almost two o'clock."

"No forced entry. Dr. Everly confirmed time of death around midnight. Did she know her attacker? She didn't have an alarm system. The perp could've broken in somehow."

"Since we ruled out the boyfriend, I'm liking one of the guys from the strip club. He gets a little too attached, starts following her, and things get out of hand. She lets him in, then he tries to make a move and gets angry when she denies him."

Sauer pondered that scenario for a few beats. "Yeah, but would she let in some guy from a strip club? Unless they've been to her house before, how would he know where she lived? I think she would've called the cops."

"True. Well, the list of regulars her boss Tony gave us is our next avenue. Gravitating towards her too much or getting kicked out for getting a little too friendly. They could've easily taken that infatuation too far and followed her home. Five guys. Not a lot, but for a suspect list, kind of."

Newman scratched his chin. "I can see why Shawn didn't like Tony. He seemed a little too controlling about his ladies, but he obviously didn't kill her."

"Nothing better than a solid alibi. Unless *his ladies*, as you put it, are covering for him and he really wasn't at the strip club working."

Newman chuckled. "Hey, just using the words he used. He said it in front of the ladies, too. They didn't seem to mind."

"Most of them didn't. Some looked at him like he was a slimeball." And Sauer had to agree. Tony acted like an arrogant creep, but he didn't kill Vanessa. "I need a refill of my coffee before we head out. You want one?" Sauer stood up, grabbing his to-go mug from the corner of his desk.

Newman declined. Sauer quickly walked to the break room, refilling his mug with the sludge that would probably make his stomach cringe, but he needed a pick-me-up. He didn't sleep much, then the call came in for the murder. He generally fueled up on tons of coffee when that happened.

He turned around, nearly running into Zeke. Great. Not something he wanted to deal with right now. Or ever. He didn't do well with confrontation. Hated it, in fact. Probably had to do with school and the many times kids picked on him. Things were easier when he ducked into his shell rather than fight back. Even as an adult, he avoided conflict by normally agreeing with the other person. He couldn't help it. He liked to keep the peace.

"I just wanted to apologize for last night, Sauer. I never meant to hurt your feelings or make you think you're not good enough for Dee, because you are."

"No worries. I'm over it." And he was. That wasn't just a line to move the conversation along. He accepted the fate of never dating Dee. No big deal. He knew it had been a long shot when he asked her out. They were two different people. It probably wouldn't work out. Newman was always saying he had to work on his shyness with women. Well, that's what he did. He considered it a step in the right direction. Maybe the next time he'd actually get the words out in the correct order.

"You sure?"

"Do you wanna sit in a circle, hold hands, and express our feelings more deeply?" Sauer asked with a grin.

Zeke laughed. "No, I'm good. I already express my feelings too much to Ben. We're thinking of having another baby and Ben's back on his kick teasing me what pregnancy is like. Been there, done that, so it's not bothering me this time." A devilish grin started to form. "Can't wait for Rina to get pregnant. I'm going to torture him like there's no tomorrow."

He laughed with Zeke as he pictured the two of them bickering back and forth about it. It was comical. Making jokes and giving each other shit in the precinct was their forte. Everyone could always count on Zeke and Ben to keep it interesting.

"Are they thinking about having a baby? They've only been married about three months."

Zeke shrugged. "He isn't saying. And trust me, I've tried to weasel it out of him."

Sauer slapped him on the shoulder, chuckling. "I just bet you have. We're headed out for some interviews. I'll talk to you later."

"See ya."

Sauer took a sip of coffee as he walked out of the break room.

"Hey, Sauer?"

He turned around. Zeke looked pensive. "I think Dee

would be the oddest choice for you just because you're quieter than her. Sometimes, opposites attract, which makes me believe you just might be the perfect guy for her."

If only it were true.

"Doesn't matter. She never said yes."

3

HE MADE a fool of himself at the Super Bowl party. Two days had gone by and he hadn't seen her to clarify whether it was a yes or no. He took it as a no. He needed to accept it as a no. Wishing it to be different wasn't helping him. He told Zeke it was no big deal. At the time, he meant it. Now, part of him wanted to know for sure. What did *you're so adorable* really mean? That could mean anything. Not necessarily a no.

These past two days had been difficult to get through, constantly thinking about her, the idiotic way he tried to ask her out. Thinking about her instead of the case going nowhere was easier. They had interviewed four of the five guys on the list that Tony had given them. They each had a solid alibi the night of the murder. They were home in bed with their wives. Every single one. Two of the men received death glares that said their asses were in trouble as soon as they left. They didn't know their husbands had been going to a strip club.

The other two men fared better in the wife department. They knew about the trips to the strip club, yet he could see it bothered the women. Maybe they were too timid to speak up. Kind of like him. Always so timid and scared.

The last guy on their list, Marvin Tannor, was making it difficult to locate him. So far, his last known address had been occupied by an elderly couple that said they'd been in the apartment for the last five months. They checked a few other addresses listed for him, coming up empty. They informed Tony if he showed up at the club to call them. They were still waiting.

That didn't mean they didn't have other avenues to work with. Still, despite how busy he was with the case, his mind liked to wander and think about Dee, especially after Zeke said he'd be the perfect guy for her. Maybe that was just his way of apologizing and making shit up. Sauer didn't know. But he liked the sound of it.

Newman was right. He was more shy and reserved, whereas Dee was loud and outgoing. Too beautiful as well. Women like her didn't go for men like him. Thinking he had a chance with her was ridiculous, even with the comforting words from Zeke.

It wouldn't hurt to say hi, though. Maybe his luck was finally changing. He never ran into Dee.

Blowing out a deep breath, he crossed the street to the small café where Dee stood outside near a table. Running a hand over his hair, already missing the thickness of it, he drew in a deep breath this time.

"Hey, Dee."

Turning around, her forehead puckered as her eyes narrowed. "Do I know you?"

His heart plummeted as he tried to gulp for a breath of air as if he'd just been sucker-punched. Just having left the barbershop, he knew he looked a little different, considering he chopped off most of his hair, but not *that* different. He still didn't know why he did it. A change, maybe. Appear more confident when he was anything but. Instead, she left him speechless, the confidence disappearing like the leaves from a tree on a windy day.

He had needed a change, or more like a break. Instead of grabbing lunch with Newman, he decided to get his hair cut. It was a spur of the moment, let's-do-this-before-I-change-my-mind sort of thing. Now, he regretted it. She didn't recognize him. He was so low on her list that she didn't even recognize him with a haircut.

Suddenly, her face lit up with delight, a deep roar of laughter as she touched his shoulder. "Oh my God, Sauer, you should see your face. The confusion is just too damn adorable."

He cracked a smile, even though he didn't think it was that funny. She seriously scared him that he was forgettable. Words wouldn't form. Partly from the shock of her joke. Partly from her hand resting on his shoulder. Her light touch was heating up his body like never before.

His desire for her spiked to a boiling point when she reached up toward his hair and rubbed his head. "A buzz cut. I likey, Sauer. Makes you look a little more rugged." Her hand smoothed back and forth. The action made him want to pull her into his arms and kiss her breathless. "I kinda miss the long hair you had. This is cool, too."

Her hand dropped to her side. Just like that, he wished for another reason, any reason for her to touch him again.

"Um...thanks." Shit. Again with those two words. Could he never form anything more coherent with her?

A sweet, low chuckle filled the air. "You're welcome." Her head tilted to the side. "What's your first name? I've only ever heard people call you Sauer. Why do guys call each other by their last name? It's weird."

Shrugging, he grinned. "An air of mystery."

God, that didn't even make sense. Did it?

She laughed again, touching his arm as her beauty filled his soul. "So mysterious. Does that mean you won't tell me your first name? I'll just ask Zoe or Rina. They'll totally tell me."

Her hand still rested on his arm. What could he say to keep it there? He leaned closer. "I might tell you."

Her slender body moved closer as a few curly tendrils of hair floated in front of her eyes. "If I didn't know any better, I would think you're flirting. Most men have a tendency to be complete douches when they do."

He couldn't move away from her. Her lips were inches from his, her hand still holding his arm. Was she calling him a douche? That was her favorite thing to call men. Zeke and Ben had both worn that badge of honor until she decided they were decent enough for her friends. What made her think that about men? All men. Who hurt her? He wanted to hurt them back for damaging her in any way. She deserved so much.

A surge of bravery zapped him. His hand swiped the locks of hair in her eyes behind her ear. He felt a tremble in her hand. "Am I a douche?"

For once, she appeared speechless. Her eyes stayed glued to his, yet she didn't answer his question. He was mesmerized by the stare. Unnerved even. What would she do if he suddenly kissed her? He slowly moved closer.

"Yo, babe, you ready?"

Both of their heads jerked to the voice coming a short distance from them. With all her talk about douches, this guy looked exactly like one. Full of muscle on every inch of his body, Sauer was a tad nervous this guy would kick his ass for standing so close to her—and provided him the reason she never accepted a date from him. She wasn't available.

"Yep," Dee said quickly, then turned toward him. "You've never been a douche. You're too good for me. That's what you are."

With that, she walked away.

Well, shit. She wasn't available. Which meant he needed to stop thinking about her.

That was easier said than done as he walked back to meet Newman with nothing but Dee on his mind.

"Who was that?"

She didn't hide the eye roll at Raul's question. Oh, she heard the jealousy in his tone. Raul was one who didn't mind when she called him every now and again for some fun times between the sheets. But when it was his time, he didn't like to share. At all.

"A friend."

"Yeah. What kind?"

Her feet halted. "I need to get back to the office." Which interpreted into 'we aren't having sex today.' Or any other day.

Dumb. She really thought it was a good idea to sleep with one man to get her mind off another. The one she couldn't have. Because it was a horrible idea. Thank God, Raul had been busy when she originally texted him the other day. Otherwise, she would've already taken the plunge, trying to erase Sauer from her mind.

What was she doing wasting her hour lunch trying to have a quickie with a guy who acted so jealous right away? She was only saying hi to a friend.

She sure knew how to pick some winners.

Sauer asked her out. So adorably. Why didn't she just accept his date? Then they could—

No. She'd never just sleep with Sauer and boot him to the curb. He was too sweet to be treated that way. She needed to focus right now, especially with the way Raul was looking at her so strangely. A hard glint had entered his eyes. Obviously, he wasn't happy with the change of plans.

"All right. I'll see you later. I don't have to work at the club tonight."

She squeezed his arm and gave him one of the best smiles she could, lacing it with a touch of sexiness. "I have plans tonight. Maybe another time. I gotta go." She placed a chaste kiss on his cheek and walked away.

There wasn't a reason to give him time to argue. And Raul would argue. He had never gotten physical, but he could get angry with her sometimes. That was one reason she never went exclusive with him. Quick sex, and that's it. That's all she needed from him. Well, not anymore.

If she couldn't work out her frazzled nerves about what to do with Sauer, she wasn't sure when she would be having sex again. Because the idea of sleeping with anybody but him didn't sound appealing.

All it took was a handsome detective asking her out in such a charming way.

"Whoa. You cut your hair. You said you were getting a coffee."

Sauer rubbed the top of his head, still reeling from the fact he saw Dee. "Yeah, I don't know what came over me."

Newman tossed the leftover paper from his sandwich

into the trash and pulled out a bottle of hand sanitizer from his pocket, pouring a small amount out. "You look good. I like it."

"Thanks."

"Are you ready to head to Vanessa's brother's house?"

"Think he'll be there? Since we notified her parents, we haven't been able to connect with him. It's odd."

Newman slid into the driver's seat and nodded. "Way too many possible suspects right now. He's on our list just for that reason. Hell, I'm willing to add her parents. They weren't too broken up their daughter was murdered."

Sauer shrugged. "She was a stripper. Not to mention, she left home when she was sixteen. Seems to me they already mourned the death of their daughter when she didn't follow their wishes to be the perfect daughter."

"Yeah, they were pretty judgmental. I blame the money. They have plenty of it."

Sauer was silent the rest of the drive. There wasn't much else to talk about concerning her parents. They were furious when she ran away from home at sixteen. At twenty-one, she became a stripper. That's when they officially disowned her. Her father was a doctor and her mother was an assistant principal for one of the local schools. Having a daughter in such a profession ruined their image.

He couldn't imagine not having a relationship with his parents. Sometimes, especially when he was younger, they smothered him a little too much. They didn't want to see their only child being bullied. Who would? He didn't like to talk about that stuff, or tell on the kids who picked on him. Hence, the smothering when they found out. They wanted to make sure he was okay. He was. As much as kids bugged him, he always tried to let it go. Coping as an adult was much easier, but he survived.

Newman pulled up to a two-story brick house with the landscaping looking immaculate even in the cold, brutal winter months in Minnesota. There was a light layer of snow from a week ago, but it all looked so organized and perfectly done. It was snow. Just shovel it to the side and be done. Not this yard.

They waited on the porch as the loud ringing of the doorbell echoed throughout the house. The door opened to a young man dressed in a fancy suit, not a wrinkle in place.

"Vince Colton?" Newman asked.

People tended to think because he didn't always do most of the talking that he was the good cop in the typical good-cop bad-cop routine. Definitely not true. He was the bad cop. A very silent and deadly one when upset. The cocky look on this guy's face made him want to bring out the bad cop immediately.

"Yes."

Newman flashed his badge, as did he. "Detective Newman, and this is my partner—"

"Look, I haven't spoken to my sister in over two years. I can't say I'm heartbroken or anything. I decided after the millionth time her begging me for more money that she wasn't worth my time anymore. That's all I was to her—a bank." Vince looked bored, yet annoyed they were bothering him with something he considered inconsequential.

Sauer held himself in check, making sure to keep his fists unclenched. Vince reminded him of the worst kind of bully.

"Where were you around midnight Sunday night?"

Vince's brow rose, as if he couldn't believe they were questioning him.

"At home with my wife. We had a Super Bowl party. I

didn't kill my sister, if that's what you're insinuating. She was useless. I don't even think about her."

Sauer grinned. "That's pretty harsh. We'll need to speak with your wife, as well as the guests that were at the party."

Vince smirked—the cockiest smirk yet. "Sure, detective. Anything to help out two hardworking men like yourself."

Without removing his grin, and his hands still hanging loose by his side, he nodded. "Great. I'd ask if you knew anyone who would hurt your sister, but I'm going to guess and say you have no idea."

"Like I said, I haven't talked to her in over two years."

Vince left them standing on the front porch, closing the door without inviting them in while they waited for him to write down a list of names and numbers so they could verify his alibi.

"What an asshat," Newman muttered under his breath, just to make sure Vince couldn't hear him.

"The worst kind. He seems a little too indifferent to kill his sister. Almost like he'd hate to waste any time thinking about her, let alone killing her."

"I know. Who does that leave us with?"

These were the cases he couldn't stand. The ones that made him scratch his head. Too many possibilities. Too many suspects. No evidence. It made for many sleepless nights. At least for him. As far as he knew, Newman always slept like a baby. But him, when they had trouble solving a case, he rarely slept. Add in the situation with Dee and sleep was nonexistent.

Scratch that. Dee wasn't a concern anymore. She had a boyfriend. Damn, if that didn't suck.

THE DRAWER SLAMMED.

"Everything okay, Deena?"

Dee turned around to Mr. Young, her boss and owner of the company, and smiled. "Yep."

He nodded and walked back into his office. Typical. If she seemed upset in the slightest way, he made sure whatever was upsetting her was fixed. He knew she was invaluable and didn't want to lose her. She'd never leave, of course. She loved her job. The freedom she had, and a little bit of power at her fingertips. Sure, she was just Mr. Young's secretary, but she was the best damn one in the office. She got shit done without batting an eye.

Her job was the only thing in her life that was right. That was perfect. That made sense. Everything else, well, just call it a complete cluster. Her dating life—laughable. Her family life—she wasn't even going to think about it. Her friends—all married and happy. She was all alone. She never felt more alone, almost to the point she wanted to hate Zoe and Rina for finding great men and leaving her so alone.

After that thought rolled in, she banished it just as quickly. They were her best friends for a reason. She would never hate them. They were the only happy thing in her life, besides—

No. She wasn't thinking about Sauer. How could she even think that? He wasn't in her life. Seeing him at a party and running into him today did not constitute being in her life. Pure coincidence she saw him today. Something she had to avoid from now on.

Her life was a mess. She wasn't going to drag a good man like Sauer into it. As much as she wanted a good man and a happily ever after like Zoe and Rina, she knew it would never happen.

Deena O'Malley. Nothing but a slut. Just like her mother. At least, that's what everyone always told her when she was younger. Instead of disputing the fact, she made it true. She slept with guys without having a relationship. What else could everyone call her other than a slut?

"Dee, everything okay?"

She looked up from her computer. Rina stood next to her with a worried expression. Why did everyone keep asking her that? Did she look that bad?

"I'm fine."

"You don't look fine."

"What's up, Rina? I have tons of stuff I need to do."

Rina sighed softly. "I was walking by to drop off some reports to Donaho and—are you sure you're okay?"

Pushing a few curly strands of hair out of her eyes, she tried not to huff in indignation. "You worry too much."

"Zoe's looking into some tickets to the Twins opener. Are you in?"

Just like that, Rina changed the subject. Dee was surprised she pressed the point as she had. Rina always let things go when she knew it was upsetting the other person. Maybe she did look terrible enough to make Rina so concerned.

"Yeah, sure."

Rina started to fiddle with her fingers as she shifted on her feet. "Well, Ben's coming with. Of course, Zoe and Zeke are going. So..."

"So I'm the fifth wheel, basically."

Rina bit her bottom lip. "Not exactly. We thought you could ask someone to go with you. This way it would be even."

"And who am I supposed to ask? That's still, like, two

months away." She couldn't resist rolling her eyes. "Just scratch me off the list."

Rina looked appalled. "No. We'd never do that. You're coming with." Her voice was firm, yet soft, in that vicious way that said she wouldn't be arguing with her. Rina was the only person she knew who could do that so effectively and not raise one part of her voice. She'd never tell Rina, but it scared her sometimes. Generally, nothing scared her.

"Who are you expecting me to ask?"

"Sauer."

Dee slumped back into her chair as she groaned in dismay. What were Rina and Zoe trying to do? Didn't they know a relationship between her and Sauer would never work?

"You don't like that idea? You really don't like him?"

Pumping her hair a little, she shrugged. "It's not that I don't like him. It's just...it's a bad idea. I have tons of stuff to do. Can we talk about this later?"

A beautiful, sweet smile crossed her face. "Of course." Then her brows dipped. "And we will talk. You can't keep avoiding the issue, whatever it is. We're your friends. Talk to us. My secrets ate away at me. Don't ruin this potential relationship because you're afraid to talk about it. I almost ruined it. Now I'm the happiest I've ever been."

Dee watched as Rina walked away. Talk to them about her secrets? Not likely. Although, Rina looked serious. It wouldn't do well to tempt her anger. Maybe she would be spilling her guts.

4

He leaned back in his chair, rubbing his temple as his head throbbed with pain.

"You okay, man? You don't look so hot."

Sauer dropped his hand as he met Newman's gaze. "My head's pounding. I feel a little stuffy as well. We've been on this case for the past two days like crazy, working late nights. I don't know if it's starting to get to me or what."

Newman chuckled. "I think it's or what. When we interviewed Doug Grayson, Vanessa's neighbor, he had a cold. He even sneezed. Maybe he passed that lovely virus to you. Go home, dude. You look like shit and I don't want it."

The idea was sounding great. Everything he felt indicated a cold was coming on. Why him? Why now? The case wasn't going anywhere. Doug didn't have anything pertinent to add other than Vanessa didn't have many visitors besides her boyfriend. Which several neighbors corroborated. So the idea she was bringing men home from the club went out the window.

They still couldn't locate Marvin. Tony from the club

hadn't called either, which meant Marvin hadn't shown up yet.

No helpful evidence at the crime scene. No witnesses. No good suspects, unless they wanted to count Marvin since he was being difficult to track down. They had nothing to go on. Sometimes, the sad reality was cases went cold. It was looking like Vanessa's case was going cold.

And he was getting a cold.

"I think I am going to go home. This case..."

Newman nodded, knowing what he was saying. They had run into a dead end until they could talk to Marvin. The strip club was looking like the best place for their suspect. Everyone in her family had a solid alibi. Which didn't surprise Sauer. They had written her out of their lives years ago. To them, she had been dead for a long time.

Sauer left work. He took some cold medicine when he got home, grabbed a warm washcloth, and laid down on the couch, placing the cloth over his forehead. He fussed around on the couch for a while trying to find a good position. The pain in his head made that a difficult task. Eventually, he fell into a semi-decent sleep.

The ringing of the doorbell ricocheted around his head. The dull, throbbing pain behind his eyes had just started to recede and someone had to visit him.

Flinging the now-cold washcloth that had been resting on his forehead onto the coffee table, he rolled off the couch in a very ungraceful manner. Not that he cared. He didn't care about anything at the moment, except for the couch and closing his eyes and making the pain go away.

Two feet from the door, the doorbell rang again.

"Stop. It hurts my—" His throat went instantly dry. Why did he open the door? He should've just pretended he wasn't home.

"Wow, Sauer, you look like shit. I brought soup." Dee lifted a small clear container filled with something colorful in one hand, then flicked her other hand at him. "Back up. I don't want what you have."

Too stunned, and a little surprised to see Dee, he stepped back automatically. Her smile almost made him forget his head pounded like a bunch of tiny elves were driving nails everywhere. Almost, but not quite.

"Go lie down, Sauer. You seriously look horrible. I'll heat up this soup for you."

She walked away. Although his head was killing him, his curiosity took over. He followed her to the kitchen where she started to open and close cupboards. Not gently either. He couldn't hide a wince every time she slammed a door closed.

"What are you doing?"

Brow rising in the delicious way she did, she wiggled her finger. "Nope. You go lie down. No asking questions like you like to do."

"How did you—"

Her lips stretched into a tight line. "Stop asking questions. But to answer that one, Newman told Zeke you weren't feeling well, who told Zoe, who told Rina, who then told me." She jerked her finger toward the living room. "Now go."

He couldn't stop it. The way his head felt, the small pinpricks of pain echoing everywhere, nothing should've made him smile. But her thoughtfulness did.

"Why are you grinning like that? And why aren't you listening to me?"

Don't say it. Don't do it. Just walk away. "I just never pictured you making soup." His smile grew, then slowly melted into a frown. "Wait. You did make it yourself, didn't you?" *God, please say yes.*

The thought of Dee slaving over the stove cooking soup for him made his heart beat double time. Made him a little hopeful she might actually like him.

"Are you implying I'm not domesticated enough to make soup?"

Like always, he screwed up. He never did or said anything right when it came to women. "No." He didn't know what else to say. Since he already failed miserably at speaking, it seemed better to say as little as possible.

She turned around, opening another cupboard. "I made the soup myself."

He watched as she continued to open and slam cupboard doors. Each time the door connected with the frame of the cupboard his head pounded with it. The picture in front of him—he loved it. He didn't care he was in so much pain from the nasty cold that came out of nowhere. She was so beautiful. And fussing over him. He never thought he'd see the day.

"You're beautiful."

Oh, man, he just said that out loud. Her hand stalled on the last cupboard door that finally held the bowls she had apparently been looking for.

"I don't think I've ever seen you look so beautiful and—"

"Go lie down—"

"I really want—"

"Before I seriously—"

"To kiss you."

Silence.

He said it. Just blurted out he wanted to kiss her. She still looked gorgeous as hell staring at him dumbfounded.

"You're sick. I don't want to get sick."

"So when I'm not sick..." He stopped before he made things worse. "I forgot. I'm sorry. You have a boyfriend."

Her hand wobbled as she pulled a bowl down from the cupboard. "I don't have a boyfriend."

"The guy at the café the other day..."

She rolled her eyes. "Just a guy."

Soup slopped into the bowl, looking strangely like chicken noodle soup. He loved chicken noodle soup. Did she know that? Or a lucky guess?

"I don't do boyfriends, Sauer. I just sleep with guys. That's all you'll ever get from me, so just stop. Go lie down and I'll heat up your soup."

Maybe it was the sickness. Maybe it was the pain over-riding his common sense. Maybe it was the honesty surrounding them.

"I have a feeling I'm going to get more than that from you. You made me soup when you normally don't do that. Admit it. When have you ever made soup for a guy—a guy you never even slept with? I think I will lie down now. My head's killing me."

He walked out of the kitchen with her jaw hanging down in surprise. For once, he got the last word in. He probably wouldn't get any other words in for the rest of his life. Where did that bravery come from? His sickness? The medicine? Complete delirium?

As he laid down on the couch, his head started to feel oddly better.

Dee came to his home. To take care of him. And she didn't have a boyfriend. That had to mean something good for him, right?

DEE STOOD FROZEN in the kitchen as she tried to process Sauer's words. She wanted more with him. For the first time in her life, she wanted more than just sex from a guy. Problem was she didn't know how to do relationships. Her longest relationship, if one could call it that, lasted four months. It wasn't anything she'd ever brag about. The sex was great. Probably why it lasted so long.

Shoving the soup into the microwave, she then leaned against the counter. Why did she come here again? Since Rina put the thought in her head to ask Sauer to go to the baseball game, she couldn't stop thinking about him. Who was she kidding? She couldn't stop thinking about him since the adorable way he asked her out.

Even now, he was still adorable as hell.

She should learn to stop messing with him. The way his face jerked in surprise when she asked if she didn't seem domesticated enough was too damn cute, and somewhat insensitive of her. She was only kidding. With Sauer, she needed to remember to be less abrasive. He was sensitive. Well, okay, maybe not sensitive.

Shy. Yeah, he was shy. He probably wasn't comfortable with a woman like her. Because, like an idiot, she was making him uncomfortable with everything she said.

Nearly dropping the bowl as she grabbed it from the microwave, the sides incredibly hot to the touch, she wondered why she was here again. What could she offer Sauer? What kind of girlfriend would she make? A horrible one. They had nothing in common. They were wrong for each other.

When, or if, she found a man, he'd need to be more alpha-like for her tastes. That's what kind of guy she wanted. Not the shy, quiet kind.

Placing the bowl onto a plate with a spoon on the side,

she walked to the living room to give Sauer his soup. Then she was leaving. She came to a decision.

No more pursuing Sauer, if that's what she even wanted to call this. She wanted more from a guy, and Sauer didn't live up to what she wanted. He was a nice guy, so she wouldn't lead him on.

"I'm not sleeping with you. Nothing is ever going to happen between us. We're just friends." She almost slammed the soup down on the table to make sure she got her point across.

He was lying on the couch, his arm resting over his eyes. He slowly lowered his arm and looked at her. Nothing about his expression gave away what he was thinking. Just a blank stare. It unnerved her. More than any other expression she'd seen from him so far. He tended to blush a lot, especially for a guy. Anytime she talked to him, even before he attempted to ask her out, he always got red from his neck to his cheeks. She found it so cute, especially since she never made guys blush. Right now, she expected so much redness to cover him, she was a little taken aback that he wasn't. He needed to blush.

Wait? Was she purposely trying to provoke that reaction because he looked so damn adorable when he did it?

Absolutely not! She was being honest with him. Nothing more. They'd never work out as a couple.

He sat up, rather slowly, and reached for the soup. Why wasn't he saying anything? She needed him to respond. Was he still acting shy with her? He didn't know what to say?

Taking a small bite, his face finally lit up with some expression, a handsome smile that always made him appear so unlike the shy guy he really was. She loved his smile.

"This tastes great."

"Did you not hear what I said?"

He scooped another bite, blowing on it before shoving it inside his mouth.

"Sauer? Quit ignoring me."

Why was he ignoring her? It was driving her nuts. She just told him she would never sleep with him or date him and he didn't say anything.

"I don't know what to say." He shrugged. "That's fine."

That's fine? That's all he had to say.

"You can't just say that. You have to say something else."

He looked perplexed. "Um...like what?"

She gestured in the air. "Like...like...ugh, you try my patience." She turned around. She was leaving.

"That's what you want me to say?"

Swiveling back toward him, she scoffed. "No. That's me telling you that you try my patience."

He grinned. The man had the audacity to grin. "No one's ever said that to me before."

"I can't argue with you right now."

"Is that what we're doing?"

"Eat your soup. Feel better soon. I'm leaving." She started to walk out of the living room.

"Dee?"

Slowing her steps, she was afraid to turn around, but she did. "What?"

"Thanks for the soup."

She stared dumbfounded at him. Why did he have to be so damn nice? She never dated nice guys. Never! No way in hell she was about to start. She liked her guys a little rough around the edges, a little challenging. Not sweet, endearing, and always saying the most wonderful things.

Her eyes glossed to the coffee table, unable to hold his penetrating stare she swore saw straight to her soul. Damn him! What was he doing to her? A simple look and she was ready to crash on the couch next to him, not leaving until she knew he felt better. Even then, the thought of leaving didn't sound appealing. That's not how she wanted to feel.

She stalked to the coffee table and snatched his phone. "Do you have a passcode?"

His eyes moved from her to his phone, the confusion clear. "Um...yeah."

She held out her hand. "Unlock your phone."

"Why?"

"You know, for such a shy guy, you like to argue with me way too much."

He smiled. A sweet, handsome smile that almost made her weak in the knees. Who was she kidding? That smile did make her knees weak. Made her weak everywhere inside. She didn't want to want Sauer. That was her problem. A huge problem. He wasn't the right guy for her.

"I forgot we were arguing. I guess because it doesn't feel like it to me." He set the bowl of soup on his lap and grabbed his phone. A few taps later, he handed it back to her. Although, she didn't give him a choice as she kept her hand hanging in the air waiting for him to place it back into her palm.

She scrolled to his contacts, saved her number, then called herself so she had his number as well. For the life of her, she couldn't figure out why she just did all that.

"Call me if you need more soup." She set his phone down and started to leave once again.

"Dee?"

Holding in a groan, she paused in her steps again. Why wouldn't he let her leave? Why did she love it every time he said her name in such a soft way? Why did she come here to begin with?

This time she didn't turn toward him. "Yeah."

"I respect your decision, not wanting to date me. I would like to be friends."

Damn, he had to be such a reasonable, nice guy. She didn't date reasonable, nice guys. Maybe that was her problem. No maybe about that. That *was* her problem. Yet, she was afraid to give in, to give Sauer a chance.

Probably because out of every guy she dated, he'd be the one to potentially break her heart.

"Get some rest, Sauer."

She left.

5

_____

Sᴀᴜᴇʀ sʜᴜᴛ the passenger side door with a bang. His head, for the first time, didn't pound with agony. He woke up this morning still feeling a little stuffy in the nose, but his head was ten times better. When he left for work, the slamming of the door bothered him. Now, several hours later, he could slam a door and it didn't even make him flinch.

He liked to think it was because of Dee and her soup. Her magic touch cured him because, normally, when he got hit with a cold, he was out for days. This one, he was back and ready to go the next day, albeit the slight stuffiness still lingering. Even that was getting better as the day wore on.

"What do you think he'll have to say?"

Sauer glanced at Newman as they made their way to the door of the Dancing Slipper. "A bunch of lies, if he's our killer."

Newman laughed. "Good point."

Sauer opened the door and let Newman walk in first. They spoke briefly to Tony, who then pointed out where Marvin was sitting. The guy finally showed up at the club. It was Friday, his regular day to come, according to Tony.

Almost an entire week had passed since Vanessa was murdered. The case was going cold, unless Marvin suddenly heated it up.

Without an invitation, Sauer sat down in the booth on Marvin's right side as Newman took the spot to his left. Marvin glanced between the two, eyes looking like a deer in headlights. His Adam's apple bobbed crazily, signaling how nervous they made him.

"Shit. I told him I'd have the money to him by tomorrow."

Sauer and Newman shared a look, then Newman plastered the biggest, fakest smile on his face as he displayed his badge.

Marvin's face drained of all color as he started to fidget a little more. "Never mind what I just said."

"I'm Detective Newman. That's my partner, Detective Sauer. We just have a few questions for you."

"What about?"

"Do you know Vanessa Colton?" Sauer asked as he leaned back into the booth, relaxing his posture, making it appear as if they intended to stay for a while. The gesture made Marvin fidget even more.

Very interesting. He was definitely nervous about something. But what?

"Never heard of her."

Newman snapped his fingers. Marvin jumped from the sudden movement. "Our bad. She goes by a different name here. Do you know Cherry?"

Not one of the men who frequented the strip club had recognized Vanessa's real name, but the minute they asked about Cherry, her stage name, they knew exactly who she was. The same could be said about Marvin. His eyes lit up with delight as soon as Newman mentioned that name.

"Cherry's a beautiful woman. If you fellas stay for a while, you'll see her soon."

Sauer couldn't make out whether he was being sincere or not, or if he really didn't know she was dead. Her death had made the news. Perhaps he didn't watch the news. Maybe he wasn't their killer. Or maybe he was just that good at faking it.

"She was murdered this past weekend."

Marvin's eyes bulged as his mouth fell open at Sauer's words. "She...what...are you...can you repeat that?"

"What part didn't you understand?" Sauer asked, his bad cop persona coming out with a flare.

Newman coughed to hide a laugh, then said, "You had a few interactions with her. How well did you know her?"

"We weren't friends or anything, just friendly, you know what I mean." Marvin shifted in the seat, going from shocked to nervous again.

"When's the last time you saw her?" Newman asked.

"Last Friday."

"Did you ever have any problems with her? Did you ever get a little too touchy-feely?" Sauer asked.

"Absolutely not! I respect every woman here!"

"Where were you Sunday night around midnight?"

Marvin looked away from Sauer. "Asleep."

Newman's voice went soft. "You're not lying to us, are you? If you're in trouble, we can try to help you."

Marvin glanced quickly between the two, keeping his attention on Newman more than him. He made him nervous, which was the point. Newman was there to make him feel safe and hopefully give them something good.

"I was asleep. That's what you do at midnight."

"You didn't watch the game?" Sauer asked.

"Game?"

Sauer knew then, he was lying. The way he twisted his hands in his lap, the way his eyes went round with fright, the way the word 'game' left his mouth. He had watched the game. In all likelihood, he made a bet he lost, which would explain the first thing that came out of his mouth when they sat down. He must owe a bookie a heavy price.

"Where do you live, Mr. Tannor?"

Marvin looked frightened by that question. "Why?"

Sauer leaned closer. "Because we need your contact information if we have any more questions, and your last known address wasn't an accurate address."

"Yeah, sure."

Marvin rattled off his address. They asked a few more questions about Vanessa that proved to be fruitless and then left. Sauer slammed his door hard again, this time in frustration.

"Well, that was pointless. I'm not feeling him as a killer."

Sauer nodded. "I wonder how much money he lost on the game. I bet he owes someone lots of moola."

Newman laughed. "I think he thought we were there to break his legs if he didn't pay."

"So we officially hit a coldness in this case."

"We did." Newman pulled out of the parking lot. "On a brighter note, your cold's gone."

Sauer smiled, as his mind conjured Dee's beautiful face. His cold was gone, and he didn't care how crazy it seemed, but it was all because of her and her magical soup.

It didn't matter that she didn't want to date him. That she tossed him into the friend zone. He'd take it. A friend was better than nothing. Maybe somewhat pathetic to think, but for him, it was what he called progress. He was actually talking to a beautiful woman without stumbling over his words...much. He just needed a little more practice.

"What's with the crazy smile?"

He jerked his head toward Newman. "Nothing."

"Definitely something."

Sauer shrugged. "Dee brought me some soup yesterday."

"No shit. Nice job, buddy."

"It doesn't mean anything."

"Pretty sure Dee doesn't bring soup to just anyone."

He shrugged again. Call it pride. Call it nerves. Call it something, but he wasn't about to tell Newman what she said. It'd sound so much worse if he voiced it. Although he and Newman were friends, Newman had a tendency to pick on him, tease him a little too much. He didn't always like it, but he wasn't going to tell him that. Sometimes, it was just easier to keep it in.

"Did you ask her out again?"

"No."

Newman tapped him on the shoulder. "Come on, man, give it another go. She might say yes this time. Brought you soup. Very nice." He laughed as if he couldn't believe it.

"What's going on with you and Chrissy?"

Sauer didn't mind changing the subject, especially when he didn't want to talk about Dee. Newman hadn't said much about Chrissy, and normally he talked about her all the time. Since they broke up, he'd been tight-lipped about everything.

"Not much to say. I'm moving out."

"What happened?"

He turned on his blinker to take a left. "You hungry for a burger? I'm hungry."

"Sounds good."

So Newman wanted to drop the subject. Fine by him. He

didn't want to talk about Dee. It only seemed right he didn't press about Chrissy.

Weren't they a fine mess? What kind of friends didn't want to talk about their girl problems? Ben and Zeke didn't have that problem. Sauer could hear them chatting all the time about their relationships.

Sometimes, he was jealous of the great friendship they had. He got along well with Newman. They were pretty close as partners, but if they didn't work together, he didn't think they would've been friends. Newman reminded him of a few of the guys from his high school days who liked to pick on him just because it was easy and fun. Newman had a tendency to do that, thinking it was funny. Sometimes, Sauer did get a good chuckle, but mostly, it bothered him.

Story of his life. Even as an adult, he let people run all over him. Confrontation wasn't a strong suit of his, and Newman was his partner. Besides the times he went too far in his teasing, he liked him. There was no sense in creating tension when it might just make him look sensitive. Not something he wanted to portray, especially to everyone else in the precinct.

DEE TOOK a large gulp of her beer, then signaled for one of the floor servers.

"A night out on the town, huh?" Zoe asked with a laugh. "You just ordered that beer."

"It's time to tell us what's going on."

Oh, Dee hated when Rina used that soft tone on her. Rina talked softly all the time, but when she really meant business, she talked even softer than was possible. It unnerved her every time. She took another swallow of her beer.

"Dee, we know Sauer isn't your typical guy, which is why we think he's perfect for you. He'll mellow you out a bit," Zoe said softly, although, not as softly as Rina. It didn't have the same effect. In fact, it had the exact opposite.

"Mellow me out? What the hell does that mean?"

Zoe didn't have the gall to look sorry. "You know what I mean." Then she decided to go for the jugular. "Acting like a bitch—like that's going to work with us—isn't going to drop the subject."

"Did you just call me a bitch?"

Rina chuckled. "Dee, you know she didn't mean it in a bad way. Stop trying to avoid us by deflecting. We're your friends. You can tell us anything."

Dee primped her hair, annoyed that her two best friends couldn't even pretend to be mad at her for her outbursts. She knew Zoe didn't call her a bitch in a bad way. She was right. Acting like one didn't make the problem go away. It was a lot easier to pretend it didn't exist.

"Sauer's nice. He's just not the kind of guy I date."

"Exactly." Zoe pounded the table, gaining a few glances from some of the other patrons at Rockster's, their normal hangout bar on Fridays. "You need to stop dating so-called douches and date a nice guy for once. I think that's your problem...and ours. We've been trying to find a guy who could match your personality, when really, we should've been trying to find a guy who will complement your person- ality. Loud and crazy with sweet and calm. He's perfect for you."

Dee hated how much that sounded true. He was sweet and calm to her loud and crazy. Oddly enough, he did calm her. Although, he drove her crazy when he refused to respond to her. Other men had gotten right in her face when they got into a heated argument. All it did was make her laugh and dismiss them quickly as something unimportant. With Sauer, when he ignored her, it made her angrier, fueling her desire to get a rise out of him. Anything but silence. Even a hint of red on his face. She loved when he blushed.

"Relationships are not my forte. Never have been."

Rina smiled sweetly. "They weren't mine either, and now I'm happily married. You just need the right guy. Sauer could be the one. You don't know if you don't try." Her voice dropped to almost a whisper. "What are you afraid of?"

Dee let loose a huge breath. "Becoming my mother. Sadly, I already have become her somewhat."

"In what way?" Zoe asked, leaning closer.

Dee never talked about her family. Yeah, they knew her mother was dead, passed away five years ago from a heart attack, but besides that, nothing. She never said a peep about her. Just like how Rina rarely talked about her family. Zoe had no problems with her family, and why should she? Out of the three of them, she had the most normal upbringing. It wasn't hard to talk about it when she had nothing horrible happen.

"She always gravitated towards losers, kinda like I do. She always had to have a man in her life. I hate to say I do, too. She..." Dee shuffled another hand through her hair. "Let's talk about something else."

Zoe and Rina shared a look, which fueled Dee's annoyance more. If she didn't want to talk, she sure in the hell wasn't going to. End of story.

"Dee—"

"Enough, Zoe."

"No." Zoe pounded her hand on the table again. "You

never let up on me when I first started dating Zeke. Do you know how many times you got into my face about him? You can't just expect me to stop because you say so. I'm not scared of you. I'm your friend and I care about you."

So true. All of it. It was always easier to dish it out than to take it. That's for sure. She just wasn't in the mood to take any more crap from her friends. She stood up and grabbed her purse. Damn good thing the server took her sweet time coming to their table.

"Don't leave, Dee," Rina said.

"I'm not in the mood for drinks anymore. You guys have a great weekend with your husbands."

She left before they could talk her into staying. She heard Zoe's voice trailing her the entire time, but it did nothing to stop her from leaving. Yeah, she just acted like a bitch. She had no problem admitting that. Yeah, she could even be called hypocritical. She did give Zoe tons of shit when she first started dating Zeke. Who wouldn't? He had treated her like a damn prostitute. He didn't deserve a second chance. Of course, Zoe gave him one and now they were happily married. So she was wrong. He did deserve a second chance.

So much easier to dish it out. Way, way easier.

As she drove home, she knew she needed to call them tomorrow with an apology. She acted way out of line. Sometimes, it was difficult to see their happiness when she had none. She had no one to blame but herself. She could have a little happiness if she gave one guy a chance. One sweet, sensitive, handsome man a chance.

What *was* she scared of?

Part of it was becoming like her mother. Part of it was just fearing the day when the happiness would be ripped away. It always happened.

Every time a new boyfriend of her mother's rolled into her life, she thought, *this is the one*. This was the guy who would stick around and be her new dad. It never took that long for the guy to roll back out. When she first started dating, she held that same hopeful anticipation. This was the guy she'd spend the rest of her life with. It never took very long for them to leave just as quickly as they entered. Part of that was her fault. She was loud and outgoing. Not every guy wanted a woman like that.

Even her happiness with her friends was slowly drifting away. They were married. They were starting a family with kids. She was waiting for the day they decided their weekly drinks on Fridays would end. She knew it had to be coming soon. Zeke and Ben probably didn't like them coming out every Friday with her. They probably didn't even like her much. Not many people did.

Whatever. When the time came, she'd suck it up like she sucked up every other disappointment in her life. That's what she did. Sucked it up and moved on.

Dee pulled into her driveway, sighing. Maybe she should call them tonight to apologize. She shouldn't have left like she had. They both had a husband to go home to and they chose to hang out with her instead. What did she do? She acted like the biggest bitch ever to them.

Her steps slowed as she neared her front door.

Another rose, like earlier this week, sat resting on the mat in front of her door. Picking it up, she read the white note next to it.

I'm sorry.

Who kept doing this? She hadn't seen her neighbor Mathias all week. Did he think his first apology didn't work? Did he honestly expect her to knock on his door?

It had to be him. Right?

Of course it was. Who else would leave her a flower and a dumb note?

She threw the flower and note into the trashcan on the side of the house as she had the first time and then went inside.

She roamed around her kitchen for a minute or two before she decided it was bedtime. At seven thirty at night. Talk about pathetic.

Having another drink wouldn't solve her problems. Only make them worse. If people thought she was crazy sober, watch out when she was drunk. She was a million times crazier.

The lights flickered off as she walked out of each room, plunging the house into darkness. The dark never bothered her. Even now, after those dumb flowers and notes left on her porch, it didn't bother her. She refused to be scared. To allow anyone to frighten her. If that's what the person was trying to do. Why did she think that? It had to be her annoying neighbor trying to be his obnoxious self.

Turning on the small lamp on her nightstand, it cast just enough glow for her to be able to read a few chapters before going to bed. She didn't always like to read, but some nights she needed the help to fall asleep, and a good boring book always did the trick.

Seven thirty was way too early to go to bed. Having a drink was out. She needed to stop using shots of whiskey to chase away the pain, the anger. She should apologize to Zoe and Rina, but she'd wait until tomorrow. Her temper was still up a bit and she didn't want to take any more out on them than she already had. That's why reading a book was the perfect solution. It would calm her down. Or she could pull the bottle out. Just one little shot.

She knew what else could calm her down. One person.

A door creaked.

Her head whipped to her bedroom door tightly shut. What was that?

Another creak. This time, she thought it sounded like the second board in front of the hallway bathroom that always squeaked.

She set the alarm. She was positive. There could be no doubt since she checked it three times to make sure. As she punched in the numbers, she couldn't even figure out why the obsession to make sure it was set hit her. She didn't scare easily. Maybe it was because she didn't trust Mathias. Sometimes, he had the weirdest look in his eyes. Could he be that upset she didn't acknowledge the flowers he left?

Swiping her phone from the bed, she cut off the lamp and dashed to the closet, closing the door as quietly as possible. Crouching behind her long dresses, which she didn't have many because she preferred the short, sexy kind, she tried to hide as far back in the corner as she could.

"Keep your shit together."

The phone shook in her hand as she scrolled through her contacts. Why? She was always calm and in charge. Her hand shouldn't be shaking even a tiny bit.

She hit dial. After three rings, relief swept in she hadn't realized she needed.

"Sauer, I need you."

"Dee, why are you whispering? What's going on?"

"He's in my house."

"Who? What is..."

The closet door swung open.

The phone fell.

Clothes rustled.

"You stealthy little bitch. Come out, come out, wherever you are. I only want to play."

She *was* a bitch. How many times did people call her that? Didn't she just act like one earlier tonight?

She didn't give two shits what people thought about her. She was confident in herself and everything she did.

So why was she crouched in the closet just waiting for this douche to find her?

Her hand brushed a heel. Her favorite heel, if she wasn't mistaken. It gave her a good three extra inches to her height. And in her sexy black dress that scooped low in the front and barely reached her ass, the red high heels added just the right mixture to the outfit.

Wrapping her hand around the shoe as tightly as possible, she lunged forward, crashing into the man. "Then let's play, asshole." There was no hesitation as she swung the shoe, connecting with his thigh.

6

BLOOD RUNNING DOWN. Screams filtering in the air. Grunts of pain. The sirens in the distance. It all replayed in her mind what happened only minutes ago. Mere seconds had to have gone by as she rolled around her bedroom floor fighting off a man whose strength scared her. If not for nailing him in the thigh with her heel, he would've overpowered her with ease. Thank God she had such great aim. Although, her target had been his face, so her aim was actually pretty bad.

One second he was wrapping his hands around her throat, and the next he was jumping up and running out of her room. She didn't understand why until someone burst into her room, a gun waving in her face. She almost picked up her bloody heel to whip it at his face until she realized he was in a uniform. Officer Spencer. Decent guy, most of the time.

He had helped her outside to the ambulance that arrived rather quickly. Or maybe more time passed than she realized. She didn't know what was going on. Her head pounded. Her nerves were wired high. For the first time in her life, she felt truly afraid.

"What are you doing?"

Dee glanced up to a face filled with so much agony, if she hadn't been sitting, she would've fallen to her knees. "Sauer?"

He looked panicked before stepping into her space, his lips getting precariously close to hers. "You called me. You... put that damn gauze back on your head." He grabbed her hand and shoved the gauze back to the small cut she received fighting with her attacker.

Well, he didn't exactly shove it, but the touch of his hand anywhere on her was a serious jolt to her body.

"You're bleeding. Don't you dare take this off until it stops."

"Most of this isn't my blood."

He leaned closer again, his eyes directly on hers. She noticed he couldn't take his eyes away from her. Was it because he enjoyed looking at her so intensely? Or was it because he couldn't stand to see the blood covering her body?

"Dee..."

"I'm fine."

"You are not fine. You were attacked in your home. You're bleeding—"

"I'm fine."

"And the man—"

"I'm totally fine."

"Got away before—"

"It's not a big—"

Lips covered hers, effectively cutting off more of her protests that she was fine. Who was she kidding? She wasn't fine. She wasn't even close to being fine. Not when Sauer's lips were anchored to her as if she would sink to the bottom of the ocean unless he kept her afloat.

And she needed him to keep her afloat. To keep her sane. In the same token, she didn't want him to know anything that happened. She could take care of herself. Why did she call him? She could handle this problem on her own. She always did. She couldn't be scared anymore because she had to take care of herself. Relying on a man like her mother had would not happen. Not to her.

Oh, but this kiss. She couldn't get enough.

She increased the intensity of the kiss. If that was possible. Winding her arms around his neck, she pulled him closer. A soft groan echoed around them. He liked that. She liked it more. And she needed more.

She attempted to pull him even closer, to align herself to every hard contour of his body when he pulled away. He grabbed her hand holding the gauze and slapped it back onto her wound.

"You kissed me."

"I did."

"You stopped."

His hand increased the pressure on her wound. "Stop talking."

She grinned wickedly. "And here I thought you were this shy guy. You're very demanding right now."

Eyes narrowing, he leaned closer, his hot breath enticing her to close the distance. "You scared the shit out of me. This is what happens."

"Maybe I'll do it more often. I like this side of you."

He groaned right before he kissed her again. A kiss as sweet as the first, but so much shorter. He pulled away, resting his head against her forehead.

"What happened?"

She itched for his lips to touch hers again. Kissing was better than talking. Talking sucked, actually.

"Dee..."

"I don't know. Some guy broke in and attacked me."

He stepped back as a paramedic cleared his throat behind him. "I'll be right back."

She watched as he walked away without another word.

What the hell? He kissed her and just walked away. God, the man could aggravate her without effort.

And damn if she didn't like it.

———

SAUER TOOK a deep breath before stepping into her home. It felt so wrong to be entering her house without her permission, without her to be the one inviting him in just because. So wrong on so many levels.

Officer Spencer stood by her bedroom door glancing in his direction as he got closer.

"Yo, Sauer, what are you doing here? This isn't a homicide."

Thank God for that. "Dee and I are friends. She called me right before he..." He couldn't even finish that sentence. The minute he heard the muffled scream and what sounded like fighting, his heart stopped beating. He didn't hesitate as he rushed to his house phone and called it in as he listened with bated breaths to the struggles on his cell phone. It was the worst thing he'd ever experienced in his life.

Spencer nodded. "Susan's here already. Dee's okay. She's one tough woman."

"Who got here first?"

"I did. I was about two minutes away. Nobody was here when I arrived, except for Dee. The front door was wide open. I found Dee in her room just sitting on the floor. She didn't say much to me when I tried to ask her questions. It was sorta strange. The few times I've interacted with her, she's always been very talkative."

Susan popped her head out of the room. "She was attacked, Spencer. What do you expect?" She glanced at him. "Hey, Sauer."

"Hi, Susan. Find anything good?"

Her brow rose, yet her eyes twinkled with tenderness. "Blood. She got him good in the thigh. He'll probably need medical attention."

He could've figured that out on his own with the blood covering Dee's clothes. It'd probably take years to erase that image from his brain.

"Anything other than blood?"

She smiled. "You'll be the first to know. He disarmed the alarm somehow because Dee said she set it. I haven't looked at it yet."

Sauer left them, deciding he'd better get back to Dee. He wasn't sure why he walked away from her. Probably because he would've kept kissing her and kissing her until his heart stopped racing from the adrenaline rush. He never wanted to feel this panicked again in his life. He lived on the outskirts of Waite Park, a smaller town that merged with St. Cloud. He liked living in the country. The peace and quiet. The wide expanse of outdoors. The beautiful nature surrounding him.

He sure in the hell didn't like how long it had taken him to reach her house. It took him nearly twenty minutes to get here, and that was with him speeding the entire way.

He approached Dee, immediately grasping her face. She didn't shove him away. If anything, she tried to scoot closer. He held her face gently as he rested his forehead against hers. The wound near her temple had stopped bleeding, now patched up. He heard the paramedic say it didn't require stitches, but it bled like a gutted pig to Sauer. Maybe it was just seeing any amount of blood on her that made it appear that way.

Sighing deeply, he then inhaled the sweet scent he couldn't get enough of when he was near her. She smelled faintly like vanilla and a splash of lavender. Perhaps from her shampoo. He loved it. He rarely got this close to her to enjoy it as he was doing now. How long would she continue to let him hold her?

He couldn't believe he was holding her to begin with. Where had this bravery come from?

"Sauer?"

He placed a soft kiss to her forehead.

"I'm okay. As much as I enjoyed the kisses, you don't have to do that anymore."

She was effectively telling him to back off. But she said she liked this side of him. His dominant side. Shit. He didn't know he had one of those.

Then he saw her.

All of that blood covering her.

He went into a panic. He wanted to strip her down to nothing. Needed to remove the evidence that someone attacked her. That someone tried to hurt her.

Damn. He wanted to kiss her again.

"Are you reverting to your shy self? Talk to me."

His lips left another kiss on her forehead. She shivered. A sign she liked that? *Don't hold your breath.* Didn't she just say he didn't have to kiss her anymore? More like she meant, don't kiss me anymore. Then why wasn't she shoving him away?

Her hands tightened around his waist, her fingernails digging in slightly. The pain was nothing. He'd endure any amount of pain just to have her hands on him. Her getting attacked was all it took to get her into his arms. Why? This wasn't right.

"Sauer, please..."

He tilted her head to meet his gaze and answered her soft-spoken plea to talk to her—with a kiss. The kiss was gentle. Light and feathery. She needed tenderness right now, even as his body screamed to pull her roughly against him. The shock was close to consuming him. She needed to change her clothes. He couldn't look down and witness the blood.

And the guy got away. As soon as he heard sirens in the distance, he fled. The only consolation was Dee got him good in the thigh with her shoe. Hence, the blood covering her. As soon as he got his hands on the bastard—

Dee moaned.

He slowed the kiss, unaware he had turned it more passionately than he intended. Nibbling her bottom lip, he then soothed the spot with his tongue before pulling away.

He sought her gaze, waiting for her to open her beautiful brown eyes.

"Why do you keep kissing me?" Her face turned stiff as she raised a brow. "You better start speaking before I get pissed."

"Do you want me to pack you a bag or can you handle it?"

She jerked back, her brows dipping in confusion. "What?"

"We have no idea why this man attacked you or if he plans to return. You're coming home with me."

Sweet laughter filled the air. "Don't be silly. I'll be fine."

Leaning in, he got nose to nose with her. "You said you liked this side of me. Well, here it is. I'm not leaving you alone tonight. Not until I can calm down. I just might need a few more kisses to make that happen."

Her eyes clouded with desire. "You make it hard to argue with you."

"Then don't argue."

She sounded breathless as she said, "Okay."

He nodded, so glad she decided to stop arguing. He didn't know if he could take it. He couldn't even believe he told her what to do, to pack a bag. But he didn't lie. This was what ensued. The fear took a hold of him and made him act crazy. Just thinking about leaving her by herself sent him into a panic.

"Can you tell me what happened?"

"Like I said—"

"Don't give me that short version you gave last time. What did you do tonight?"

The cringe that crossed her face confused him, but he waited patiently for her to talk. He had the most patience in the world, something that irritated people, especially suspects.

"I went out for drinks with Zoe and Rina, and left early." She hesitated, like she wanted to say more. "I came home and there was another dumb rose and note on my doorstep. I threw that shit away and went inside. I decided to go to bed because..." She stopped talking again. "And I went to my bedroom. Not a minute later, I heard a noise in the hallway. A noise I should've never heard unless someone was walking, so I grabbed my phone and hid in the closet. You know the rest."

"What do you mean another rose and a note? From who? What did it say?"

He didn't mean to whip out question after question to

her, but the panic that entered back at home ratcheted up another notch. Almost painful, dropping him to his knees.

"I think it's from my neighbor, but I'm not sure. It didn't say who it's from. It just said I'm sorry."

The air left his body as he almost staggered back in excruciating pain. A quick sucker-punch to the gut. I'm sorry? No. It couldn't be.

"Did you keep the note?"

She rolled her eyes. The gesture should've annoyed him, but it only made her look so damn adorable.

"I said I threw the note away with the flower."

"Where?"

"In the garbage."

He grabbed her face, breathing in deeply. "Not the time to be sarcastic."

Her lips turned up into a sweet grin, devilish in a way, but sweet, nonetheless. "Are you going to kiss me again?"

"Are you trying to make me kiss you by acting this way?"

"Maybe."

He was tempted to wipe that cocky smirk off her face with another kiss; instead, he dropped his hands and took a step back. If she knew why he wanted to see that note, maybe she'd act scared for once.

"What garbage can did you throw the note away in?"

"You're stuck on that note, aren't you? Why?"

"What garbage can?"

"Tell me why."

"Garbage?"

She huffed in indignation and then crossed her arms as her brows rose.

He could play that game as well. She thought he was a shy guy. Yeah, he wouldn't dispute that. But his job—just call him a bulldog. Nobody messed with him, especially the bad guys. He wasn't about to let some asshole, some killer out there, hurt her. She wanted to be difficult? Well, he could be, too.

He turned around and started to walk away.

"Where are you going, Sauer? You can't just walk away from me. I didn't tell you what garbage can I threw it away in."

He looked back at her. "I need to do my job, whether you're going to cooperate with me or not. I'm not going to let anyone hurt you. I'll search every damn garbage can if I have to."

She deflated right before his eyes. Her posture slouched, her eyes turned down, her smile slid away. "On the side of the house."

"Thank you." He cursed under his breath when he realized he didn't ask one of the most important questions of the night. "Did you get a good look at his face?"

"No. It was dark. Maybe he has dark hair, that's all I can really say. It happened so quickly."

"Not enough for a sketch?"

"No. Why would a simple break-in require a sketch artist?"

"You're hurt. Nothing about this was simple. I'll be right back." He started for the house again to tell Susan the new developments.

"Sauer!"

He stopped walking. Before he could turn around, she asked, "You know who did this, don't you?"

"I have an idea, yes." He kept walking before he gave in and pulled her into his arms again. It wasn't his shyness that had him walking away. It was his determination to find this killer and keep Dee safe at all costs.

DEE LOOKED around Sauer's foyer, more so than the last time she came here, liking the simplicity of it. He had a small coat rack in the corner, probably because there was no closet to hang coats. A long green rug that matched the gray walls ran a pathway down the hallway that she knew led to the kitchen at the end and the living room to the right. She assumed the opening a short ways down to the left led to the bedrooms.

A cute house. No neighbors surrounded him as he lived a few miles out of town in the country. It was very quiet. Kind of like him. His silence sometimes grated on her nerves. Got her so fired up. No man could ever fire her up the way he could.

He just didn't listen to her either. No matter how many times she tried to tell him she'd be okay on her own, even as the thought disturbed her a bit, he argued in the silent way he had perfected that she would be going home with him. End of discussion. He actually said those words to her, then remained silent while she badgered him with question after question after question about who attacked her.

Nothing. Zilch. Sauer refused to say anything. It royally pissed her off. She wasn't some meek, mild woman who needed saving from a man. Of course, she didn't say that to him. Deep down, she liked the attention he was giving her. She liked that he seemed to care enough to want to keep her safe. No one had ever made her feel safe like that before. No one had ever seemed to care like he did.

"I'll show you the bathroom. I'll put your stuff in the spare room. And then you can take a shower."

"A shower?"

He pointed up and down her body.

She followed the path. She had changed clothes at her house, gladly handing them over to Susan as evidence. Then she saw it. A smear of blood on her arm.

So disgusting.

Evidence of the man attacking her sucked the life right out of her.

"Come on. Shower."

For once, she silently followed Sauer. Or more like, he dragged her by the hand to the bathroom. There wasn't much she could say. A shower sounded like the best damn idea ever. She needed to wipe every speck of that man off her. Suddenly, she couldn't stand it. It was as if a million tiny bugs were invading her skin. Prickling goose bumps scoured over every inch.

She practically slammed the door in his face, and with jerky movements, ripped her clothes off. Each article of clothing hit the trashcan next to the toilet without hesitation. They weren't the clothes she had been wearing when she was attacked, but still. She couldn't stand the sight of them anymore.

Jumping into the shower, she twisted the knob and let the water rain down. Cold. Hot. She couldn't tell. All she knew was she needed to feel clean.

Grabbing a bottle from the corner of the tub without checking if it was soap or shampoo or conditioner, she poured an enormous glob into her hand and started to furiously rub everywhere. Her chest, her arms, her legs, her hair, her face. Every single inch of her body.

She just kept pouring and scrubbing and pouring and scrubbing before she realized nothing more came out of the container. Nothing but air.

The bottle fell from her hands.

As did the tears. Slowly at first, then a little heavier.

Slumping down, she wrapped her arms around her waist. The tears wouldn't stop. She wasn't a crier. Tears signaled weakness. An emotion that solved nothing.

How many times had her mother cried when another man walked out of their lives? Every time. Did the tears do anything? Did they magically make the man reappear? Did it mend her mother's broken heart? No. They did diddly-squat.

Why was she crying? Besides a bump on her head and a few aches and pains from tussling around with him, she was fine. She hurt him. She jabbed him good in the thigh. Tears were useless. Yet, she couldn't stop them as the water poured over her head.

Nothing registered. Not the water. Not the tears. Not the voice calling to her. Just complete numbness.

A pair of warm hands grasped her shoulders. Then suddenly, Sauer cocooned her in a warm embrace.

"Shit, Dee. This water is freezing."

She buried her head into Sauer's chest, the rough material of his shirt almost soothing. He had stepped into the shower clothed. To comfort her. To help her. Why did he always have to be such a nice guy?

The water stopped flowing. His warmth disappeared, then just as quickly it was replaced with a towel. So soft and inviting. Without warning, he had her cradled in his arms, his clothes soaked to the bone.

"You're shivering like crazy." He kissed her head.

He smelled divine. Or was that her? She smelled like him now after using his stuff from the shower. She could get used to this if she let herself. Why couldn't she? Would it be so wrong to give in to her feelings?

Everything was wrong. Didn't she learn anything when every time her mother let in a new man and he waltzed out just as quickly? Life was easier when she just dated and got rid of the man first. No broken heart. No tears. No reason to feel anything remotely bad.

As soon as he laid her on the softest bed she'd ever felt in her life and the covers yanked over her body, she missed him.

"Sauer..."

Her eyes pleaded with him with what she couldn't say out loud. She needed him to hold her just a little longer. She needed his strong, warm arms around her. That was all.

He hesitated, but only for a second before he started to disrobe right before her eyes. She imagined he would've never done that in front of her if his clothes hadn't been wet.

Just like that, he was naked like her. She didn't have time to revel in his hard body as he quickly joined her in bed, nestling nicely under the covers. He grabbed her immediately. She didn't hesitate to rest her head on his chest. His warmth instantly soothed her.

"You're shaking. It's okay. Everything's okay now."

Until he said that, she hadn't realized she was shaking. But she was. From the cold. Because she didn't even take a warm shower. From the attack. Because she'd never been attacked before. She could've died tonight.

"Who was that man?"

He rubbed his hand up and down her back, his quiet breathing calming her. His lack of words, not so much.

"Sauer?"

"I don't know."

She lifted her head. "You do, too." Suddenly, her timid behavior from moments before disappeared. She couldn't believe she acted so weak. That wasn't her. She was strong and in control of her emotions. She wasn't starting to feel better just because he was comforting her, his hands roaming her back and soothing her. Not the reason at all.

"Tell me now, Sauer."

"I don't know. If I did, I'd be arresting his ass for even thinking about you."

"What are you leaving out? You're not telling me something."

He kissed her forehead. "Nothing for you to worry about."

She slapped his chest. "I'm not some meek and mild woman who needs to be taken care of. Tell me."

He laughed. The man had the audacity to laugh. "You're the strongest woman I know." His hand glided down her back and up again as he kissed her forehead once more. "But I'm still not saying anything."

"Why not?"

"Because it's my job. It's your job to stay out of it."

She bent her head, inhaling his musky scent, relishing in the heavenly smell. "Why do you even care?"

"Why wouldn't I? You're amazing. I've known that since the moment I met you..." He chuckled. "Even if I only said one word to you. I always get tongue-tied around beautiful women. But you, it's like ten times worse."

"It's rather cute when you blush and stutter over your words."

"I don't blush."

Her eyes lifted. "You do. I wouldn't be good for you. We're so mismatched."

His brows furrowed. She had to admit, she didn't like it when he looked sad. "Why would you say that? You're perfect."

"I'm a bitch."

"I wouldn't change one thing about you."

She slapped his chest again. "Oh my God. Did you just agree I'm a bitch?"

He laughed. "Of course not. So you don't hold back what you say. That doesn't make you a bitch. Some people can't stand that, but I like everything about you. I wouldn't change one thing."

"I need you to start acting like a man I hate. Not one who makes me wish for things I can't have."

"Is this you trying to maintain only friends between us?" He lowered his mouth, kissing her gently. "We are naked in this bed."

"Why aren't you doing something about that?"

His mouth moved away, making her wish he never had. "Because you're still shivering. Because I'd never take advantage of you. What happened tonight affected you. You never responded to the comment about being friends, which makes me believe you still want to be *just* friends."

"We *are* naked, Sauer."

"And?"

Her head fell to his chest once again. "And sometimes you're almost too perfect. You know exactly what I need even when I don't. I like you holding me."

His hot breath flowed down her neck, making her shiver for an entirely different reason. "I like it, too."

Her head jerked up. "You're sick. You've been kissing me and you're sick."

"I'm much better. That soup did wonders."

She gave him a stern look, trying to make him squirm as most people did under that look, but he just stared back at her. She couldn't decipher the emotion in his eyes. He had kissed her. Shy, sweet Sauer, who couldn't even string together a fluid sentence when asking her out, had kissed her. Each kiss was better than the last. She couldn't be mad at him for kissing her, even if she did get his cold from it.

"You better be because I don't want to get sick." With that, she lay back down, resting perfectly on his chest. Small, jerky movements rippled below her head. He was laughing. The man had the nerve to laugh again. Damn, if she didn't want to laugh with him. Instead, she snuggled closer, letting his warmth seep into her bones.

Then silence rented the air. She didn't know what to say to the friends comment. It'd be much better if they stayed friends. She liked Sauer. Like, really liked him. More than friends could ruin everything. She didn't want to lose him from her life. He hadn't been in her life that long and she didn't want to lose that. Becoming more than friends would make her lose him. She knew it with complete certainty.

Every relationship she had always failed. Just like her mother. Being more than friends would never work.

Lying naked together was completely normal. Friends could do that. Of course they could. There was nothing weird about this.

Talk about temptation, though. Every time his hand wove up then down her back, she wanted him to keep going lower. He never did. He was the utmost gentleman. Just one more reason why Sauer was one of a kind. She could be naked in his arms and not take advantage of the situation.

Or shit. Maybe he didn't find her attractive. Maybe he didn't want to have sex with her.

No. Dumb thought. She could feel his hard erection against her leg, because she obviously liked to torture them both by draping her leg across him. He was feeling plenty at the moment, but wasn't straying into that territory. One, because he knew that's not what she needed right now. She just needed his comfort. His warmth to surround her.

Second, because he knew she only wanted friendship. He wouldn't cross that line even if he wanted to.

Ugh, but they were naked. She had never in her life laid with a man like this and something sexual didn't happen. So weird and unusual. But she loved it, just lying here quietly with him as his hands calmed her down.

For the first time in her life, she found a man who understood her, who liked her for her, crazy bitchy tendencies and all.

Sauer was making it hard not to fall in love.

Oh, shit.

She couldn't afford to fall in love with the man. But like the idiot she could be sometimes, she did.

She just fell in love with the sweetest, shyest guy on the planet.

7

IDIOT! Who sleeps with a beautiful woman—a naked beautiful woman—and doesn't do anything other than hold her? Him. That's who. Only shy, awkward Sauer would do something like that.

He imagined most men would've taken her up on her subtle offer of going further. She insinuated that he could've if he wanted to, because they had been naked.

But he heard her voice loud and clear. The pain, the slight fear. That man attacking her had affected her more than she wanted to admit. He would never take advantage of her like that, no matter how badly he wanted her.

He opened the oven door and shoved the bacon in. Did she like bacon? Maybe she didn't eat meat. Was she a vegetarian?

No. That was a dumb thought. She made him chicken noodle soup.

"Calm down. There's nothing to be nervous about." He blew out a breath and grabbed some eggs from the fridge.

He couldn't stand the temptation lying in his arms. He had hopped out of bed the moment he woke up and decided to make breakfast. Seeing her sleep so peacefully had made his control almost snap. He wanted to wake her up, his hands roaming to places they didn't venture to last night.

Only friends. That thought stopped any movement from him and made him flee from the bed. Last night had taken a toll on Dee. She was always so strong and in control. Last night, she needed comfort. He provided it as best as he could. Like a good friend. Which was something she still obviously wanted to maintain between them.

She claimed that she wouldn't be good for him. He laughed as he whipped the eggs. That was clearly her way of saying he just wasn't the right guy for her. She wasn't attracted to him. Because she was perfect in every way. She'd be perfect for him.

"Damn it."

"What's the matter?"

Sauer whipped around, almost flinging eggs everywhere as the whisk shook in his hand. "You're awake."

Dee smiled, the sleepiness still evident in her eyes as she brushed her hair back from her face. "Is something wrong?"

"Nope." He shook his head. No way in hell he was going to share his feelings. A guy could only handle rejection so many times. "I'm making breakfast."

Her brow rose. "I know. I could smell the bacon."

"Right. I didn't mean to wake you up yet."

Oh God. He couldn't handle it. He was reverting to his shy, awkward self. He had no idea what to say to her, so he did the only thing he could think of. He turned back toward the stove and poured the egg mixture into the pan sitting on the front left burner.

"You sure you're okay, Sauer?"

He flashed a smile. "I'm good." He started to spoon the

eggs around. He should pop some toast in, too. Did she like toast? All he had to do was ask.

Not exactly tension, but something stretched between them in the kitchen. He was afraid to turn around and ask her even a simple question, like, did she want some toast.

He shivered as a pair of arms circled his waist. She rested her head against his back.

"What's the matter? You're barely talking to me."

"I apologize."

She chuckled. "I am not mad you made bacon. I love bacon."

He set the spoon down and turned around. Her arms fell away as she took a step back. "I was talking about last night."

"You didn't do anything wrong."

"I...the bed...naked..." He ran a hand over his face as he managed to take a deep breath. Now wasn't the time to stumble over his words.

Her soft fingers brushed his cheek. "I should thank you for last night. I needed that. This morning, I feel rejuvenated. Let's find this bastard. Nobody attacks me and gets away with it."

His jaw clenched. "I will find this bastard. Not you."

"Whatever."

"You'll listen to me, Dee." He took a step closer, a breath away. "I don't want to see you get hurt. Let me do my job."

She bit her lip as a sneaky grin emerged. "Every time it comes to your job, you get so dominant and assertive. Then, in the next breath, so shy. You are a very complex man."

"No. I'm pretty simple. I'm good at my job. You leave this to me."

Her lips brushed his. "I never listen well." She laughed as she backed away. "You're cute when you get upset."

He groaned and turned back to the eggs. She was going

to be the death of him. Some man, most likely the killer he was looking for, attacked her, and she wanted to argue with him about who would catch him. Why did every little thing about her make him like her more? Even when she was annoying the hell out of him. Refusing to listen to him.

"Who is this guy?"

He gave a few shakes of the salt and pepper into the eggs.

"Sauer?"

He pulled the bread from the cupboard and untied the bag, pulling two slices out. He'd make some toast and she could choose herself whether she wanted one. He decided he wasn't going to ask. She was really starting to piss him off.

"I know you know something about this guy. Just tell me."

Scratch that. He was passed pissed off. She just wouldn't let it go.

"I hate it when you ignore me like this."

He slapped two pieces of bread into the toaster and hit the button.

"Sauer!"

Slowly, he turned toward her. "Did you want butter, jelly, or peanut butter on your toast?"

Her lips fell into a tight line. "Are you kidding me right now? Tell me—"

"Butter, jelly—"

"Take your toast and shove it."

He smiled. "Duly noted. You don't like toast." He grabbed the jelly from the fridge and tried to ignore the rising tension in the kitchen.

He didn't care how mad he made her. He wasn't going to share any information about the case with her. Not one tiny bit. It was his job to protect her, and by giving her information, he knew she wouldn't stay out of it. That wasn't her style. To protect her, he had to find this killer on his own, whether or not it made her mad. What did it matter? They were only friends. Friends got mad at each other and moved on. Now, if he were her boyfriend, perhaps that would make him a little more nervous. Good thing they were only friends.

"If you don't start—"

The doorbell rang.

Sauer set the spoon down after scrambling the eggs some more and glanced at Dee, who looked ready to explode. God, she was so beautiful angry. He walked out of the kitchen without a word. Surprisingly, she didn't speak or follow him.

He opened the door to Ben and Zeke and gestured them inside. "Hey, guys. I hope you found something good."

"Not really." Zeke sniffed, pleasure lighting up in his eyes. "Bacon."

Ben chuckled. "Dude, we just ate. How's Dee?"

Sauer cleared his throat. "Pissed. I won't tell her about the case. She'll just try to do things on her own and I won't let that happen. Did you interview her neighbor?"

"Yep. He didn't send the roses or notes. Although, he was creepy as shit. He has a real thing for her. Ben and I put the fear in him."

"She barely saw her attacker, but I don't think it's her neighbor. I think she would've recognized him. Maybe the guy who broke in is different from the one who sent the roses and notes. It'd be better if he left those things."

Ben nodded in understanding. "We hear ya, Sauer, but we don't think he gave her that stuff. Like Zeke said, he's creepy. He watches her. He mentioned seeing a guy stop by Sunday night. Knocked on the door and then bent down.

Which was him probably leaving the rose and note the first time. He didn't get a good look at the guy, though. Said he was tall. That's about it."

"Damn it." Sauer blew out a deep breath. "This isn't good. Vanessa...it was a messy crime scene."

"Dee's tough. Don't worry." Zeke clapped him on the shoulder. "Just curious. How come you didn't call Newman last night? Not that Ben and I mind helping you, but he is your partner."

Sauer shrugged. He was still trying to figure that out. Last night, he just knew he wanted Zeke and Ben on it if he couldn't do it himself. "You guys are close to her. Zoe and Rina...I just thought it'd be best."

"Newman okay?" Ben asked, the concern prominent.

"Yeah, he's good."

"Are *you* okay?" Zeke glanced around the hallway. "Dee still sleeping?"

"She's in the kitchen. Want some breakfast?"

"Bacon!" Zeke's smile grew.

Ben rolled his eyes. "We just ate."

Sauer laughed as he led the way to the kitchen. The eggs were probably burning right about now. Dee sat on a stool by the island in the center of the kitchen.

"Oh, look who it is. Start talking." Dee's hard glare didn't waver once from Zeke or Ben. "Because Sauer ain't saying shit."

Zeke glanced between him and her, his brows high. "How do you stay strong under that scary gaze, Sauer?"

He didn't smile. Not even a small grin as he stirred the eggs. "Because I prefer her to stay safe. Not run right into trouble." His eyes softened as he glanced at her, hoping the anger would disappear. It didn't.

"Well?"

Ben shook his head. "I'm not saying anything. I don't wanna be on Sauer's bad side. I've never seen it before, but I'm slightly worried it'd be really bad."

"Worse than my bad side?" Dee stood up and slammed her hands to her hips.

Zeke chuckled. "Actually, now that I think about it, you're all bark and no bite. I'm going to respect Sauer and leave it to him what he wants you to know."

Her head whipped to him, the fury blazing like heavy flames. "I am not amused. This man tried to hurt me. I want to know who it is."

Sauer dropped his eyes from her, unable to handle the pain he saw behind all the anger. "You can hate me, Dee. As long as you're safe, I'm okay with that."

"Damn you, Sauer!" Dee stalked out of the kitchen.

"Wow. Everyone, and I mean everyone, always caves in. How do you do it, man?" Zeke asked with a small laugh.

He shrugged, pulling the eggs off the hot burner. "I won't compromise her safety just because she gets upset." He looked at them. "You know as well as I do that if she gathers information, she'll head right into the danger. She's not like Zoe and Rina who prefer to let you guys handle things. Dee likes to handle things all on her own. This is one thing I'm not willing to let her handle. Last night..."

"It's hard to see the one you love hurt, isn't it?" The words left Ben's mouth soft and low, reminding him of Rina.

He averted his eyes. Love? Could he love Dee already?

Well, that was a dumb question. Of course he could. He did. Last night had cemented that decision with ease. It was hard to see her hurt. Hard wasn't even the right word. He couldn't explain even to himself how that made him feel last night.

"Does she know?" Zeke asked quietly.

"Know what?"

Zeke glanced at the hallway, then answered in a whisper, "That you love her, Sauer. It's kinda obvious. I never saw it before, but it's not hard to see now."

"Rina said one time that we should've tried to set you up with Dee. I dismissed the idea because you're a shy guy and Dee is...well, Dee is the exact opposite."

Zeke nodded at Ben's words. "Strangely, it kinda makes you the perfect guy for her. You handle her like I've never seen anyone handle her."

Sauer's jaw clenched. "I wasn't *handling* her. I just refuse to let her get hurt."

Zeke held his hands up in apology. "You know what I'm saying. Not many can withstand an argument with Dee."

"You should tell her."

Sauer whipped his eyes to Ben. "I think not."

"She's mighty pissed right now. Telling her you love her might lessen that," Zeke said with encouragement.

"Did you guys talk to Susan? She get any prints off the note? What about the alarm system?"

Ben and Zeke shared a look at his change of subject. He didn't care. He wasn't going to talk about his feelings for Dee with anyone. If he wanted to broach the subject, the only person he'd be doing that with was Dee.

"We talked to her this morning. She got two prints. She needs a sample of Dee's. Could be hers." Zeke tossed his head toward the hallway. "Can you swing by the lab this morning with her?"

He nodded.

"Nothing was damaged with the alarm. We called her company and the code was entered to disarm the alarm. He got her code somehow." Zeke shrugged. "Or he's a seasoned criminal. He could have a device that disarms alarms."

Sauer hoped that wasn't true because then it could mean they had more victims they weren't aware of yet. He turned toward the oven when the timer went off. The bacon was done.

"Ready for some bacon?"

Zeke clapped his hands. "Am I ever!"

Ben chuckled, then nodded. "Well, I'm not gonna pass it up. But maybe we should take it to go."

Sauer looked questioningly at them. He saw them communicate silently together. He had always been jealous of their relationship, how they could communicate with just a simple look. He and Newman could never do that. Simple things, sure, especially concerning a case. But things like this, never.

"You can stay for breakfast."

Zeke smiled. "Na, you made breakfast for Dee. Maybe she doesn't know it yet, but you're perfect for her. Start showing her just how perfect you are. I'd love to see her happy with a great guy like you."

He cracked a grin. "Thanks, Zeke, but we're only friends."

———

HE PAUSED in front of the closed bathroom door and listened to the shower. The food was going to get cold. If she did what she did last night, crumbling into pain in the shower, the food would go Arctic cold. After thirty minutes of waiting, wondering, he had knocked on the door last night. Nothing. No words echoed back. Not even a quick, "be right out." He didn't realize he had the strength, but so much concern for her had him twisting the knob. He had called her name a few times, and when no answer came, he peeked behind the curtain to see her kneeling on the tub floor in so much agony. He didn't hesitate once to step in and comfort her, clothes on and all.

His eyes grazed to the door handle. Would he have to do it again this morning? He would. He'd do anything for Dee. Even make her hate him by refusing to share information about the case.

Zeke and Ben left five minutes ago. She hadn't been showering long. He'd give her more time before he breached the threshold.

Walking away, he sat down on the edge of his bed, running his hand over his head. Getting used to the buzz cut would take time. He never cut his hair this short before. Maybe it hadn't been such a great idea to cut his hair. He'd rub his head raw with stress. Back and forth. Back and forth. The worry, the nerves, the pain in her eyes. It all poured out of him as he rubbed his hand over his head.

"That is sexy as hell."

His hand dropped as his eyes popped to the doorway. Dee stood with a towel wrapped around her slender body, her fiery-red hair a wet mess. She looked so beautiful he lost his breath for a moment.

And naked. Just a tiny towel covering her gorgeous body.

She glided to him, rendering him even more speechless when she rubbed her soft hand over his head.

"I love this feeling. What does it feel like to you?"

Words still wouldn't form. Why did he always revert to his shy self when it came to matters of the heart? She was right. When it came to his job, he wouldn't hesitate to get into her face about it. But this, he was putty in her hands. A geeky, shy guy.

"Stop ignoring me, Sauer." Her hand slid down his head, grazing his cheek, then went to the simple knot at the towel and undid it with a flick of her wrist. The towel fell to the floor.

He had finally died and gone to heaven. What virile man could ignore a naked woman twice? Not him. If she expected him to, she was in for a rude awakening. He stood up.

"Breakfast is ready."

Who was he kidding? He couldn't make a move toward her when he knew all she wanted was friendship. If she wanted more, that was a different story. Only problem: he couldn't seem to voice it.

"Don't you want me?"

What kind of question was that? Of course he wanted her. He wanted her so badly sometimes it hurt to breathe.

"Yes."

DEE SLOWLY LET out the small breath she had been holding.

"Then what are you waiting for?"

He had stared at her with such passion—intense passion —when she stepped into his room. His eyes had followed her the entire trek from the doorway to where he sat on the bed. His breathing had become heavy when she rubbed his head, his cheeks turning a rosy red. When she dropped the towel, she saw the desire in every facet of his body, especially the thick bulge in his pants.

Yet, he stood up and said breakfast was ready. What was she doing wrong? She never met a man who didn't want to eat her up right away. How much more blatant could she get? So she asked the question she feared to hear the answer to. His answer was yes. Then why was he still standing there not touching her?

"Sauer?"

His jaw clenched, then unclenched, his features softening. "We're just friends. I don't sleep with my friends."

She pointed to the bed and laughed. "You slept naked with me last night."

"Naked, sure, but that wasn't sexual. That was comfort. I can't fully define what that was last night." He groaned. "I'm not a guy who sleeps around with just anybody. I want you. I have for a very long time. But I want more than friendship. If you can't give that to me, then you better put your clothes on."

Wow. That was sure putting her in her place. He was the only man capable of doing that. All. The. Time.

Not once did he stutter. When he was passionate about something, generally his job, he never faltered. His words came out strong and fierce. He was serious with what he just said. He didn't sleep around. What did that make her? Granted, it'd been a while for her, but still. She had her fair share of men between the sheets. Thank God, she didn't give in to Raul. She didn't want any other man anymore. Only Sauer.

But he wanted more than friends. Could she do that?

He nodded, as if her silence was her answer, and started to walk away. She grabbed his hand before he was out of her reach.

"Don't go."

His eyes refused to turn her way. "It's okay, Dee. We'll just be friends."

"No, it's not." She whispered it so softly she was surprised the words even left her mouth. Where was strong and tough Dee? She needed that woman to come out.

He turned her way, his grip becoming stronger. "What are you saying?"

"I suck at relationships, Sauer. Like, really suck at them."

"Me, too." He chuckled. "Shy guy, remember?"

She bit her lip with a sassy smirk and pulled him closer. He didn't hesitate in his steps. "I like your shyness. It's just one of the many reasons you stick out among the rest. In a very good way."

"I like everything about you. I've never had a woman affect me the way you do. Hence, all my garbled words half the time."

She let go of his hand and gripped the edge of his shirt. "I can't promise I won't screw up whatever this is. I don't even know how to define it. What I do know is I don't want to be *just* friends."

His hands curled around hers. "The definition part is easy. Exclusive." His eyes glided to the bed, then back to her. "I won't share with another man."

"Not a problem." A silky smile lit up her face. "I haven't had another man on my mind since you asked me out."

"Umm...guy from the café."

"Lame attempt to try to forget about you. Please, don't remind me. I didn't sleep with him."

He smiled. "Breakfast is ready."

She shook her head as she pushed him a little, his hands still grasping hers firmly at the edge of his shirt. "I want a different kind of breakfast right now."

"Good. So do I. I was just...I don't know...making sure."

She leaned in, kissing his lips lightly. "Don't get shy on me now."

He lifted his hands, hers gliding with him as he pulled his shirt off and tossed it to the floor. "Never." He nodded to the bed. "Lay down. I'll go grab a condom from the bathroom."

"Condoms."

His brows rose in surprise, a little bit of delight mixed in. "Of course. That's what I meant."

She chuckled as he walked out of the room. Jumping on the bed, she settled into the middle, the anticipation rocking her body. She was about to sleep with Sauer. Sweet, caring, loving Sauer.

Did she even deserve such a great guy? Would a relationship work between them? Or was she setting him up to break his heart and hers with it?

When he walked into the room not even a minute later, she decided he was worth the risk. Every single worry that plagued her mind.

This was Sauer. And he was all hers.

8

DEE SHIVERED as Sauer brushed a hand up, then down her stomach. She was still reeling from him walking into the bedroom completely naked after grabbing some condoms. She had asked where he put his clothes. One simple answer echoed around the room. "In the hamper in the bathroom." Sauer was such a sensible guy. She enjoyed watching him walk into the room like that. She almost asked him to walk out and back in again. Like rewinding a good part in a movie.

She was glad once they decided to have sex that he wasn't shy. She liked his shyness. She really did. But in the bedroom, while getting it on, was definitely not something she wanted.

"What are you waiting for?"

A sweet grin punctured his face as he lightly blew on her nipple, then sucked it briefly. "What's the rush?"

"Oh, so you're trying to torture me with anticipation."

"Maybe I'm just enjoying every little sensation, every soft spot on your body, every little cute noise you make as I do something like this." His finger circled her areola, and her breath hitched a little at the contact.

God, every little touch from him made her body crave more. Sauer knew what the hell he was doing. He was making her wild for him and he had barely touched her yet.

"I'm hungry."

"Me, too." His lips grabbed her nipple, tugging, nipping, and devouring it as if it were a delicious cinnamon bun with extra icing.

Oh, yeah, he was hungry all right. So was she. She was so damn ravenous for the man lying next to her. She didn't want him next to her. She wanted him on top, claiming her, branding her, penetrating her. What was he waiting for? She couldn't take this teasing anymore.

"Please, Sauer. I want more. I need more." She turned toward him and tried to grab for the rock-hard erection that had been resting against her thigh, but he was quicker. His hand wrapped around her wrist, stalling her movements.

"You're a force of nature, Dee. Trust me, I like that about you. A lot. But here, in this bedroom, I want to savor you. Just let me have my way right now. Just lie still."

Her brow rose slowly as a grin emerged. "Me, lie still? Did you lace something in your coffee this morning?"

He brought her hand above her head as he rolled her to her back, hovering above her. Finally, he nestled into her body the way she wanted.

"You will lie still until I say so."

"Is that right? Shy Sauer is gonna make me, huh?"

"He's hibernating right now. You get dominant Sauer at the moment." His mouth inched closer to hers. "I've wanted you for a long time." A kiss touched her lips. "Last night scared the shit out of me." Another kiss. "You know how I get when I'm worried about you." One more kiss. "So, yeah, you're going to let me touch every inch of this gorgeous body and lay perfectly still."

For a man who stuttered and screwed up a simple question like asking her out, he sure knew how to make her insides melt. Could this man get any sweeter?

"And if I don't?"

His mouth crushed hers, his tongue diving in with intensity. She matched his pace, letting the kiss consume her. The man knew how to kiss. Before she knew it, he was backing away, lifting his body up.

"Then you get nothing."

She shivered from the cold that hit her body, wanting, needing his body against hers again. "Okay, you win. I won't move."

Without another word, he lowered himself and started to kiss her. A tender peck to the right cheek, then the other. His lips made a path down her neck and up to her ear, his teeth nipping her earlobe, sending tingles everywhere. A man of his word. He didn't forget the other ear as a trail of kisses made their way to the other side.

Her body zinged to life, even more so than before, as he made his way to her breasts again. Time slowed to a stop as he doted on each one, taking his time to kiss, nibble, and suck as if he'd never get to do it again. Never in her life had she let a man take his time like this. Sex was normally a way to have fun, release a little tension. Not this. Not so much passion.

Even if she would've let a man have his way like this, she didn't think they would've put in as much attention and devotion as Sauer did. He didn't miss one spot on her. Kisses sprinkled on her belly, up and down, around her belly button. The entire time, his hands brushed her arms, her breasts, and teasingly down near the spot that was dying for him to touch. Yet he never did. He was building her up so sweetly, she knew when she exploded it would be the best orgasm of her life.

His mouth finally made it to the ultimate prize, his hot breath telling her the best was yet to come. When his tongue licked and suckled faster than the kisses that had covered her body, she couldn't stop herself from arching off the bed and moaning in delight.

His tongue danced, pulling every emotion out of her that was possible. He touched her in more ways than just physical. Tears started to well in the corner of her eyes as the desire hit her. She cried out, grabbing his head, wanting to pull at his hair, yet settled with rubbing it as her orgasm shot through the roof.

She continued to rub his head as he moved back up her body and planted a kiss to her lips. Normally, she hated when a guy did that—kissed her down there, then kissed her on the lips. She didn't want to taste herself like that. But Sauer. Hell, no. She wanted his lips on hers no matter where they were before. Her hands tightened on his head as the kissed turned intense.

She loved it when their kisses went from slow and sweet to passionate and unbridled. Only Sauer could ever manage to pull that deep emotion out of her.

A few crinkles sounded as Sauer shifted around her, then suddenly, he slid into her. For the first time in her life, she felt complete. Whole. Where she belonged.

He extracted his mouth from hers, his breathing heavy. "God, you feel so good." He kissed her lightly. "You taste so good."

"Can I move yet, or do I still need to lie still?"

He grinned as he pulled out, then back in with delight.

"We might need to work on you lying still. You didn't listen so well just now."

She bit her lip coyly. "Practice makes perfect. If we have to do that again, I guess we have to."

Chuckling, he cupped her face, brushing his thumbs across her cheeks. "I want to do that again and again and again. I think I might've even missed a few spots."

She slid her hands down his back, relishing in the way he shivered. "We can't have that. Next time make sure you hit every single spot."

His lips met hers once again as they started to move together as one. Thrust for thrust. He felt divine and wonderful and something she couldn't even define correctly. What she did know was she never felt like this before. The way his body moved over hers, in and out, the passion, the desire, it said the one thing that kept beating in her heart.

Love.

She loved this man. It sure felt like he loved her, too.

It scared and excited her, a mixture of tumbling emotions. Their movements became more frenzied as the kiss turned hotter and fiercer. Her body started to tingle once again, burning flames of ecstasy everywhere. She almost wanted his lips to douse the flames. Yet, she also didn't want him to disconnect from her.

Just like that, it hit her. She moaned into his mouth as she grabbed his ass and held on as the orgasm crushed her. Sauer continued to pump into her, then swiftly followed suit, groaning into her mouth. His body relaxed into her, the kiss slowing to a brief peck. He moved his face to the crook of her neck, his warm breath soothing her frayed nerves from the powerful lovemaking.

"Dee..." A soft kiss hit her neck. "Are you ready for breakfast yet?"

She chuckled, not expecting that to come out of his mouth. Surprisingly enough, she was hungry. "Yeah, breakfast sounds good."

He lifted his head, his eyes sparkling with humor, desire, and what she swore was love. His features dipped a little, then sprang back to his sweet smile she loved. What was that? Did he suddenly regret what they had just done? Was that why he wanted to eat suddenly?

"I—"

"Go shower and I'll heat up the food." She swatted his ass playfully and then nudged him to get off.

Hesitation warred on his face, then he grinned and rolled away. Plucking the condom off, he stood up. "I'll be quick." He walked out of the room.

She had no idea what he was about to say and didn't want to hear it. Was he about to say he regretted sleeping with her? Was he about to profess his love? Well, that was a dumb thought. Of course not. She knew he liked her, but what man could love an outrageous, loud woman like her. She annoyed most people. She didn't endear them to her.

It didn't matter. What she did know was she loved him. Everything that just happened was too much for her. She couldn't tell him how she felt.

As she stood up and went to her suitcase, she realized she was still angry with him. Yeah, definitely angry. He wouldn't share any details of the case with her. Someone tried to hurt her. Sauer knew who it was, or at least had an idea. It pissed her off she didn't get a good look at the guy's face. If she had, she'd have her own answers. But she did see one thing.

Little did he know, she had a starting point to find out who it could be as well. If he wouldn't share what he knew with her, she wouldn't share what she knew either.

SAUER QUICKLY WALKED to the bedroom, hoping against all hope that Dee was still gloriously naked in bed. What had he been thinking? *Are you ready for breakfast yet?* Who said that after having the best sex of their life? An idiot, like him.

He couldn't describe it as anything other than pure panic. The way they moved, the heat they created, the intensity that spurred between them was too much to even convey in words. It was...everything.

Like he normally did, he acted like a moron. What he should've done was profess his love. Which was what he tried to do when she cut him off. Probably for the best. Dee might seem like the toughest woman out there, where nothing fazed her, but he knew better. She was fragile. Like a delicate flower among a bed of weeds. Telling her he loved her would only do one thing: send her running in the opposite direction.

He stepped into the room, his mood dipping further down south, even though he knew she wouldn't still be in bed. It didn't stop him from wishing it. Dressing quickly in a simple pair of jeans and a red shirt, he almost ran to the kitchen. He acted like an idiot, but now he'd make it up to her. They'd eat breakfast as fast as they could and then he'd whisk her back to the bedroom and start the process of covering every inch of her skin with kisses.

Just thinking about the first time had him hard as a rock. Maybe breakfast could wait...again.

"I was thi—" Glancing around the empty kitchen, he froze for a second. "Dee?"

Well, shit, where was she?

A quick look in the living room had him developing the

worst kind of panic. Did the killer grab her while he was in the shower? Did he find her that quickly?

"Dee! Where are you?" He started rushing through the house once again, just in case he missed her. Not likely, because his eyes always zoomed straight to her whenever he walked into the same room as her.

Another search still came up empty of Dee anywhere. No sign of a struggle either. If the killer did come in here and take her, Dee would've put up a fight. He had no doubt about that. Which meant he would've heard it. Where could she be?

He sat down on the edge of his bed, rubbing a hand over his head. No Dee. No struggle. No clues. Where did he begin to start looking for her? She couldn't have just disappeared on him. Maybe the killer had a gun. Threatened her somehow. That made some sense. She wouldn't fight back if he had a gun. Or not. He could actually see Dee fighting back even if the perp had a gun.

He couldn't lose her. Not in that way. Not to a sadistic killer.

His hand dropped to his lap as his eyes glossed to his dresser. Where were his car keys?

Rushing from the bedroom, he yanked open the door to the garage and almost stumbled down the two steps.

Shit! No. She didn't. She wouldn't.

He raced around the house again, this time looking for Dee's purse. Gone. Just like her.

She took his car and left.

He tried to call her. Three times. Each time it went to voicemail. He wasn't sure how he was feeling at the moment. Scared. Irritated. Teetering on pissed off. Each crazy emotion mingled together, making it impossible to leave a message. Angry words wanted to come out, mixed with words of love. Saying nothing seemed like the best option.

Slinking down into the couch, he dialed another number. His fingers hesitated, knowing quite well it wouldn't be good. But he had to deal with him sooner or later.

"Hey, Newman. Can you come pick me up?" He let out a heavy sigh. "Dee had trouble last night and stayed at my house. She's gone. She took my car."

Twenty minutes later, Newman walked inside and met him in the living room. "How come she didn't tell you she was taking your car? Stealing, really." He chuckled.

Sauer tried not to roll his eyes. "She didn't steal my car. She borrowed it."

"Without asking, dude."

Rubbing a tense hand over his head, he sighed. "Maybe I scared her."

Newman sat down on the recliner. "Um, pretty sure that woman does not scare easily." Sauer avoided eye contact, which was the wrong thing to do. "Holy shit! Did you sleep with her?"

"And if I did?"

"I'm proud of you then." Newman laughed as he slapped his knee. "It's about damn time. Wrong woman, but good for you."

Sauer stood up, his features taut with tension. "I've had enough with the shit you say about her. What's your problem?"

Newman jerked to his feet as well. "My problem? Maybe I should ask you the same thing. Why the hell didn't you call me last night about what happened? We're partners, yet you called Zeke and Ben. What the hell, dude?"

"I can't explain why I did. I have no good excuse. You've

been acting weird lately and I...Dee was attacked. Zeke and Ben are close with her. Closer than I am. Maybe I just thought it'd be better if they helped."

"I'd say you're pretty close with her now."

"You're such an asshole."

Sauer walked out of the living room to the kitchen, grabbing a water bottle from the fridge even though he wasn't that thirsty. He needed to keep his hands occupied, otherwise he'd be sorely tempted to sock a fist into Newman's face. He would never do it. But he was oh so tempted.

"If you're so pissed at me, why'd you call me now?"

Keeping his back to Newman, he twisted the cap off the bottle. "Because you're my partner and friend. It's not like I was going to keep this from you. Last night...shit, man. The bastard almost hurt her..."

"She means a lot to you, doesn't she?"

"More than I can express. Go ahead, keep saying more shit. We're not right for each other. We're complete opposites. I'm not good enough for her."

"Dude..." Sauer finally turned around when Newman paused. "I don't...how do I say...I'm jealous, all right."

"What?"

Newman shrugged as he shuffled his feet. "You have your shit together. You're comfortable with yourself no matter what anyone says. The ladies, even as shy as you are, they notice you. You just don't see it. This thing with Dee... I'm sorry for everything I said. Breaking up with Chrissy...it's messing with me. She cheated on me. Like, shit! Why would she do that to me, man?"

Not what he expected to hear. A complete surprise that threw him off balance. Especially the part about Chrissy. They seemed so in love.

"I'm sorry." His eyes bulged, realizing what he was

saying. Those words. He never wanted to hear or say those words again. "I hate those words. I feel like getting sick right now."

Newman nodded. "We're sure this is the same guy that killed Vanessa?"

"It has to be. He left a note on her porch with those words on it. Twice. A few days later and she's attacked." Sauer set the bottle and cap down on the counter. "Chrissy's an idiot for doing that. You deserve better. I apologize for not calling last night. It was shitty of me."

Newman grinned, then chuckled. "All right, girl talk's over. We're good, man. At least, I'm ready to forget it all. You?"

"Yeah. I just need to find Dee."

"Where do you think she went? She's not answering her phone? Did she call Zoe or Rina?"

"I called Zeke before you got here. She hasn't called anyone. He'll call me first thing if she calls one of them."

"Did something happen this morning? You said you might've scared her. How?"

Sauer glanced away, raising a hand to rub his head, then dropped it just as quickly. "Maybe scared was the wrong word. More like, I probably pissed her off." He lifted his eyes. "You know me and words. I sound like an idiot at times."

"Shit, man, you didn't tell her you love her already, did you?" Newman's eyes got round with shock. "Because I'm getting this feeling you do."

He slowly shook his head no. "I wasn't smooth with my words, though, after we...you know...anyway, she said to take a shower and she'd heat up breakfast. After my shower, she was just...gone." He propped himself against the counter as a huge sigh escaped. "I've done nothing but piss her off, too, when it comes to the case. I refuse to tell her anything. All I keep doing is pissing her off at every corner, or saying the dumbest shit."

"Red flag."

Sauer met Newman's gaze.

"This is Dee we're talking about. She's not a person who's just gonna idly sit by and let you figure this out."

His stance straightened as his gut twisted with unease. "You think she left to find this killer?"

"Dude, Dee and intrigue equals, hell yeah."

"She's in so much trouble when I find her."

Newman grinned wickedly. "The naughty kind of trouble? I didn't know you had that in you, you sly dog."

Sauer chuckled, despite the fear racing through his veins. "Yeah, well, I found out when she scares the shit out of me, the dominant part comes roaring out. She knows it, too."

"Yeah, knowing Dee, she purposely did it then."

"Let's go." Sauer headed for the front door, swiping his jacket from the coat rack before going outside.

"Where are we going? We have no idea where to start."

"Let's keep working the case. That's all we can do right now."

Newman paused on the front step as Sauer locked the door. "We could put an APB out on your car."

Sauer gave him a look that said not to say anything like that again. "She didn't steal my car."

"No, of course not. She just took it without asking." Newman laughed as he slid into the driver's seat. "You know that deserves at least a good spanking."

"Dude, I don't...let's go interview Dee's neighbor again."

"Not the spanking kind of guy. Gotcha." Newman laughed, then frowned a little. "We don't talk about our relationships much. I know I give you shit about talking to women, but we don't really talk. Thanks for listening."

"Anytime."

"You know, I'm here if you ever need to talk."

"Thanks, man."

And he meant it. It was nice to know he could go to Newman if he wanted. He was right. They didn't have too many moments like this. Not like Zeke and Ben did. He liked it. It wasn't something he experienced growing up. Of course, he had a few friends, but not a best friend. Not someone he shared secrets with about anything and everything. He wanted that. He wanted it with Newman. Because he was the closest thing he had to a best friend. He trusted Newman with his life. Being partners, he needed to have that level of trust. Because, like it or not, there could come a time when they had to depend on each other.

Right now felt like one of those times. So many scenarios were running through his head, even though he knew Dee left on her own accord.

She left him.

A part of him withered away inside. She didn't trust him enough. So she left.

9

"STITCH, my man. How's my favorite hunk with the ink?" Dee sauntered up to the counter at Tat Me Tattoo Shop to a man built like a truck with tattoos up and down his arms, legs, neck, chest, and she'd never seen his ass, but she imagined that part was tattooed as well.

"Well, if it ain't Deena O'Malley, sweetest chick I know."

Her brow rose. "Me? Sweet? I'm pretty sure you're the only person on this planet to say that."

"That's because all those other people don't know you like I do. I do recall in third grade you socking Jimmy Thomas in the nose because he pushed me off the slide. What's not sweet about a girl sticking up for a scrawny ass little boy?"

"Nothing scrawny about you now."

Stitch leaned on the counter, his biceps bulging slightly. "It's been a while. You finally getting a tattoo? I've been dying to get my hands on that gorgeous body of yours."

"And ruin this perfection? No way. I like looking at your beautiful designs, but I'll never get one."

"Pity." He winked, then turned serious. "What's up then?"

"I had a small incident last night and—"

"Back it up." Stitch held up his hand as he walked around the counter and stood right next to her. "Define small incident. When it comes to you, nothing is ever small."

She wanted to huff and puff, but she knew she would never get anything by Stitch. She never had before. If there was anyone in her crazy, mixed-up life that she could always fall back on and trust, it was Stitch. She had to agree with him. It had been a while since they had seen each other. Time never mattered between them. Ten years could've gone by and it would feel like just an hour had passed. Their childhood, well, they went through a lot together. That created a thick bond that couldn't be broken. As much as he enjoyed teasing her about dating, or having sex, there was never any sexual attraction.

"I'm waiting."

Rolling her eyes, she scoffed just a little because she could. "Some jackass broke in and attacked me. The police have no clue who it is, but I thought maybe you could help me."

"How so?"

Just one of the many things she loved best about Stitch. He didn't ask if she was all right. If she wasn't all right, she would've told him. He bypassed all that mushy, how-are-you-feeling crap and got straight to the point.

"The guy had a tattoo on his arm. He was wearing gloves, but his sleeve rolled up a little and I got a glimpse of it. Thought if I described what I saw, you might be able to identify it. I'm no expert on tattoos, obviously, but it's nothing I've ever seen."

Stitch nodded his head and started to walk past her. "Let's have a seat and do some drawing."

"I knew I could count on you."

"Anytime, doll. Anything for you."

Stitch took a seat on his stool, then rolled to his desk and grabbed his sketchpad. Dee tossed her purse onto his desk, then took a spot on the tattoo chair and lay back, relaxing.

"Are you sure I can't convince you to get a tat? It'd be sexy as hell." He rolled back over to her, his grin wide and wicked looking.

"Focus. Don't make me remind you how you got your nickname."

He laughed heartily and held his hands up in surrender.

She had ceremoniously dubbed him Stitch in sixth grade. They had been on the playground playing around on the swings when the 'meanies,' as she named them to avoid getting caught saying bitches, showed up. Not much affected her, or Stitch. But when the meanies showed up, most people avoided them rather than deal with their antics. They vacated the swings without issue because her patience as a child was just as horrible as an adult. One meanie, Tiffany, had started to swing. Stitch turned back to grab his jacket and Tiffany's feet connected with his head at just the right time. He went down hard, hitting his head on the pavement. He had to get ten stitches that day.

He had felt like an idiot getting hit like that, not paying attention. Although, Dee thought Tiffany did it on purpose, because that's how the meanies were. Just plain old mean. Nobody messed with her friends. Nobody. So she had a little chat with Tiffany after school. Dee was very proud of herself that day. She didn't throw the first punch, but she threw the last one.

Dan—Stitch's real name—came up to her the next day

after hearing what happened. He grinned, put an arm around her shoulder, and squeezed. That was his way of saying thanks. Her response had been, "Anything for you, Stitch." And it stuck. She never called him Dan again. Neither did anyone else.

Pencil poised for action, Dee started to describe what little she had seen of the tattoo. Very, very little of it. A small flame, black and white with a hint of orange. That didn't seem unique at all. Although, the lines looked fine and accurate. Not some of the choppy stuff she'd seen. Which helped. Stitch knew all the great artists in the area, him being one of them. Now, she just had to pray her attacker had his tattoo done around here.

What stuck out in the tattoo was the dagger embedded in the flames with the letters I and S sketched on the blade. It was the strangest thing. IS. What did it mean? Initials, perhaps? She still didn't know how she managed to capture even that tiny picture of the tattoo. Maybe she was getting it all wrong. Then again, maybe she wasn't. She normally didn't get things wrong. Like, ever.

"Look familiar?"

Stitch raised a brow. "You didn't give me much, doll."

"So."

Laughing, he stuck the pencil behind his ear. "It's not one of my designs, but I'll ask around."

She stood up and grabbed her purse as Stitch slung an arm around her. They walked back to the front. "Something else is bugging you."

She wanted to play it off as if nothing was wrong, plaguing her mind since the moment Sauer asked her out, but Stitch could always read her. Almost from the first time they met. He didn't phrase it as a question either, meaning he knew something was bugging her and wanted her to confide in him. Maybe coming about the tattoo wasn't the only reason she came to see him.

"Deena…"

The way he said her name. So softly. So sweet. With so much concern. He was one of the few people who called her by her full name. Most people wouldn't look at Stitch and see soft and sweet. More like rough and dangerous.

"Spill, doll."

Huffing a little, just to give him a hard time, she finally muttered, "I kinda met someone."

Stitch stopped walking, impeding her steps as well. He turned her toward him with a tender smile. Something he rarely offered to display. "That scares you."

It was crazy scary how well Stitch could read her. Maybe it wasn't such a great idea to come.

"Did the asshole hurt you? I'll fu—"

"No!" Dee laid a hand on his chest to calm him down. His breathing had skyrocketed, and his face was contorted in rage. "Sauer would never hurt me. Ever. He's the sweetest, shyest guy to ever exist. I…"

Stitch's heavy breaths dissipated as fast as they started. "Shy, huh?"

"In a very sweet, endearing way. We are the complete opposites. We don't match at all. Barely have anything in common. I'm loud. He's quiet. I'm crazy. He's normal. I'm—"

"In love with him and it scares the shit out of you." Stitch shook his head as he chuckled. "Just say it out loud. Just once. It might calm you down."

"Don't be silly. Sauer and I…love is…Stitch…"

"Did you tell him?"

Dee let loose a strangled laugh. "He probably hates me. I left this morning."

"Guys do shit like that all the time. He won't hate you for it."

She puckered her brows, a deep frown forming. "When I say I left, I mean I left his house...right after we...while he was in the shower...and I took his car."

Stitch appeared to process everything she said, even as cut off as it was, then started to laugh. A deep, boisterous laugh that made her smile despite the turmoil swimming in her veins.

"It's not funny."

"It kinda is."

"I hate you."

His smile grew as his laughter got a little louder, if that was possible. "You always have the craziest stories. I'm not sure I have one to top that. I was with this chick, Corianna, and she could do—"

She lightly punched his arm. "I don't wanna hear one of your sexual escapades. I'm having a crisis. Fix it."

"So you want me to kick this guy's ass when he didn't do anything wrong?" Brows high, eyes sparkling with mischief, he nodded. "All right. I'm on it."

Another reason he was one of her best friends, and always would be. His ability to make her laugh no matter how horrible she felt.

"Probably not the best idea. He's a cop. I wouldn't want you to get arrested for beating a cop."

"Wow, he's definitely not your normal type of guy you date. A cop? And you stole his car?"

"Borrowed."

"You took it without asking."

"Totally borrowed."

"The very definition of stealing is—"

"Stitch..." Sounding whiny, even to her own ears, she

started to panic a little more than before. Did Sauer think she stole his car as well? Maybe his feelings were beyond hate. Would he slap handcuffs on her the moment he saw her?"

Throwing her a tender smile, he said, "Don't worry so much, Deena. Wanna grab a drink?"

Dee laughed. "At ten o'clock in the morning?"

"Never stopped you before."

"Rain check. I should probably go back to Sauer's. Call me as soon as you find something."

"Assuming I do."

"I know you will."

"Ah, the faith you have in me."

Stitch walked with her the rest of the way to the front and hugged her before she ventured outside his shop and debated on her next move. Head to Sauer's to deal with his wrath? Or keep running?

Did Sauer have wrath? Maybe he wouldn't be that mad at her.

No. She was just trying to pacify herself. He was pissed. Any sane man would be pissed.

She started to step off the curb when a car came squealing to a stop in front of her. A man in a dark hoodie jumped out, grabbing her by the arm. Dee froze, shock over-riding any other reaction.

Stumbling toward the car as the man tried to shove her inside, she hit her head on top of the doorframe. Her purse fell from her grasp. Snapping out of it, she swung her leg up, connecting with him. She turned around to get another good kick in when Stitch came barreling out of his shop.

The guy pushed her into Stitch, making them both stagger backwards. Her breath hitched as Stitch lightly shoved her behind him and then ran after the car as it raced away.

The bastard tried to kidnap her. What was going on? First he tried to kill her, and now he tried to kidnap her.

She fell against the door, almost slithering to the ground when a pair of strong hands grabbed a hold of her.

"Shit, doll, was that him?"

Nodding, she tried to regain her equilibrium. She needed to stay strong and in control. Letting this asshole get to her wouldn't help her.

Stitch started to let go. All her strength left, her stance faltering. His hands instantly went back around her.

"Come on, Deena." He opened the door and walked her inside, pushing her to sit down on a tiny leather couch near the door. "What's your cop's number?"

It took a moment for his words to sink in. Sauer? He wanted to call Sauer. That was a very bad idea. The last time she was attacked, he didn't take it well. Well, if one considered kissing her not taking it well.

Grabbing her chin firmly, a scowl on his face mixed with concern, Stitch said again, "His number."

"He hates me." Three little words said in a whisper, yet reverberated around the room. Sauer had to hate her for leaving the way she had. He wouldn't be happy to hear she was attacked again. She had no one to blame but herself.

"I'll kick his ass if he says one hateful word towards you." Stitch stood up, looking outside the shop window. He started walking to the door.

"Where are you going?"

"Your purse is on the sidewalk. You said the guy's name was Sauer. I'll find his number on my own."

Dee made no move to stop him. It was better this way. So much better to let Stitch talk to him. Sauer didn't want anything to do with her. He had to hate her. No man ever stuck around for very long. Which was why she always left them first. Her heart could survive if she walked away first.

So why did it feel like her heart would never recover?

"MOVE."

"Who are you?"

Sauer looked the guy up and down, deciding whether he wanted to take him down. The dude was big. Really big. Muscles lined his arms and chest, tattoos as well. He clearly worked out often. He also towered over Sauer by a good few inches. He wasn't short, almost six feet, which made this guy well past six feet.

Six feet of an angry, tattooed, muscled man stood in his way to Dee. He might be shorter, but he could knock this guy to the ground. He worked out as well. Almost every day. For at least one hour, lifting weights, doing exercises, working on defense moves. Not only was he picked on and teased, but he had the misfortune of getting beat up as a kid. He swore to himself he'd never let that happen as an adult. So yeah, he could totally take this guy.

But should he?

Obviously, he was a friend of Dee's, considering he called him from Dee's phone, not Dee herself. The question he didn't want to answer was what kind of friend was he? If he kicked her friend's ass, what would Dee say about it? Would she hate him?

Did it matter anymore? She left this morning. Without a word good-bye. She probably didn't hate him, but she didn't like him as much as he liked her.

He had to quit thinking about that. She was attacked

again. Almost kidnapped. He needed to see her. Pull her into his arms. Hold her. Regardless of how she reacted. This dude needed to step out of his way. He was prepared to do that by any means necessary.

"Move."

The guy cocked his head to the side, his arms crossed. "Who are you?"

"Gentlemen, we could be here all day." Newman smiled at the guy, producing his badge. "Detective Newman. This is my partner, Detective Sauer." Newman tossed his head toward him. "And if you don't move, he will kick your ass. It's written all over his face. Not something I've seen before. I'm a little worried. You should be, too."

The guy leaned closer, his scowl deepening. "You hurt Deena and I hurt you." He turned around and opened the door to the shop.

Sauer followed him inside, even more curious about his friendship status with Dee. Deena? Not many people called her that. What did it mean?

Dee sat on a leather couch near the front door, head down, hands in her lap. She looked...broken. The only word he could think of. He didn't want to think of her like that, but the way she sat there looking lost and sad and maybe a little confused, all he could think was the word broken.

Where was his strong, forceful Dee?

Newman stayed by the front door as her friend took a spot near the counter, leaning against it, crossing his arms again with a fierce scowl on his face. Sauer ignored the warning vibes flowing off him and knelt down in front of her.

"Dee?"

Her eyes shot to his. Panic, fright, and just a little bit of defiance gleamed his way. "Sauer..."

"Are you okay?" She nodded once, her eyes glossing to her friend behind him. That pissed him off. "What the hell happened?"

Probably surprised by his tone, she looked at him again. "Didn't Stitch tell you on the phone?"

"Stitch?"

She lazily tossed a hand toward the massive dude standing by the counter. So his name was Stitch, which fit the total picture of the badass he appeared to be.

"I'm asking you."

"Why haven't you kissed me yet?"

"Kiss you?"

Dee frowned. "Yeah. Kiss me. The last time something happened, you kissed me. I'm waiting."

His anger, boiling steadily since the standoff with her friend, started to inch closer to the surface. Was she playing games with him?

"Oh, so was that your plan? Leave this morning and find another way to get me to kiss you. I'm pretty sure all you would've needed to do was ask instead of leaving."

"You're mad?"

"Brilliant deduction." He slowly breathed in and out, trying to calm down. Even though she upset him, hurt him more than anything else, he didn't want to take his anger out on her. "Just tell me what happened."

Defeat started to form in small increments until, just like that, she steeled her features and gave him a blank expression. "I was leaving. Just standing on the sidewalk when this car came out of nowhere. He jumped out and grabbed my arm, pulling me toward the car. I kicked him and started to kick him again when he shoved me backwards. I fell into Stitch. The guy drove away."

"Why were you here?"

She stared at him, as if debating what to say. "Visiting an old friend."

"That's all?"

"Are you accusing me of something, Sauer?"

"No. I'm waiting for you to stop lying to me."

When she said nothing, he knew she was lying. "Did you get a good look at his face?" She didn't see his face great the night before, but he was hoping she got a better look this time.

"Not really. He had a hoodie on."

"Anything useful about him that would help me identify him?"

"I...don't think so."

She hesitated. Why was she trying to make his job harder? Why couldn't she just let him do his job? She was still lying to him.

He stood up and took a step back, then turned toward Stitch. "Did you catch the license plate or what he looked like?"

"I saw the license plate."

"Great. What is it?" Newman pulled out his little notebook from a pocket inside his jacket.

"It's getting a little hazy now."

"Excuse me?" Now this jackass was going to start lying. What the hell? "Did you catch the license plate or not?"

"I'm not sure I like you. Deena said you were shy. I don't see an ounce of shyness."

Sauer glanced at her, confused why she talked to this guy about him. Was that good or bad? Then he turned his full attention back to Stitch. "Nobody jerks me around, especially when it comes to my job. All I'm trying to do is find this bastard who's trying to hurt Dee and you're preventing me from doing that. Even Dee is."

"Just tell me what you know. I hate being left out."

Sauer swiveled his gaze to her. Dee now stood, hands on her hips, the anger prominent. "It's not your job. It's mine. I don't have to share anything with you."

"Well, I don't have to share anything with you then. Fair is fair."

"Do you enjoy getting attacked? Do you enjoy—" He stopped talking. He wasn't about to ask if she enjoyed messing with his heart in front of an audience. It'd also give her the knowledge he cared about her more than she cared for him.

"I just want to help."

"It's not your job!"

Dee staggered back by his outburst. He rarely yelled, and at a woman, forget it. That never happened. But the thought of her getting hurt scared him.

"Okay. Uh, let's all take a deep breath." Newman walked closer and placed a hand on his shoulder, leaning in to whisper, "Yo, partner, you good? Maybe we should step outside for a moment."

"I'm good." Looking at Newman, he nodded for added reassurance. "It was never going to work out. You were right."

Newman frowned. "What does that mean?"

Ignoring him, he stepped closer to Dee. "Why did you come here?"

"I told you. To visit an old friend."

Sauer looked at Stitch. "Why did she come here?"

"To visit."

"What did the license plate say?"

"The letters and numbers are all jumbled."

He glanced back and forth between Dee and Stitch, his heart pounding, aching, and falling apart into a million pieces. He didn't want to do it. She was leaving him no choice. He refused to be jerked around—by anyone.

Clearly, Dee didn't care that much about him. She left this morning. Maybe she didn't care at all. Maybe sleeping with him had been a distraction from the beginning.

He was such a guppy. Falling for it. She used him.

"Fine. I guess I just have to lock both of you up for obstruction."

"What?" Dee screeched.

Sauer saw Stitch out of the corner of his eye stand a little straighter but said nothing.

"You can't be serious, Sauer? You're not a jerk, so why are you acting like one?"

"I take my job seriously. I won't see you get hurt again."

"Locking me up will keep me safe, huh?" She took a step toward him, her hands still propped on her hips. Her red hair, bouncy as ever, curls framing her face, made him ache to brush them back. He ached so badly to touch her for just a moment.

"Maybe it'll teach you a lesson as well. You're impeding my investigation."

"What's so wrong with letting me help?"

"You're not a cop." How many times would they go around in circles about this? "What's so wrong with letting me handle it all?"

"I don't need other people handling my problems."

"Really? Yet you came here to let *him* help you." He jerked a hand in Stitch's direction. "How come he can help, but I can't?"

"I...came to visit."

"You're still lying to me. Good to know."

"What's good to know?"

"Where we stand."

She trembled, her eyes glistening. Was she about to cry? "So I mean nothing to you?"

"You should know how I feel about you."

"How? You're about to arrest me. Doesn't sound like you care about me at all."

"Damn it, Dee, I love you! I never would've slept with you this morning if I didn't."

Silence descended.

Shit. Why did he say that? With people around them. He was worse than an idiot. Just call him stupid.

He turned away from her and walked out.

10

LAST TIME SAUER was scared about what happened to her, he kissed her senseless, starting them on a path that was probably inevitable. This time, instead of kissing her, he declared his love. Then walked away.

Why did he walk away?

Would he arrest her?

Why didn't she run after him and declare her love back?

"Can you just put him out of his misery and tell us why you came here?"

Dee turned away from the window, trying to see where Sauer walked, and looked at Newman.

"Just tell him, Deena."

Her gaze trailed to Stitch. Then Newman and Stitch shared a look.

"Giving us the license plate would be helpful as well."

Stitch continued to look at Newman as he walked over to her. "I know why you feel like you have to take care of it yourself, but it might be better to let them handle it."

"You're just saying that because of what Sauer said."

"Are you saying that didn't affect you, doll?"

Dee ignored that loaded question and looked at Newman. "He won't really arrest me, will he?"

Newman shrugged. "I've never seen him act this way. I have no idea what he'll do. He should arrest you for taking his car."

"Borrowed."

Newman laughed. "If you say so." His laughter died quickly. "Quit jerking him around, Dee. He doesn't deserve to hurt like he is."

"I'm not."

"You're shitting me, right? You can't see how much you hurt him?"

"Watch your tone, dude." Stitch tensed beside her.

"Start talking. I'm almost to the point I'm not going to wait for Sauer to arrest both of you."

"Whoa, what's going on here?"

Dee turned toward Zeke, who had just walked into the shop with Ben.

"Dee's withholding information about our investigation, and so is her friend." Newman didn't bother to keep his annoyance and disgust out of his voice. She couldn't be mad at him. She deserved it.

"Come on, Dee…" Zeke said, cocking a brow as if she were acting like a child not getting her way.

Wasn't she a little? Was it a big deal if she told them what she knew? She hated to admit that it felt like she would lose control of the situation if she told them anything. The situation was already uncontrollable. This asshole had tried to hurt her twice. How many times would something have to happen before she let Sauer in—in more ways than just the obvious?

"Fine." She folded her arms as she almost stomped her

foot to add to her petulant child act. "As soon as Sauer comes back, I'll tell him."

"You jerk him around again about this investigation and I'll slap the handcuffs on you myself." Newman pointed an accusing finger at her.

"I said watch your tone."

Newman glared at Stitch. "You don't scare me. How about you watch your tone?"

Ben cleared his throat. "How about I find Sauer and move this along? Let's all calm down."

"I'll be in your room." Dee touched Stitch's shoulder as she passed him. "I'm bound to explode if I stay around all of you."

"Hey, Sauer."

He looked up, his knee bent, leaning against the alley wall around the corner of the tattoo shop, and didn't even attempt to smile at Ben's friendly face.

"When did you guys get here?"

"A few minutes ago. You okay?"

He bent his head and shrugged. "Sure. I'm used to acting like an idiot. No big deal."

Ben took a spot next to him. "Dee's ready to talk to you. Newman mentioned what happened. Probably not the way you wanted to tell her, but I think it's a good thing."

"It doesn't matter."

"It does."

He lifted his head, meeting Ben's gaze. "I don't know what to do. Dee...she's complicated. I keep screwing up at every turn. Now she knows how I truly feel and I probably ruined my chances."

"I screwed up plenty with Rina. Do you want to know the one thing that worked?"

Sauer nodded, eager to soak up any advice he could get. He wasn't ready to lose Dee, even though he probably lost her before he even had her.

"I didn't give up."

Not the advice he was expecting.

He didn't want to give up. Giving up wasn't his style. No matter how many times life brought him down, he always got back up.

Dee just made things so difficult. Of course, one of the many reasons he loved her. It made Dee, well, Dee.

"You're right."

Ben chuckled. "Of course I am. Remind Zeke. He forgets all the time."

Sauer laughed with him and started walking back to the tattoo shop with Ben by his side.

"So, you threatened to lock Dee up?"

"If she doesn't tell me what she knows, it's not going to be just a threat." He laughed with no humor laced in it. "How's that for trying to endear her to me?"

"I've never seen anyone match Dee in an argument. You're doing just fine winning her heart, threats and all." Ben couldn't hold in his laughter.

Sauer walked into the shop first, eyeing Stitch right away, who was still leaning against the counter as when he left.

Newman looked at him and nodded at Stitch. "Got the license. The car was reported stolen last night. Doesn't help us much. Zeke offered to interview the victim. He and Ben will head that way, we'll head to the precinct. Susan still needs Dee's fingerprints."

"Sounds good." Sauer glanced around the shop. "Where's Dee?"

Stitch stood up to his full height, obviously trying to intimidate him somehow. It did nothing but piss him off. He still wanted to hit the guy just because he was friends with Dee. When did he become so jealous?

Since he fell in love, apparently.

"She's in the back. One tear touches her eye, you'll be sorry."

Sauer stepped closer. "Just what do you think I'm going to do?"

"Arresting her would be the dumbest thing you ever did."

"Wouldn't be the first time I've done something dumb in my life."

Stitch took a step, a punch away. "I care about Deena. She's the best friend I've ever had. Once you're her friend, she's there for a lifetime." He sighed heavily. "It might not be obvious, but she cares deeply. She hides her feelings well, but she hurts so easily. I'm just telling you not to hurt her."

Sauer's anger toward him slowly dissipated. "I'd hurt myself before I'd ever cause her any pain. Arresting her isn't about hurting her, it's to protect her. I'll do anything to protect her."

Stitch took another step closer. Sauer almost backed up, but held his ground. If the guy was going to punch him, he'd jump in with both arms swinging.

His voice was low. Low enough where only Sauer could hear him. "She ever talk about her childhood to you?"

"No."

"Don't give up on her." Stitch cocked a brow. "Ain't saying I like you or anything...but...she's worth it."

Twice now, someone said that. *Don't give up.* Never. He

might develop an entire head of gray hair before it was all said and done, but he'd never give up on her.

For the longest time, they stared at each other before Stitch finally backed away and gestured down the hallway. "Last door on the right. And don't touch my shit."

Sauer nodded and walked away. Each step he took felt like the last steps he'd ever take. Like a death sentence. It shouldn't have felt that way. He didn't know what awaited him. Probably, "It's over. I don't want to see you again." Just line the needle up to his vein and inject him. It'd kill him if she said those words to him.

Why did he shout out he loved her? So soon in their crazy, messed-up relationship? It was the worst thing he could've done.

Focus on the case. That's what he'd do. Pretend he never said a word. He didn't imagine she'd bring it up.

He knocked once on the door, then opened it. Dee stood across the room, her back to him, staring at the designs on the wall.

"You should've never said that, Sauer."

The pain ricocheted everywhere, almost staggering his balance. How did she even know it was him? She still hadn't turned around. What did he say to that? While he regretted jumping the gun on telling her, he was glad she knew he loved her. It would've been difficult to hide.

"It's the truth."

She turned around, her eyes blazing with fury.

"You got a funny way of showing how much I mean to you when you wanna lock me up."

His brows dipped. He thought she was talking about his declaration of love. She still thought he was going to arrest her? Well, he would, if she didn't cooperate. Might be a weird way to show 'I love you' but he wouldn't see her get hurt. She needed to let him do his job without inter-ference.

"Well? You gonna slap on those cuffs?"

Okay. So she was going to ignore the love confession. Maybe a good thing. He didn't want to broach that subject yet. Especially in a tattoo shop with everyone waiting for them up front.

"Are you going to tell me what you know?"

Her anger depleted, replaced with despair. "Would you really arrest me if I refuse to tell you? That's not you. You're not a mean guy."

He moved closer, within reach to grab her into his arms if he wanted to. "How many times do you want me to say it? I take my job seriously. It's not about hurting you. It's about keeping you safe. I will find this guy. I need you to stop looking yourself." He couldn't stand it any longer. His hands wrapped around her waist and pulled her flush against him. "He tried to hurt you again today. Dee...you know how I feel. I can't—won't—see you hurt. Once was enough."

She lowered her head against his chest. "I don't know how to let go. Don't be mad at me."

"I'm slowly getting over it. Just, please, tell me why you came here."

"He has a tattoo. I saw part of it. Stitch drew the details for me. He's going to ask around to see if anyone recognizes it. Maybe it's nothing. Maybe it's a lead."

"Can I see the drawing?"

Dee lifted her head, but didn't move out of his embrace. "Can I have a kiss yet?"

"You don't play fair."

"Duh."

The laugh fell out before he could stop it. "You drive me a crazy kind of nuts."

"The shy, quiet guy going crazy?" She brushed a hand over his head. He loved it every time she did that. "Just don't ever match my crazy."

He lightly grazed his lips against hers. "Drawing?"

"A man of few words yet said with such a punch." She chuckled as she stepped out of his arms and grabbed a sketchpad from the desk near them. "It's not much."

He looked at the drawing, impressed by Stitch's skills. The man had talent. He didn't have any tattoos, but eyeing the small, yet detailed sketch made him want a tattoo. What would Dee say if he got her name tattooed on him?

Oh, man. He wasn't that crazy. Or was he?

No.

"I guess he didn't recognize it."

"No. But I'm hoping somebody else does. We'll find this guy."

Arching a brow, the anger flooded back in. "I'll find this guy. Let's not keep arguing about it."

"I like arguing with you." She flashed him a smile and walked past him.

"Dee..."

She opened the door, her smile widening. "Make-up sex later?"

"Are you serious right now?"

"What? You've never had make-up sex before?"

Of course he never had that. He didn't argue with women. He never had the gumption. With Dee, it came so easily. Plus, she loved to provoke him.

"I'll take that as a no. I've never had it either. Something new we can try together." She winked and walked out.

She was going to be the death of him. Or break his heart into a tiny million pieces. Either way, Dee loved to pull the emotions out of him in every direction. Nonstop.

It should scare him. Send him running in the opposite direction. When, really, it was sending him straight to her. Did she realize it? With Dee, it was hard to tell.

Make-up sex? Could sex get any more powerful between them?

Sex with her suddenly scared him. Nothing else frightened him, but that did. Last time they slept together, she ran. Would she run again?

Don't give up.

Sound advice. Repeating it might give him the courage he needed.

Neither apologized. Oddly enough, he was okay with that. He didn't like those words anymore. They were only words. Showing an apology with actions sounded like the best plan. He'd apologize with his hands, his lips, his entire body later tonight for his outburst. He should've never hollered at her. Never again.

He loved Dee.

Did she love him?

Zeke took a left, passing a woman walking her two dogs. They were two minutes from their destination driving through a nice neighborhood that had a neighborhood watch. People were out and about walking or running, even in this cold weather. Although, they were actually blessed with a decent enough day where the cold didn't bite you in the ass.

How did this guy steal a car in broad daylight without anyone noticing?

The victim, Tracy Stenson, had called the police shortly before suppertime last night to report her vehicle missing. She had parked it in the driveway, doors and windows closed and securely locked. Nothing of value was visible. She had to leave for her daughter's gymnastics practice around five, only getting home at three. A two-hour window. This killer wasn't only smart and skilled, he was brazen.

"What do you think about Sauer and Dee? Think they'll make it?"

Zeke took another left and shrugged. "For Sauer, I hope so. Dee's always been difficult. Since the moment I met her."

Ben laughed. "Dude, she had a reason to hate you."

"Whatever. You know what I'm saying. They're cute together, I guess. She's just an odd pick for him."

"Rina said she's been trying to talk to her about what's going on and she isn't talking. I hope she'll be okay."

"Nothing brings Dee down."

Ben sighed. "There's always something that can bring a person down."

Zeke pulled into Tracy's driveway and shut the vehicle off. "Should we help somehow? Dee might be difficult, but she is Zoe's best friend. She's like family."

"I'm all for helping, but how?"

"Let's interview this witness and then get the ladies involved. Maybe they'll have a great idea. I haven't got a clue how to play matchmaker."

"You barely had a clue how to win Zoe's heart." Ben laughed. "And wait until baby number two is here. Even more clueless."

"The whole baby thing is getting old. It doesn't bug me." Zeke knocked on the door. "Rina pregnant yet?"

"Is Zoe?"

"I bet we get pregnant before you."

"What? You wanna race? I'm down with that. Making the baby is the best part."

Zeke chuckled. "Damn right it is. Need any tips—" The door swung open. "Mrs. Stenson?"

A blonde-haired woman, early thirties, with a toddler in her arms, looked at them with confusion. "Yes. How can I help you?"

"Detective Chance and Detective Stoyer with the St. Cloud Police Department. We have some questions about your report of a stolen vehicle yesterday." Zeke smiled to help ease the worry lining her face as he showed her his badge.

"Sure. Come in." She held the door open and closed it as soon as they stepped in. "I told the officer everything I know yesterday."

"Of course. We understand. There was an incident today where a man tried to hurt a woman, and he was driving your car." Ben said each word softly. Zeke wanted to chuckle but, of course, wouldn't dare since it'd be highly inappropriate, but it reminded him so much of Rina. She was obviously rubbing off on him.

"That's terrible. Is she okay?"

"She's fine, but he managed to get away. Did you hear anything? See anything strange when you got home from school?"

She shook her head at Zeke. "Same routine every day. Drop the kids off at school. Drop this one off at daycare," she said with a nod to the toddler in her arms, who was wiggling like a worm on the end of a fishing pole. "I came home because I work from home, then I went and picked the kids up when it was time. I didn't notice anything weird. I have no idea what to do. I need a car."

Her eyes started to glisten. "My daughter missed gymnastics and was in tears last night because they have a big event coming up. I have no idea how I'm going to get them to school on Monday. I wish I could help you somehow."

Zeke didn't know what to say, or how to comfort her. Not once did she mention a husband, yet she didn't correct him when he called her Mrs. Stenson. He got the impression she was a single mother. Ben clearly didn't know what to say either because a long, awkward pause happened.

"Have you contacted your insurance yet?" Zeke finally asked.

"Can you believe there's a waiting period to see if the car is recovered? Two weeks. That doesn't include waiting to get a check and then trying to find another vehicle. I can't live without a car for two weeks. I can't afford to rent one for that long either."

"We're doing everything we can to find your vehicle. I promise. You notice anyone strange hanging around the neighborhood?" Ben asked.

"I'm sorry. I wish I could help you more." She switched the toddler to her other side. "Maybe Barry will be more helpful."

"Is that your husband?" Zeke asked, feeling slightly better she wasn't alone. He hated to think of her struggling on her own.

She pressed her lips together as the tears gathered in her eyes. "No, my husband passed away last year. Barry's the head of the neighborhood watch here. He's like a hawk. Sits outside every day, just watching. He's retired."

"He sits outside in this cold weather?" Zeke asked, surprised, and back to feeling awkward and like an idiot for bringing up her husband.

"Off and on, about five to ten minutes at a time. Long enough to smoke a cigarette. Or he sits by his window and watches out. I feel safe knowing he's watching. He's three houses down."

"Thank you, Mrs. Stenson. As soon as we find something out about your vehicle, you'll be the first to know." Zeke smiled, hoping to wipe those tears away.

She smiled weakly and nodded. "I appreciate that, detective."

"Thanks, Susan."

Dee took the wet wipe from Susan and tried to get all the fingerprint ink off her fingers.

"You okay?"

"Peachy keen."

"It's not every day someone breaks into your home and attacks you, then tries again. I repeat, are you okay?"

Dee tossed the wipe into the trashcan, sitting in the corner not far from the desk. She and Sauer had driven in his car, while Newman followed them to the precinct after leaving Stitch's shop. Sauer walked her to the crime lab, which was on the second level of the building, and left her with Susan. Her office was tiny but immaculate. Susan was very organized. Her desk was clutter free, filing cabinets closed with nothing on top. Everything appeared in its place. Not even a piece of paper sat askew. Dee was just as organized. Sort of. She left some crap lying around her desk, especially while she worked. Not Susan. She pulled out everything they needed to take her prints, then just as quickly, put it all away. She handled a few phone calls while Dee waited patiently. Each time, she wrote down a note on a small Post-it. Then she quickly pulled a notebook out of the top drawer, jotted down a notation, then tossed the note away. All very efficient-like and with a speed that said she did it every day, all day.

"Ignoring me doesn't help me think you're okay."

"I'm okay. I'm more confused about my social life." As soon as she said that, she regretted it. Why was she talking to Susan about her personal life? Sure, she occasionally saw her here and there, but she wasn't someone she talked to about private things.

"Men. Tell me about it."

Dee jerked her head up.

"Oh, I know you and Sauer got a thing going on. He's a great guy. You're lucky. I'm sure it'll work out." Susan plopped down into her chair. "Men are just so confusing... and aggravating."

"They are. I think that's what has me so messed up in the head. Sauer's a nice guy. I don't date nice guys."

"He's the best. I have to admit, Zeke and Ben are my favorite. But Sauer, he's like his own kind of special. You're right. He's always so nice, so considerate."

"What guy has you in knots?"

Susan blushed and hesitated as she wrung her hands on top of the desk.

"Come on. Tell me. What's said in the crime lab, stays in the crime lab."

Susan chuckled as she stopped fidgeting. "Will you keep it between us?"

Dee leaned closer, totally intrigued. "Of course. My lips are zipped."

Biting her lip, Susan hesitated again. "You could call it a crush. I work with him, but I don't think he knows I exist and...God, I feel like I'm in high school right now telling you this."

Dee slapped her knee as she laughed. "I hated high school. Gossip was the worst." She tapped her chin. "Can I guess who it is?"

"Sure."

Dee sat there thinking hard. She didn't know Susan well at all. On occasion they all went out for drinks. Susan sometimes showed up. It didn't happen often. The normal crew was her, Ben and Rina, Zeke and Zoe, Sauer and Newman, and a few other guys from the precinct. It couldn't be Ben or

Zeke because Susan wouldn't sleep around with married men. It wasn't Sauer, because she didn't think Susan would be stupid enough to try and take him away from her.

Whoa. That seemed territorial of her. Since when did she react like that about a guy? Like, never.

Didn't matter. Sauer was hers. Any woman who dared to try and steal him away would see her wrath.

Hmm. Who could it be? Newman? He was dating Chrissy. Susan didn't strike her as the type to fool around with unavailable men. The other guys in the precinct she just didn't know that well. Maybe it was Tray. He could be loud and obnoxious when he showed up. He tried to get in her pants one time. Of course, she shut him down immediately without saying much.

"I'm stumped. That never happens."

Susan giggled. "I'm shocked." Then her face turned red. "I'm embarrassed to admit it. He's not even available."

Dee sat straighter. She still didn't believe Susan would mess around with a guy who was unavailable. Who cared if she had a crush? There was nothing wrong with looking. She just couldn't touch.

She cocked a brow. "Well?"

Sighing, her face bloomed a deeper red. "It's—" The phone rang.

Dee could've groaned in dismay. She wanted to know so badly who Susan had a crush on. Damn the phone. Dee leaned back in her chair as Susan went about her business once again. The woman never took a break just to breathe. She had no idea how Susan stayed so chipper and in control, as busy as she was.

"Mrs. Stenson didn't have much to add other than the fact it sucks when your car gets stolen. Did you know her insurance is waiting two weeks to see if it's recovered before they do anything?" Zeke propped his long frame against the desk across from Sauer's.

"I think every insurance is different. My neighbor, a few houses down, had their car stolen a year ago. I'm pretty sure they only had to wait a week. The car was never recovered," Newman said.

"We did talk to the neighborhood watch guy, Barry Jenkins. He didn't notice anything at the time, but he's a suspicious dude. He has security cameras outside. He said he went through them and he has the guy on video driving away. It wasn't helpful. The guy had a hoodie on and you couldn't see his face. It was time-stamped at 4:05 pm. The question is, did he stakeout her house, or was it random?" Ben said as he stood near Zeke.

"I'm hoping for random. He's only killed one woman so far. Vanessa and Dee have nothing in common, so he really has no MO. I might ask patrols to step it up in her neighborhood, just in case." Sauer leaned back in his chair, trying not to think about Dee and how she was doing with Susan.

"That's a good idea," Zeke said. "Anything else you two want us to do today?"

Sauer shared a look with Newman, then said, "Na, I think we're good for today. Thanks for helping."

"Well, it is Saturday. Let's call it a day. Be back here bright and early Monday morning." Newman stood up and chuckled. "As long as Dee doesn't create another fiasco and steal your car."

"Borrowed." Sauer stood up as well. "I'll see you guys later. Thanks again."

He walked away without waiting for a response. Getting

into whether she borrowed or stole his car wasn't on his to-do list. He didn't care what anyone said. She borrowed it... without permission. No doubt, it had to do with the fact he scared her.

She wanted make-up sex. The thought terrified him. Would she get scared again afterwards? Would she borrow his car again? Would he survive another attempt of her fleeing? Geez, would she even go home with him? He was assuming she would.

Yeah. He had a tough heart. It survived so many pains, not much could damage it anymore.

As he stood outside Susan's office, eyeing Dee through the small window in the door, he realized how foolish that thinking was. His heart wouldn't survive another round of pain from her. She was too deeply embedded inside him. She was his everything. So quickly, too. He knew the exact moment it happened. This morning when they made sweet love.

Maybe he jumped the gun on that. He always took sex seriously. It wasn't a casual thing to him. He went in with his heart on display and it got trampled on the minute she walked out. Could he offer his heart like that one more time?

She was expecting sex. Dee didn't like to be denied anything.

Well, at least his courage with her was getting better. He wasn't stumbling over his words as much. If anything, his words were getting more aggressive than they ever had with a woman.

Taking a deep breath, he knocked once on the door and stepped inside.

"How's it going?"

Susan hung up the phone and smiled. "Great. We're

done. I'll run these prints as soon as I can. I still have to run the DNA on the blood I gathered as well. When I know, you'll know."

"Anything pan out with the car?" Dee asked as she stood up.

Sauer hesitated. He didn't want to answer that. She knew he didn't want to, yet still asked. The more knowledge she gained of the case, the worse it would be. Honestly, could it get much worse? If he didn't tell her, she might go out on her own again and try solving the case. He felt damned if he did, damned if he didn't.

"You're really not going to tell me?"

The annoyance was plain, as was her pain. Did she think by not telling her he didn't trust her? Trust wasn't the issue. Well, not really. He didn't trust her to not go off on her own.

"Ugh, you're the most aggravating man ever, especially when you don't speak." Dee brushed past him and walked out of the office.

Guess he took too long to answer the question.

"I would've never thought you'd look so happy."

Sauer looked at Susan, no smile on his face. "What?"

"It's in your eyes. The minute you looked at her, I saw it in your eyes. I know it's hard, but telling her small things about the case might help. She just doesn't want to feel useless." Susan held up her hand. "I know it's your job, not hers, but come on, Sauer. This is Dee. She isn't someone who idly sits around. She gets antsy. Telling her something rather than nothing might show her you trust her to leave it to you."

Trust.

How did Susan guess what he was thinking? He did trust Dee. Mostly. Either way, Dee would do her own sleuthing if he didn't give in a little. That couldn't happen again. She was the most fearless woman he ever met. Getting attacked twice didn't appear to affect her as it would other people.

"You might be right. I just don't want to see her get hurt."

"You're a good guy, Sauer. She's lucky to have you." Susan smiled. A sweet, bright smile that finally made him offer one back.

"Thanks, Susan. I'll see you later."

He walked out, curious where Dee sauntered off. If she left... He wouldn't think about it. She wouldn't do that to him twice.

He made his way back to his desk, hoping that's where she wandered off to, and sighed heavily with relief when he saw her lounging in his chair.

"Ready to go?"

She looked up at him. "Where are we going?"

Such a loaded question thick with an intense emotion. With such pain. A wrong answer was possible. He wasn't too confident in the answer lingering in his mind.

"Home."

Brow cocked, she tilted her head. His heart pounded as he waited for her to say something to his brazen word. He obviously meant his house, which she knew. But that's not what he said. There was a distinct difference, at least to him. A house you dwelled in, slept in, did your normal functions. A home signified love, a place to feel wanted and cared for. Would she finally acknowledge his love just a little?

"Can we pick up fast food on the way? I'm starving." She stood up, her winter jacket already on, and started walking. He snagged his jacket from behind his chair and followed her.

She was ignoring his words of love again. Or maybe he was reading into a simple word too much.

At least she didn't argue about staying with him. Until

this guy was caught, he felt better with her under his roof. In his home. How long would she stay?

Best not to think about it.

"You're ignoring me again." She stopped and turned around, a flicker of surprise on her face as if she didn't think he even followed her. Or it could've meant something else. His nerves were wired so high he didn't know what to think anymore.

"Whatever you feel like is fine."

She nodded, then grabbed his hand and started walking again. Hand-holding? That was new for him. He wasn't much of a public display kind of guy. Yeah, chalk it up to his shyness. He liked it, though. He liked it a lot. Probably because it was Dee holding his hand.

They walked out of the precinct in silence, holding hands until they reached his car. He opened the door for her, waiting until she slid inside before closing it, then walked to the driver's side. He smiled at the sweet grin on her face that he did that. Had no man ever done that for her?

He liked the thought he was the first guy to do it. It put him in a special spot. Something he did that nobody ever considered to do for her. He wanted to be special. Needed to be. Anything to keep her in his life for the long term.

They swung by McDonald's, scarfing their food down on the way home. By the time they reached his house, they were both full and he had no idea what they'd do the rest of the day and night.

Dee obviously had more of a plan than he did because she went straight to his bedroom, changed into comfier clothes, then took a spot on his couch, switching the television on.

"Put a movie in. I wanna cuddle. I've never cuddled before. Have you?"

The innocent question swirled around them. He felt like it was very significant she admitted that. Cuddling wasn't much, but it said plenty. Some might even say it was above casual sex. It was developing a closeness that suggested strong feelings. Especially after having sex. At least in his mind. He'd semi cuddled before. Meaning, he never really let his guard down with the few other women he dated. That shyness always lingered on the top, working him up into anxiety. The cuddling never lasted long.

His damn shyness always messed everything up. Except for Dee. Each second he was with her, it slowly withered away. That never happened with his other girlfriends. His shyness was normally what ruined the relationship. They couldn't handle it. Couldn't understand it.

"Are you my girlfriend?"

Oh, shit. He just blurted that out. He was back to saying the dumbest stuff. He refused to avert his eyes as his cheeks flamed with heat.

She cracked a smile, her lips pressed together as if she were trying hard not to laugh. A small chuckle escaped anyway. "You're so adorable when you blush."

He finally looked away. "I don't blush."

She got up and grabbed his hand, pulling him down onto the couch next to her. "You do, too, and it's adorable as hell." A quick kiss to his lips. "You don't hate me? You're not mad about this morning?"

"I get why you left. Not the best timing on your part, but I understand. I'm not trying to rush you into anything. Just forget everything I said today."

Her eyes clouded over with sadness. "Everything?" Her tone dropped to a whisper. "Every word? Nobody's ever said they loved me before. Not the way you said it."

He looked away. "I didn't mean to yell."

"It was sexy as hell."

He whipped his gaze back to her.

"Are you saying you didn't mean it?"

"I meant it." He paused, taking a deep breath. "Do you... does this count as cuddling?"

Close call. He almost asked her if she loved him, too. Hearing no would devastate him.

She bent her head, resting it against his shoulder as she positioned herself to be wrapped in his arms better. "I told you I suck at relationships. I'm sorr—"

"Stop. Don't say those words. Ever again. I hate them."

"Why?" She started to brush her fingers up and down his chest in smooth, small strokes. "I know he left a note with that, but why does it bother you so much?"

He wanted to ignore that question so badly. It didn't take much for fight mode to initiate with her. He'd ignore the question and she'd storm off in anger. He didn't want that. He also didn't want to answer the question.

But maybe if she knew, she wouldn't be as eager to find this guy herself. Just maybe.

"The guy who attacked you, he..."

Her fingers stalled near his belly button, a slight pressure as she tensed. "He what?"

He wrapped his hand around hers and squeezed. "He killed a woman. A week ago. He..." Sauer raised her hand to his mouth and pressed a tender kiss to it. "He left the same note."

The shiver that wracked her body could only be interpreted in one way. Fear. Did she finally understand his persistence that she stay out of the investigation? Did she see why it frightened him so much?

"How?"

He dropped their hands to his lap and laughed, somewhat lamely. "Be thankful I shared what I did. I'm not going into details."

She lifted her head and yanked her hand from his. "I can handle it." She huffed. "Let's skip the part where you ignore me. Why don't you trust me?"

"It's not about trust."

"It is."

"You want that make-up sex now?"

She blinked in surprise. "Excuse me?"

"Well, we can sleep together and then you can leave again without telling me to go find this guy on your own. Then he can attack you and maybe hurt you a lot more this time, where I can see the woman I love—" He spoke louder. "Love—did you hear that part clearly—hurt so badly I'll probably go into a murderous rage. Do I trust you? Yes. Do I trust you not to leave? I'm a little hesitant."

She rested her head against his shoulder again, resuming the strokes up and down his chest. What the hell? She was going to ignore his outburst, because that's exactly what it was. An outburst. She brought those out of him so easily.

"I deserved that." She sighed. "You scared me."

"I would never hurt you."

She grabbed his shirt into a fistful. "You know I'm not talking physically. You make me feel things I've never felt. It scares the hell out of me, Sauer."

"Me, too." He grabbed her hand once again. "I yelled again. My bad."

She chuckled. "You're going to apologize in as many ways as you can without saying those other words, aren't you?"

"Do you forgive me?"

"No."

His heart started to beat a little faster. No doubt, she could feel it.

"You didn't do anything wrong. There's nothing to forgive. I deserved that. I need to earn that part of your trust back. I just don't know how."

"Stay." *Forever.*

Her hand swooped down his chest to the edge of his shirt, then back up. Delicious trembles touched him everywhere. Her soft hand anywhere on him made him lose his mind instantly.

"Well, it is customary for a girlfriend to spend the night at her boyfriend's house."

He couldn't help the smile that touched his face. "It is."

"Is it time for make-up sex yet?"

"I am curious to see what it's like."

They laughed together. Dee sat up and quickly removed his shirt. "Ready when you are."

He stood up and scooped her into his arms. "I've always wanted to carry a woman like this. I like the feeling."

She tucked her head under his chin as he made his way to the bedroom. "By all means, do it whenever the urge strikes you." She sighed softly. "The words are stuck." Her voice lowered even more. "I wanna say them."

He paused at the foot of the bed, his heart pounding like mad once again. She just admitted in her own way she loved him. Oddly, it was enough. That's all he needed to hear.

"Let me show you how much I love hearing that."

12

DEE ARCHED a brow as her mouth slowly opened in shock. "You want me to do what? Are you nuts, Rina?"

"Dancing lessons will be fun. Ben's so sweet. When I told him I would love to go dancing, the frightened way he looked at me told me right away he doesn't know how to dance. But he smiled and said okay." Rina moved closer to her desk. "It'll be fun. Zoe and Zeke are going to take the classes, too." She clapped her hands so giddy-like. "There's this event in two months...the King and Queen's Ball. Doesn't that sound like so much fun? The dance class is four weeks long. We'll have plenty of time to learn the dances we need to for that. We'll have to skip opening day, but we can go to a Twins game this summer."

Dee didn't want to hurt Rina's feelings. Of all people she hated to make feel bad, it was Rina. The way her face fell into sadness, her little lip pouting, the pain in her eyes. Rina was so sensitive, and one of the sweetest people she knew. It hurt to hurt her.

But dance classes? Was she nuts? Clearly certifiable. When she danced, it wasn't appropriate for something like a

King and Queen's Ball, that's for sure. More like indecent. She'd rather go to a baseball game.

Didn't Rina see how uneven it was again? Her and Ben. Zoe and Zeke. Dee and...uh, well, Sauer. Would he take dance classes with her?

No. She couldn't ask him. Their relationship was tentative at best. He still had moments of shyness. Asking him to take dance classes with her would bring out his shyness tenfold. She wouldn't embarrass him like that.

"Dee? Come on. It'll be fun. Don't look at me like that."

Dee realized she still had the shock written on her face and relaxed somewhat. "I'm not really a King and Queen kinda girl. Sorry, Rina." Adding a sweet smile, "And I hate being the fifth wheel. You guys have fun."

Rina pursed her lips. A look that was uncommon for her, but lately, since her and Ben had gotten together, the aggressive Rina had started to come out and play. "You'll ask Sauer, of course."

"You telling me or asking me?"

Rina propped a hand to her hip. She was definitely telling her.

"That doesn't sound like a Sauer-like thing. I don't want to embarrass him. You know he's a shy guy."

"Stop being afraid."

Dee jerked back. "I'm not afraid."

A brow arched. "Prove it?"

So unfair. Rina was playing dirty with her. What happened to her shy friend? This one scared her a little. Dee averted her eyes for a moment, then squared her shoulders. "Fine. Sign us up."

A slow grin emerged. "Perfect. The first class is Wednesday. I'm so excited. I'm going to tell Zoe."

Dee turned back to her computer as Rina walked away

with a pep in her step. She always gave in so easily. She hated upsetting her. And Zoe. She quit her position at Young's Accountants two months ago, wanting to stay at home with Zabrina. She agonized over the decision, but overall, so happy she left. It was times like this she missed her terribly. She enjoyed the little breaks the three of them had at work, gossiping, giggling, just acting like the best friends they were.

What was she getting herself into? Dance classes? Worst decision ever. Would Sauer say yes? Would she end up being the fifth wheel?

The weekend had gone by fast. Make-up sex was just as delicious as the first time they slept together. The entire weekend they barely made it out of bed. Exploring, devouring, and enjoying the time between the sheets. It wasn't just sex. They talked, laughed, and had fun. She never let her guard down like that with a guy. With Sauer, it was easy to do.

She saw the hesitation in his eyes, the worry whenever he walked out of the room to dispose of the condom. Would she still be there in bed waiting for him? He still didn't trust her not to leave.

She didn't blame him. He shouldn't trust her. Because every single time, the urge screamed at her to get up and run. Every little emotion he sucked out of her made her want to run. It was damn scary. She didn't know if she'd survive it.

When would he leave her? That's what scared her the most. It was always better to leave first. Not be dumped and let the guy break her heart.

He'd eventually get sick of her. Annoyed. Frustrated. Men always did. What made Sauer any different?

Everything. He was one of a kind. She had to start

believing it. He'd never trust her until she believed in him wholeheartedly.

Although, she was proud of herself. She hated the look in his eyes when she ventured off to handle the case on her own. She hated the pain, the fear, the terror that slipped out. She put it there. To avoid seeing that, she would let him do his job. It was damn hard to do.

She felt antsy. All she wanted to do was call Stitch every five minutes to see if he found anything. Or talk to her annoying neighbor Mathias to see if he saw anything strange. She wanted to do it all.

But like the good girlfriend she was trying to be, and the promise she was trying to keep, she held the urge in. Because if she broke her promise to Sauer, he'd never trust her again. She wanted—needed—his trust.

I swear I'll leave the case to you. I promise. Just tell me a little.

Surprisingly, he went over a few aspects of the case with her. Oh, she knew he left some things out, but for the first time, he didn't ignore her. She loved him a little more for that.

So no. She wouldn't break her promise. His trust.

———

"She said yes."

Zoe squealed in her ear. "I knew you'd convince her. She would've totally said no to me."

"Yeah, but she wasn't too happy about saying yes. She doesn't think Sauer will want to do it. That it will be embarrassing and hard for him because he's so shy." Rina sighed. "I didn't think about that. She might be right."

"Nonsense. Zeke and Ben wanted our help to get these

two together permanently. This will work. Dancing... dancing can be erotic. They'll fall in love."

"But Sauer is shy. He doesn't like to be the center of attention. Maybe he won't do it. Then Dee will feel horrible because he said no and it'll be all our fault."

"Rina, he won't say no." Zoe paused. "I don't think so, anyway. He's shy, yes, but I also think he'll do anything for her. Look at Zeke." Zoe laughed. "When I told him our plans, the look of terror on his face. Oh, it was priceless. Then I told him about the ball, and he nearly ran out of the room, shaking his head no. I reminded him it was his idea to get these two closer together."

Rina chuckled. "Ben reacted the same way. He wasn't fond of dance lessons, and even less so about the ball. Just watch, those two will be in competition, arguing who's the better dancer. Get your dancing feet ready. They're going to want to practice at home."

A fit of giggles rang in her ear. "Oh, God, you're so right. Well, I'm okay with that. Dancing will just lead to stuff that is too inappropriate to say in front of Brina."

"Like she knows what that means." Rina sighed wistfully, hoping to be pregnant soon. Although, after a lengthy discussion, mostly to soothe her nerves, they decided to keep it to themselves. It hadn't been long since they started trying—only a few months, even before they were married. She still wasn't pregnant yet, not as quickly as it happened for Zoe. She worried something was wrong. Ben insisted everything would work out. But it made her feel better to keep it to themselves for now. "I should get back to work. I'll sign us all up. Classes start Wednesday. Should we wait for Dee to ask Sauer?"

Zoe didn't have to think about it. "No. If anything, we'll sic Zeke and Ben on him. He won't say no."

"So, we hit a brick wall again. We can't find the car. Nothing panned out when we talked to the shops around Stitch's place to see if they saw anything useful. Did Stitch get back to you yet? Or is he calling Dee?"

Sauer looked away from his computer. "Dee said he'll call me. We...uh...we talked a little about the case. I gave in. She promised to leave the detective work to me." Sauer rolled his eyes. "Since I am the detective."

"Think she'll keep that promise?"

He didn't like to think she'd break her promise, but it lingered in his mind. The nasty feeling that she just might. "Yeah." He looked away, knowing it didn't sound as confident as it should've.

Newman cleared his throat. "You got company, buddy. Lucky dog, you."

Sauer smiled as Dee walked toward him with an equally happy smile. He stood up and almost pulled her into his arms for a kiss, sort of like Ben and Zeke did all the time when Rina or Zoe visited, but stopped himself. Did Dee like public displays like that? Would it embarrass her?

His worry went out the door when she slithered up to him, wrapping her arms around his neck and planted the sweetest kiss on his lips.

"Lunch?"

He could feel his face flaming with heat as he glanced at Newman, who waved a hand at him to go. He turned back to her. "Lunch sounds great." His brows puckered. "How did you get here? You need to be careful."

Her lips pressed into a thin line. "I can take care of myself." Then just as quickly, she relaxed. "Rina and I drove together. She wanted to have lunch with Ben."

Round and round they go. Always with her. Did she forget this guy tried to hurt her twice? Once in public, in broad daylight. He hated hearing, *I can take care of myself*. He wanted to take care of her. In every single way. Would she ever let him?

"Wipe that look off your face and stop ignoring me."

"It's called reflecting. Sometimes, I have to think of what to say because you make me so...irritated."

She smiled wide. It should've annoyed him she found that funny, but it did nothing but captivate him more and more toward her.

"Your cheeks are still red."

Newman snickered, reminding Sauer they were arguing with an audience. "Come on. Let's grab a sandwich down the street."

He quickly put on his jacket, then grabbed her hand first this time as they walked out and down the block to the sandwich shop that made the best hoagies in town. They both ordered and took a seat near the window.

"I like this."

Dee paused at taking a bite, grinning. "I'll have to try that sandwich next time. I always get the ham and turkey. I'm not a huge fan of bean sprouts and whatever else that is."

He knew he started to blush when he glanced down at his sandwich that had bean sprouts, cucumbers, onions, ham, and a few other things that just made his taste buds salivate with hunger. "That's not what I meant." He looked up. "I like that you came to visit me."

For the first time he could remember, a small hint of red emerged on her cheeks. "I like it, too." She cleared her throat. "Can I ask you something? It's no big deal. You can totally say no."

He reached for her hand that started to fidget with a

napkin. He'd never seen her so nervous before. Warmth filled him up, knowing he wasn't the only one who could get nervous. It also worried him. Why was she nervous? He had a feeling he wouldn't like the question.

"Will you take dance lessons with me?"

His sandwich dropped from his hand, the question a total surprise. He never expected that in a million years. "Dance...lessons?"

His mind drifted back to Ben and Rina's wedding, the perfect way she moved. The ease at which she danced. She obviously knew how to dance. She didn't think *he* could dance. Just assumed because he was shy, he didn't know the first thing about dancing.

"I know how to dance."

"You do?"

The shock in her tone pissed him off. Almost the same feeling he got when she refused to leave the case alone. "Why do you sound so surprised?"

"Why are you getting upset with me?"

"Why do you think I can't dance?"

Anger quickly replaced her shock. "I never said that."

"Then why do you want to take dance lessons?"

Her anger slowly morphed into pain. "I've seen you upset at me, but I can honestly say, I never expected you to get so upset at me for something like this." She stood up. "Go to hell, Sauer."

She walked out.

"LET'S GO."

Rina glanced away from Ben where they sat in the break room at the precinct. "What's wrong?"

"I'm ready to go. I have tons of shit I have to get done. You ready?"

Rina looked at her unfinished food, shared a look with Ben, then back at her. "We just started eating. You left with Sauer less than ten minutes ago. What's wrong?"

"I already told you, I have tons—"

"Stop lying to me."

Dee didn't want to admit it. She didn't want them to know how Sauer got so upset. It had been like the flick of a switch. He went from happy to mad within seconds. She had no idea why the thought of dance lessons would do that to him.

"Sauer said no."

Rina couldn't hide her surprise as Ben nearly choked on his food he just swallowed. "He would never..."

"Think again. I refuse to be a fifth wheel. You guys have fun." She suddenly had the strange urge to cry. "I want to leave, Rina. Can Ben bring you back when you're done? I'll drive back by myself."

"Shit, Dee, I'm sorry."

She turned her attention to Ben, who had cleared his throat and stopped coughing. "For what?"

He looked panicked. "That Sauer said no. Are you sure? Maybe I should talk to him. It'll be fun."

"Oh, I got the message loud and clear."

"What's that?"

Dee whipped around to see Sauer standing in the doorway.

"You shouldn't walk off like that."

Slamming her hands to her hips, she let the pain drift away and the anger sweep in. "Don't worry about me, Sauer. It isn't your job anymore."

"Whoa, whoa. What's going on?" Ben stood up, scooting

his chair back. "A simple question of dance classes caused this? We'll have fun."

Confusion crossed over Sauer's face. "We?"

"Me and Rina. Zeke and Zoe. You and Dee." Ben glanced at Rina with a goofy smile. "There's this ball these ladies want to go to and I don't know how to ballroom dance." He looked back at Sauer. "Do you?"

All sets of eyes looked at him. Dee watched as he got red in the face, a mixture of pain and rage. "I can."

"Really?" She couldn't stop the question, knowing as soon as it slipped out he'd hate it.

"Yeah. My mother said a man should know how to dance properly." He deflated right before her eyes as he looked at Ben. "Make sure she gets to work safely."

He walked out.

"I've never seen him so pissed." Ben rubbed a hand over his jaw.

Dee shook her head as the tears threatened to flow. "He hates me. What did I do?"

Rina looked away as Ben turned red with embarrassment.

"Or should I be saying, what did you two do?"

13

"Rina was in tears when I drove her back to work. Dee refused to ride with us, demanding Rina hand over her car keys. Honestly, I didn't argue with her. I just followed her to work."

"So you told her?"

"Dude, she didn't give me a choice. I'm not going to be on the receiving end of Dee's anger. And it made Rina cry."

"Zoe's not going to take it any better. This is bad."

"This is your fault."

Newman finally cleared his throat. He had enough of listening to Ben and Zeke whispering in the break room. "You ladies wanna tell me what's going on. My partner is pissed. Which is strange because he came to work with a smile on his face."

Eyes swiveled to him, the embarrassment reflected in their eyes. He tried to get Sauer to talk, to tell him what the hell happened, but he mumbled something he didn't understand, then said he was heading to the crime lab to talk to Susan. He figured if Sauer wouldn't tell him, these two would.

"Well?"

Ben sighed. "Guess you could call it playing match-maker. We asked Rina and Zoe for some help and they thought dance lessons was a great idea. It wasn't. Sauer's pissed about it for some reason."

"He can dance."

"I don't know why, but that surprises me." Zeke rubbed his jaw. "We were just trying to help."

"Well, quit it. You're pissing off my partner, which pisses me off. I'm not used to him surly and upset. Let me tell you, I don't like it."

"We didn't mean to make it worse. Why did it piss him off so much?"

Newman shrugged. He honestly didn't have a clue. Sauer didn't talk much about his childhood, but he let little things slip. He knew Sauer could dance, but never used it to his advantage when they went out looking for women. Or, more like, when he went out looking for women and Sauer tagged along. Newman doubted at times that he could dance, since he never actually went out on the dance floor.

Then one night, Sauer had one too many to drink. The alcohol masked his shyness enough to dance with a woman who could move. The energy they sparked on the dance floor was electric. Newman never saw someone with such amazing moves. Of course, when the music ended and the woman draped herself over his body with blatant sexual interest, Sauer snapped out of his stupor and back into his shyness. He never left the bar with the woman.

"Just...mind your own business."

Zeke's expression turned hard. "Don't tell me what to do, Newman. We didn't mean to upset him."

"When you mess with my partner, you're messing with me."

"You messed with him yourself. And guess what?" Zeke took a step closer. "You're messing with me when you do that."

Newman didn't like the scary glint in his eyes, but he wasn't about to back down. Or admit how much of an ass he acted the night of the Super Bowl party. He regretted it the minute he had done it. There wasn't a good enough excuse for his actions. Other than jealousy.

"Leave him alone." He took a step.

"You leave him alone." Zeke took a step.

Ben shoved his way between them, considering they were almost nose-to-nose. "Enough!" He was breathing heavily, his jaw clenching and unclenching as he stared at him. "You hit Zeke, then I gotta hit you, then I'll go home looking like I got into a fight, which will make Rina cry some more. I hate seeing my wife cry."

Newman backed away. "Look—"

"What's going on?"

Newman turned around. Sauer stood there glancing from one person to another. "Just having a friendly chat."

Zeke scoffed.

Either Sauer didn't hear anything, or he chose to ignore it. "Mrs. Stenson's car has been found."

"That's great news." Zeke's enthusiasm dimmed as Sauer continued to look at everyone with a frown. "I'm getting the feeling it's not that great."

"Walker from the fire department called me." Sauer started to rub a hand back and forth over his head. "He torched the car. Covered his tracks and destroyed any evidence."

"Shit."

Newman concurred with that exclamation from Zeke. The case loved to go from one dead end to another. When would they catch a break?

"Sauer, you and I can go speak to Mrs. Stenson. Ben and Newman can check out the car." Zeke glanced around the room. "Sound like a plan?"

Ben raised a brow with a questioning look, then nodded. Sauer looked a little confused as well, but also nodded. Newman wanted to know why Zeke wanted to split up, but refused to ask. If Sauer came back even more pissed, he'd knock a fist into Zeke's face and be damned the consequences.

His life had turned to complete shit lately. A fight sounded like a great plan. Unleash some of his anger and pain. He didn't care if Zeke would be on the receiving end. He deserved it after upsetting Sauer the way he had.

"Fine. Let's go." He gave Zeke a look that conveyed a message he better be on his best behavior. Zeke had the audacity to smirk and brush past him without one word.

SAUER WASN'T AN IDIOT. He knew they were talking about what happened with him and Dee. His anger had dissipated to regret the minute he saw her walk out of the precinct. She didn't glance his way once. He knew he screwed up. His anger got the best of him. The past swamped his mind, bringing the rage straight to the top. He couldn't have stopped it if he tried. Trying to explain it to Dee would be hard. No doubt she wouldn't want any explanation from him. She didn't want anything to do with him anymore.

He wasn't dumb either about Zeke splitting them up. He had something to say. Sauer was still waiting for him to say it as he drove to Mrs. Stenson's residence.

"About the dance lessons..."

It was about time he started talking. Sauer stayed silent, wanting to hear what Zeke had to say.

"It was our idea...Ben and I. We were just trying to help. You know, bring you and Dee closer or whatever. Although, Rina and Zoe came up with the idea to take dance lessons. There's this ball coming up...I don't have the first clue how to ballroom dance. The waltz, the fox-trot, the tango...I got two left feet for shit like that." Zeke turned to him. "How long have you known how to dance?"

Now he felt worse than before. It hadn't even been Dee's idea. A ball. What kind of ball? Since Ben's wedding, he'd been dying to dance with her. A ball was the perfect solution. But dancing...

"Sauer, man, I'm—"

"I know you feel bad. No need to apologize." Those words slipped so easily from people's lips way too often. Two words and people thought it magically fixed everything. Oh, he knew Zeke and Ben meant everything in his best interest. Nothing was done maliciously. He reacted badly. He should be apologizing. But not with those two words. They didn't mean anything. He'd say it another way. "It's not your fault. I reacted badly."

"We should've—"

"I've known how to dance since I was twelve." He turned right, glancing at Zeke. "My mom thought every man should know how to dance. My dad still takes my mom dancing. She loves it."

Zeke grinned. "Yeah, my dad's taken my mom dancing a few times. Although, she never made me take lessons when I was younger."

"I liked it. I had fun. When the first school dance, the Snow Ball, came around, I was so excited to dance." He fell silent, unsure if he could finish. Thinking about it, let alone talking about it, was hard. Kids could be so cruel. "Let's just say, the other kids didn't appreciate my dance moves."

"They teased you."

Sauer heard the question in the statement. Zeke wanted to know more.

"You know I'm shy, kind of quiet. What can I say? I was an awkward kid." Sauer shrugged. "Kids can be mean. Dancing wasn't as fun after that."

"Sauer, they were jealous."

He pulled into Mrs. Stenson's driveway, pondering that. Maybe they were. Although, he knew dancing the fancy dances at a school function probably wasn't the smartest move on his part. Not many kids could dance like that. Just one of the many ways he stuck out like a sore thumb. He was always the oddball in school. He still felt like that sometimes as an adult.

"We conjured bad memories." Zeke sighed. "I have to admit, I wasn't thrilled about Zoe and Rina's idea. Dancing... not my idea of fun. Of course, I get to hold my wife in my arms, but I have no coordination on the dance floor. Talk about embarrassing." He met his stare. "I'm envious of you that you know how to dance. I hate to admit it, but I didn't think you did."

Sauer nodded, not surprised. Another reason he got so upset. As he thought about it, he shouldn't be. Zeke didn't know how to dance. If someone like Zeke, a ladies man before he met Zoe, didn't know how to dance, why would he think Sauer knew how to, as shy as he was with women.

"I reacted badly. I don't normally do that. I was wrong."

Zeke chuckled. "She's got you tied up in knots. Love can make you act crazy. We're good, man...right?"

A smile touched his face. "Yep." Then it dimmed. "I guess I ruined the fun."

A wide smile emerged, almost twinkling with delight. "Oh, no, you didn't. Rina already booked the lessons, and the tickets to the ball. The King and Queen's Ball. It's all non-refundable. Don't worry, it's on me. Maybe you can teach me some suave moves to impress Zoe."

Laughing, he winked. "I got some moves she'd love." Looking away, he squeezed the steering wheel tightly. "Dee hates me now. She won't go with me."

"Na, you have a way with her. She'll forgive you." Zeke cleared his throat. "You ever talk to her about...the past?"

"No."

"It might help. In more ways than you imagine."

"You're probably right."

"Oh, I'm always right. Tell Ben that."

Sauer laughed hard, remembering Ben's words from the other day. "Yeah, he said he's always right."

"Only in his dreams." Zeke tapped him on the shoulder. "Come on. Let's break the news to Mrs. Stenson. I really hate to do this."

They stepped out of the vehicle, walking slowly to the door, obviously trying to delay the inevitable.

"Can you keep our talk between us? It's...embarrassing."

Zeke lowered his hand after knocking on the door and nodded. "You got it, buddy. At least let Newman know we're good. He wanted to punch me. Which means I'd have to punch him, then Ben would jump in..."

"Then I'd have to jump in..." Sauer chuckled. "Yeah, I'll talk to him."

Talking with Newman would be nothing compared to talking with Dee. Talking was not his forte. What could he possibly say so she'd forgive him?

For a guy who rarely argued with people, that's all he'd been doing lately. He didn't like it one bit.

DEE LOOKED up from her desk and groaned. She already felt bad enough Rina got so upset she cried. Apparently, she called Zoe, who felt compelled to come.

"Where's Zabrina? If you're gonna come here to ream me out, at least you could've brought her with."

Zoe rolled her eyes. "I'm not here to ream you out. She's with my parents."

She fiddled with the keyboard. "I'm so—I didn't mean to make you cry, Rina. You know I'm a bitch."

A soft hand touched her shoulder. "I have no idea why I cried like that. It wasn't anything you did. I just feel horrible we created such tension between you and Sauer. I never imagined…"

Dee squeezed her hand as she looked up. "Me either. I was shocked when he got so angry."

"Talk to him. I'm sure if—"

"Talking's overrated."

Zoe gave her *the look*. Hand on her hips. Lips pierced in a thin line. Brow cocked. She wasn't amused.

"I didn't want to go to this dumb ball, anyway, or dance lessons."

Rina's lip started to tremble.

"Oh, shit, Rina, don't start crying again." Dee brushed her crazy hair back. "Fine. I'll go. I don't need Sauer to go with me."

"That's not okay." Rina swiped a hand under her eye. "I'm not going to cry. I don't know what's wrong with me."

"Maybe you're pregnant. Zoe was ridiculous with the waterworks when she was pregnant." Dee shot up out of her chair. "Holy shit, are you pregnant?"

Rina's eyes grew large, round as saucers. "No. I don't…

think so." Small, silent tears started to leak out.

"What's the matter?" Zoe touched her shoulder. "Those are tears of joy, I hope."

"We said we wouldn't say anything, but...I can't." Rina hiccupped in disgust. "Ben would get that look if he heard me say the word can't."

Dee snapped her fingers. "Focus, Rina. Start talking."

A smirk formed as she wiped a tear away. "Talking's overrated."

That did it. Their laughter bounced off the walls. They couldn't hold it in. A few other employees looked at them in surprise, but said nothing.

"Fine. I'll talk to him," Dee said. "Now, what's going on?"

Rina rolled her eyes at the way she caved in so quickly just to divert the attention back to her. "We've been trying for a while and...and nothing. It happened so quickly for you, Zoe."

Zoe wrapped her arm around Rina's shoulder and gently squeezed. "Everybody's different. Have you seen a doctor?"

Rina nodded. "They aren't worried. Not yet. I can't help but worry."

Pushing her hair back again, scrunching it a little, Dee smirked. "With all the tears, I'd say it's finally happened. Hope you're not a yacker like Zoe was."

Laughter filled the room again.

"I haven't felt nauseous yet." Rina breathed deeply. "I'll be back." She pointed an accusing finger at her. "You'll talk to Sauer."

"Where are you going?" Dee didn't want to acknowledge the Sauer part. How many more times could she screw up and he'd forgive her? He had to be sick of her by now.

"The pharmacy." Then Rina gave her *the look*. Soft smile.

Relaxed posture. A hard glint in her eyes that said she meant business. Rina's look scared her more than Zoe's.

"I said I'd talk to him."

"Good." Rina got a giddy look on her face as she walked away.

"Can I stay with you guys? I'm not saying I'm scared or anything, but to make you all not worry, I'd rather stay with someone until this guy is caught." That was the truth. She didn't get scared. Maybe a bit apprehensive because this guy was persistent, but scared? No way. "If she is pregnant, they'll probably wanna celebrate." Dee lifted her eyebrows up and down mischievously.

"You just told Rina you'd talk to Sauer. You can stay with him."

A heavy sigh should've told Zoe everything she needed to know. "With the way I acted, he's not going to want me around, even if we do talk. Trust me. I've used up my apologies with him."

Zoe smiled softly. "You might not be afraid of this guy attacking you, but you're scared of Sauer. Of letting someone get close to you. Just let go. Let him in.

"And when I let him in and he leaves, because they always do, what then?"

"You pick yourself back up like you always do. You're Deena O'Malley. Nothing scares you or brings you down." Zoe hugged her. "Sauer loves you. He won't give up. This can be fixed. It's just a misunderstanding."

As Zoe walked away, Dee wasn't so sure she agreed. He said he loved her, but in her experience, everyone always got sick of her. What made him any different?

Would he really not give up on her? She wasn't sure. She wasn't feeling confident in the answer she wanted.

14

HE LOOKED at all the papers swamping his desk and groaned. Nothing. Still no evidence to point to the killer. Of all the cases littering his desk, he didn't want this one to go cold. For Dee's sake.

How was she doing? How upset was she?

"He torched the car good. There must've been some kind of evidence we would've found." Newman leaned back in his chair.

"Overly cautious, I say," Ben chimed in, standing near their desks. "We already know he has balls, trying to attack Dee in broad daylight. He doesn't want to leave anything to chance."

"The only saving grace from this is Mrs. Stenson can contact her insurance company, which I'm sure she did the minute Sauer and I left. That Barry dude is a great guy letting her borrow his vehicle until she gets a new one. I'm glad, actually. If not, I would've felt compelled to help her somehow."

"You're such a sucker. Aren't you married?"

Zeke straightened as Ben placed a calm hand on him. "Still got a problem, uh, Newman?"

Sauer cleared his throat, not wanting a fight. He'd be on Zeke's side. Newman was out of line—again. Obviously breaking up with Chrissy was messing with him more than any other breakup. "Let's not do this, guys."

Newman looked away from Zeke and nodded at him. "I'm ready to call it a day. Did you talk to Susan again about those prints?"

"She said she'd get to them as soon as she can, but I haven't heard back from her. She processed the DNA first. Nothing in the system popped up. Something needs to pop up with the prints, otherwise we have nothing."

Newman stood up, grabbing his jacket from the back of his chair. "I'll stop in to see her on my way out. Maybe she has something by now. See ya tomorrow." He walked away.

"What's his problem?" Zeke asked as soon as Newman disappeared through the door.

Sauer shrugged. It wasn't his business to share what happened with Newman. "I guess I should...uh...pick up Dee."

Shuffling his feet, Zeke glanced away, clearly uncomfortable about something.

"Or not."

Zeke groaned, then said, "Zoe picked her up. She's going to stay with us. At least that's what Zoe told me." He rubbed his jaw. "I think you should come pick her up. Don't take no for an answer."

Sauer stood up, portraying more strength than his legs carried. He wanted to keel over in pain from the thought of Dee leaving him. Because that's exactly what she was doing. Leaving him. Running away. He knew he upset her, but apparently, she didn't even want to talk to him anymore. She didn't even have the nerve to tell him herself that she wouldn't be staying with him. After the weekend they had. The intimacy they shared. The closeness. She broke his heart. He had no one to blame but himself.

"It's okay. Perhaps a breather between us would be good." He fiddled with his papers, trying to organize them a little more. "I don't know what to say to her."

"Yeah, you do."

Sauer jerked his gaze to Zeke. He was referring to the talk they had in the car earlier. "Just make sure she stays safe. I'll see you guys tomorrow."

He left before they could change his mind. Simple conversation was hard enough for him. Explaining to Dee his reaction sounded like the biggest challenge he ever faced. What would she think of him? A loser. A geek. Just a few things kids called him when he was younger.

He didn't want to see it in her eyes that she agreed.

Thirty minutes later, he pulled into the garage. He took the long way home, delaying the inevitable silence and loneliness that would punch him in the gut the minute he opened the door. In a short time, Dee had invaded his home and heart. He honestly wasn't sure how he'd survive the loss.

He stepped inside, disarming the alarm, and tossed his keys to the kitchen counter. Silence echoed. The loneliness slapped him in the face.

Damn, he missed her.

Grabbing a beer from the fridge, he walked to the living room and slumped down on the couch. Instead of turning on the television, he took a swig of beer and listened to the quiet. Dee loved to talk. About anything and everything. She always filled the silence with her beautiful voice. On the rare occasion they were silent, it was comfortable. Normal. He had easily gone from awkward and shy to comfortable and natural in her presence. That never happened with any of the women he dated. He could never quite lose that shyness with them. With Dee...she just made it seem possible. She accepted him for him. Shyness and all.

"It's about damn time you got home."

His eyes jerked to the threshold of the living room. Dee stood with her hands on her hips, her lips pressed tightly together, and her hair fanning out in the beautiful curly way it always did. So damn beautiful. Every inch of her.

Before he could respond, the words stuck in his throat, Dee walked to him, straddling his lap as if nothing happened between them today. She grabbed his face, pressing her sweet lips to his. The kiss was slow and lazy, and as delicious as a kiss could be. With her, it always took his breath away.

She pulled away, dropping her hands to his chest.

"Zeke said...you were staying with them."

"Yeah, and why in the hell didn't you come get me?"

So she was mad at him.

"How did you get in?" The thought suddenly jolted him. He never gave her a key, or the code to the alarm. The garage door was down. He didn't hear the front door open, which would've been impossible since it was locked.

Giving him a cocky look, the one that had mischievous intents written all over, she laughed. "I swiped your spare key from the drawer in the kitchen before we left today." She kissed the side of his lips, swiping her tongue across, teasing him. "I memorized your code, looking over your shoulder every time you set it or disarmed it. I'm a resourceful girl. Never underestimate me, Sauer." She tapped his nose. "I forgive you for not picking me up."

Confused didn't begin to describe the swirling emotions plaguing him. "Why would you swipe my spare key?"

"In case you had to work late and I needed to get in." She gave him a look that said she wanted to add the word 'duh' to the end of that statement.

"Do you also forgive me for my outburst earlier? I...I shouldn't have gotten so upset. I'd like to take dance lessons with you."

The laughter and happiness died in her eyes. "I obviously touched a sore spot. Forgive me?"

Chuckling, as a shiver of pleasure rushed through him as her hands explored his chest, he held her gaze, hoping the light would shine once again in them. "Are we about to argue who was wrong? Because I hate arguing with you."

"You don't have to take dance lessons. You can dance."

He almost averted his eyes, but he wouldn't look away as he explained why he got so sour about it. She wouldn't judge. The knowledge and trust in that came swiftly. Shortening his embarrassing story, he explained his uneasiness about dancing, but he couldn't resist adding, "I've wanted to dance with you since Ben and Rina's wedding. I ached so badly to ask you."

"Then why didn't you?"

The laugh came so easily, he was shocked she asked such a question. "Uh...you do recall the first time I asked you out and how well that came out?"

"Those girls were idiots. You know that, right?"

He nodded, unable to speak. He liked hearing Dee say that.

"So, are you going to go with me or what?" She scooted back just a little on his lap, then grabbed the beer bottle from his hand and set it on the coffee table. Turning back to him, she brushed her fingers to the edge of his pants, grasping his belt buckle. "Actually, I'm not giving you a choice. You're taking the lessons with me, then escorting me to this ball. Got it?"

Nodding again, words suddenly foreign to him, she undid his buckle, slipping his zipper down. Her hand snaked inside, wrapping around him.

"Uh, oh, is shy Sauer making an appearance?" She stroked him once as she leaned in, nibbling on his ear. "Or have words just escaped you?"

He slid his hands over her legs, cupping her ass. "You know what you do to me. I have no words right now."

Another delicious stroke. Up, then down. "Dance, ball, you and me. Got it?"

"I look forward to it. Every part." He trailed kisses down her neck as her hand started to pump faster. "You in my arms is the best feeling in the world. Dancing with you...it's been a dream of mine."

She pulled away and stood up.

He missed her touch instantly. Her sweet, soft body against his. "What did I say wrong?"

Her shirt rose slowly as she winked at him. The shirt went flying behind her. "You never say anything wrong. Ever." Her bra joined the shirt. Soon after, her pants and underwear were added to the pile across the room. "In fact, your words always get me horny."

Heart pounding, the gorgeous picture in front of him took his breath away. He watched silently as she tugged his jeans down and off, his boxers just as quickly. Straddling his lap once again, she started to loosen his tie.

"Have you ever been tied up?"

Wrapping his arms around her, his hands squeezing her ass, he raised a brow. "What do you think?"

The tie dangled in her hands. "Wanna try it?"

"Uh..." He really wasn't sure if he wanted to do that. Kinky sex wasn't his thing.

She laid the tie across her legs, then started to unbutton his shirt, her fingers grazing his chest as she went along. Trembles coated his body as the fireworks of desire attacked him. "Can I tie you up, too?"

Shit. Did he just say that?

She looked surprised as well.

"I was kidding. You really wanna try?" She dropped his shirt to the floor, leaning into him, lightly brushing his lips. "I'm not sure I could stand not to feel your hands on me."

Breathing a sigh of relief, his tongue swooped in, increasing the kiss from light and teasing to strong and urgent. She tasted so sweet.

"Good. I really didn't want to."

Tossing the tie to the floor, she laughed, then reached behind her to the coffee table and tore open a condom.

"Where did that come from?"

Offering a tsking sound, she slowly covered him. "You're supposed to be observant, Detective Sauer."

His hands splayed across her thighs as she sank down on top of him. "I lose all train of thought when you walk into a room. I lose my mind."

She hugged him close, pressing a kiss to his neck. "Why do you have to say the sweetest things?"

Was that bad? She didn't like it? He could clearly hear the pain in those words. What did it mean?

He pulled her closer, lifting his hips, pushing even farther inside her. "Because you deserve sweet words."

She moaned, as they started to move together. He met her each time she sank down. Up and down. Every time they joined as one, they moved differently. Fast and rough. Slow and sweet.

Eager and energetic. Tenderly and carefully. He wasn't sure how to classify this. Perhaps a mixture of slow and sweet with fast and rough. Her kisses went up and down his shoulder to his neck, where she nibbled on his ear. No matter the position, they could always create beautiful magic together.

"I love you, Dee. I'm probably going to screw up again, but know that I'll always love you."

"Shut up, Sauer."

Right. She didn't want sweet words.

The pleasure started to rise within. He knew she was just as close as her moans of bliss echoed in the room.

Tough. She'd get his sweet words, whether she wanted to hear them or not.

"So beautiful." Up and down. Thrust for thrust. "So sweet." A kiss attacked his lips. "So mine."

She bit his bottom lip as the strongest orgasm she ever experienced hit her. He knew it, too, by the way she clutched his head, her nails digging in, her lips bruising his. He couldn't hold back, didn't want to either. He came with her, holding her tenderly in his arms as contentment flowed through.

She rested her head on his shoulder. Her words slipped out in a whisper, with a quiver attached to each one. "You promise to love me always?"

Did she doubt his love? Well, he wasn't smooth with the ladies. Perhaps he wasn't showing her well enough.

"My love is something you should never worry about." He squeezed her tighter into his embrace. "I promise."

TAKING A SIP OF PEPSI, Dee tried not to let Rina and Zoe's stare break her. She had already told them she and Sauer would attend the dance classes and the ball with a smile on both of their faces. She didn't want to go into detail of their make-up session. Those moments, those special times, were for her and Sauer only. Normally, she had no problem talking about her sexual encounters. But Sauer was different. He was hers. She didn't want to share anything.

Call her possessive.

Yeah, definitely call her possessive.

"Why are you scowling?" Zoe shoved her fork into the salad sitting in front of her. "Are you sure you and Sauer made up?"

Primping her hair, she nodded. "We're good." Turning to Rina, she decided to deflect the attention from herself. Plus, she was curious as hell. "Well?"

Rina's eyebrows shot up. "What?"

"You left work early yesterday to do something...and you never returned."

"It was negative." Rina's eyes turned to the sandwich in front of her.

"Sor—"

"Shut up, Zoe." Dee couldn't help but butt in and stop her from saying that dreadful word. Sauer hated to hear it and now she did, too. Of course, it made her look and sound like a bitch. "I didn't mean to say shut up. I just meant... that's what the guy left on the note. Those words..."

Zoe's face went from hurt to sympathetic just like that. "I'm... Wow, it's hard not to say those words." She chuckled. "It's okay. I get it."

Dee sighed in relief, even though she still felt bad for that tiny outburst. She could've said it in a nicer way than the words shut up.

"You okay, Rina?" Zoe asked.

She nodded, fiddling with the edge of her sandwich. "I

guess I'm just impatient." She looked up and smiled. "Ben made me feel better when he got home. This helps, too. Thanks for having lunch with us, Zoe."

"Hey, I miss seeing you girls every day. I love being home with Zabrina, but I miss this."

"Are we about to hold hands and sing 'Kumbaya?'" Dee asked with a laugh.

"Geesh," Zoe said as she shook her head with a grin. "You made up with Sauer, yet you're still prickly today. What's up?"

"Don't brush us off anymore," Rina added.

They weren't going to leave her alone. At all. It didn't surprise her in the least. She knew this was coming.

"Dee..." Zoe took a bite of her salad, chomping vigorously, her annoyance plain as day.

"How long will it last?"

"What, the dance classes?" Rina asked. "It's a four-week class."

She sighed. "No. Sauer and I. How long will it last? I can't believe he forgave me so easily for everything I've done already. I haven't made anything easy on him." She traced a pattern on the table, unable to look them in the eyes. "He'll leave me eventually."

"Why do you believe that?" Zoe asked softly.

"They always leave."

"No, they don't. You always drop the guy first," Rina pointed out, making Dee cringe at the truth in those words.

"Because it's easier to survive if I leave first."

"So, who's they?" Zoe asked, confused.

Dee fiddled with the table. "My mom went from guy to guy growing up. None ever stayed." She looked up. "It'll break my heart if he leaves."

"Life's full of disappointments and things that make us

want to cry and scream and stomp our feet with frustration." Rina grabbed her hand and squeezed. "It doesn't mean you give up before it even started. You're making it difficult on him because you're protecting yourself. Just let him in. Just try a real relationship for once."

"That's my Rina, voice of reason."

"Damn right."

They all giggled.

"Go back to being my sweet, soft-spoken Rina. Since when do you swear?" Dee raised a brow as she brushed her hair back.

"Since I married Ben. He's rubbing off on me." She giggled. "And I like it."

Dee let out a breath and smirked. "Okay, my pity party is over. Thanks, ladies. As always, you set me straight."

"It ain't easy sometimes." Zoe laughed. "At least you keep life interesting for Sauer. He needs a little adventure in his life."

Oh, so right. He'd get plenty with her.

———

"Why are we heading to the strip club?" Newman asked as Sauer took a right instead of a left toward the precinct.

"Because, the cold's sweeping in. I don't like it. Let's just revisit everything one more time." He tried to keep the pressure off the gas pedal and not speed. He had no specific reason to be so anxious to get there. It was more like nervous energy to solve the case. Part of the issue between him and Dee revolved around the case. Maybe if he solved it, they could focus on their relationship. "I knew no prints other than Dee's would come back from that note. It didn't even matter she stabbed him. His DNA isn't in the system.

How ever he patched himself up, it wasn't at a hospital. I'll give him credit. He's smart."

"He'll screw up somewhere. They always do. We should send Susan a thank you card for running our stuff ahead of all the other crap in the lab," Newman said. "Finding the murder weapon doesn't seem like it's going to happen either. Susan searched Vanessa's house from top to bottom."

"Probably wouldn't find any prints on it, anyway." Sauer rubbed his jaw. "We do owe Susan big time."

Newman stretched, then cracked his knuckles. The sound grated on his ears. "Everything okay with Dee? You haven't mentioned her all day."

"We're good. We talked last night."

Sauer liked talking with Newman, bridging their friendship into newer territory. But he wasn't about to start talking about his sex life. Especially one with Dee.

Boy, did she surprise him last night. He never expected her to be waiting in his home, or snatching his spare key and memorizing his alarm code. Although, neither shocked him. Sounded like something she'd do. He wasn't upset. Of course, if he mentioned either of those things to Newman, he'd say she stole from him and broke into his home.

Yeah, best to keep that to himself. He didn't need more grief from him.

He cleared his throat. "You okay? You kinda acted weird with Zeke yesterday."

"Zeke's a little too cocky sometimes. I don't always appreciate his attitude."

"But you're cool with him now, right? At least when it concerns Dee."

Newman met his gaze. "Just sticking up for you, partner. That's all."

Sauer figured that's all he was going to get out of him

and dropped the subject. He hated tension and confrontation with a passion. He certainly didn't want it in the workplace. Especially with Zeke and Ben.

Ten minutes later, he parked the car and walked with Newman to the entrance of the Dancing Slipper. They met with Tony, the manager of the club, once more, getting no new information from him.

"Not sure what you want me to say. As long as my ladies keep the customers entertained, they don't care who is up on stage. Nobody has asked about her. I think most know she was murdered." Tony scratched his chest, then lowered his hand, making Sauer a little nervous he was going to scratch his dick next. Thankfully, his hand went to his side and hung there.

"Any complaints from the ladies about any customers? Getting a little too touchy-feely or anything like that?" Sauer asked.

"What, you think this guy is gonna hurt another one of my ladies?" His eyes narrowed.

"Just looking at every angle." He shrugged, speaking the truth. Dee had no ties to this place, but it couldn't hurt to try a new angle to find this killer.

"No complaints. Are we done?" Tony jerked his head to a booth in front of the stage. "Feel free to stay for the show coming up."

"Thanks for your time. We have things to do," Newman said.

Tony nodded and walked away before they could barrel him with more questions that would lead them nowhere.

"We still have shit."

Newman clapped him on the back. "We'll find something. It was worth a try. You wanna interview Vanessa's family again. That was so much fun the first time."

Sauer laughed at his sarcasm with a quick shake of his head. "Once was plenty."

They headed for the exit. His eyes darted back and forth, taking in the surroundings. Men waiting for the afternoon show to start, already drinking with their money ready. A low, mellow sound of music followed every step he took.

He could honestly say he'd never been to a strip club. Except for this case, of course. Personally, as a customer, never. He didn't have to ask Newman if he'd ever been to a strip club. It was obvious. His eyes had said yes to Tony's offer even as his lips declined. Sauer had no desire to stay. That was all reserved for Dee. He couldn't wait to pick her up.

He stopped walking. Newman collided with his back, almost knocking him to the ground.

"What the hell, Sauer?"

His eyes zeroed in on the man that just exited what he assumed was an employee area. Confirmed when the door swung closed and "Employees Only" was clearly written.

"I know him."

Leaving Newman standing there confused, Sauer walked up to the man who had been with Dee at the café and blocked his way.

"You work here?"

The guy's eyes thinned into slits. "You again." Muscles tensed in his arms and neck. "Who the hell are you?"

"Answer my question." Sauer stepped closer instead of retreating. This guy didn't scare him. Yeah, he was built like a truck. Didn't matter. He'd take him in a fight if he had to.

"Look here, asshole, I don't have to answer any of your questions. I think I'll just throw you out."

The guy lifted his hand to grab his shirt when Newman stepped up and swung his badge in the middle of them.

"Detective Newman. The guy you're about to lay a hand on is Detective Sauer. I suggest you back up and answer his question."

The fire in his eyes didn't diminish as he took one step back. "I work here."

"What's your name?" Sauer sensed the tension emanating off Newman. Probably wondering why he was so pissed. "What's your relationship with Deena O'Malley?"

Newman inhaled sharply. The only hint he managed to surprise him.

Cocking a brow, the guy puffed out his chest some more. "Maybe I should ask you the same thing."

The jealousy swam in his veins as he resisted the urge to slap handcuffs on this guy just for the fact he knew Dee. This was a new emotion. Never had a woman evoked such possessiveness. Anger and jealousy mixed like a deadly storm brewing. Controlling his breathing took every ounce of strength he had.

"We're investigating the murder of Vanessa Colton and two attacks against Deena. They're related." Sauer clenched and unclenched his fists. "Answer my questions before I decide we need to take this down to the precinct."

The muscles in his cheeks ticked like a time bomb. "Raul Santiago. I protect the ladies here, not hurt them. Nor would I ever hurt Dee." His eyes softened. "Is she all right?"

"She's fine. What was your relationship with her?"

Raul crossed his arms. "What makes you think we had one?"

"I saw you together outside the café. Friends or more than that?" Sauer tried to control the rapid beat of his heart, hoping against hope that Raul wouldn't hear the pounding. He didn't want to hear the answer. In all honesty, it was a dumb question. He knew the answer.

A smirk emerged. "Lovers." The word rolled off his tongue erotically.

"And she broke up with you. How did that make you feel?"

"What makes you think we broke up?" His brow cocked high. "What's she to you?"

A hand clamped onto his shoulder, stopping him from attacking Raul. How did Newman know what he wanted to do?

"How well did you know Vanessa?"

"I didn't sleep with her, if that's what you're getting at. Now, Dee, she knows what she's doing in the sack."

"Where were you Saturday, mid-morning?" Newman piped in.

Maybe he'd be better off letting Newman handle the rest of the questions. He was so close to hitting this asshole. Although, he started it with his attitude. He couldn't help it. Dee was his. Everyone, including this jackass, would know it.

Well, he could make the conclusion. Sauer wasn't about to admit she was his girlfriend. *His* girlfriend. No one else's. The less this guy knew, the better.

"Home."

"Were you with anyone?" Newman asked.

"Nope."

"How about Friday night? Where were you?"

"Working."

"And two Sunday's ago, around midnight?"

"Working."

"So you're a bouncer here?"

"Yep."

Newman growled low under his breath, probably getting as frustrated as Sauer with his one-word answers.

"Notice any customers bothering Vanessa? Notice anything off?"

"Nope."

"You ever physically hurt Deena?"

His jaw clenched. "She say I did?"

"Nope."

Sauer had to press his lips together tightly to keep from laughing at Newman's answer.

"Look, I didn't hurt Vanessa, and I'd never hurt Dee. She'd hurt me back if I ever tried." He dropped his arms to his sides. "I'm done talking."

"Stay away from Deena." Sauer couldn't resist any longer.

He stepped into his face. "Only if she says so. Otherwise, screw off, detective."

Raul walked around them and toward the front. Before they left, they verified with Tony that Raul did indeed work the night of Vanessa's murder and Friday night. Regardless of that, Sauer still didn't want to cross him off the suspect list. Probably because he despised the guy. It wasn't fair or professional. He didn't care.

Slamming his door shut with a little too much force, he sat there a brief moment.

"That was intense. Lately, I never can tell if you're going to start a fight or not."

"Dee..." He looked at him. "I just get so possessive. I don't know what's wrong with me."

"Me either." Newman chuckled. "I like this side of you, though. I'm kind of bummed you have a woman now. Who's going to be my wingman?"

Sauer laughed. "Maybe you should take a break." He started the car. "You know I'll still be your wingman. I can bring Dee with. Being the third wheel could reel in the ladies. Maybe."

Slapping his knee, Newman's laughter rang in the small confines of the car. "That's a good point. Can't hurt to try. Are you going to tell Dee about Raul?"

Good question. Would he?

He answered with a shrug.

Talk about a huge difference between him and Raul. It made him wonder what Dee saw in him. He was definitely not her type.

Would she start to see that and leave him?

Best not to think about it.

"You should tell her." Newman cleared his throat a few times. "Maybe you should ask her...ask her if she really broke up with him."

Sauer almost slammed on the brakes, whipping his eyes to Newman. "You think she's still seeing him? She was with me all weekend."

The pain reflected in Newman's eyes. "Maybe not in person. He made it sound like they were still in contact." He looked out the window. "I never thought Chrissy would cheat on me."

His nerves had calmed since leaving the strip club. Now they were back full force. Was she still talking to that jackass? Maybe he was deluding himself to think he could keep a woman like her forever. Perhaps that's why she didn't trust his love. Because she didn't want it. Didn't need it when she had a guy like Raul to go to.

Before, eager to see her beautiful face. Now, scared as hell.

15

DEE SNUGGLED into Sauer's embrace as she rested her head on his chest. The night had been awkward and stilted from the moment he picked her up from work. She had asked him a few times if everything was all right. He always answered, "It was a frustrating day."

The case was wearing on him. He wanted to solve it, more so, probably for her. She understood that, but she also didn't want him to wear himself down so much that she lost his sweetness.

That's how she felt right now. Even lying in his arms. She didn't feel his sweetness. For some reason, he was pulling away.

"Tell me you love me."

God, that sounded so needy. She didn't care. Hearing those loving words from him always fortified her heart. Made her stronger. Made her believe she could keep him.

A kiss hit her forehead. "I love you."

"Why doesn't it feel like it?"

She could feel a fight brewing. Why did she always do

this? Was she purposely creating an issue when nothing was wrong?

His hand brushed up her arm and back down. "I honestly don't know how to keep telling you and showing you that I do." His heart pounded. She could feel it under her hand. "You've never said the words yet. Maybe I should ask you that question."

Whack! Just like that, it felt like a slap to the face. Honest, but true.

"Did you get a break in the case?"

He tensed.

"You did, didn't you?"

She lifted her head, not missing the steel in his gaze. He was keeping something from her. She scooted out of his arms and sat up. He slowly joined her, leaning against the headboard.

"What is it? You wanna go round and round and round like we do about this dumb case."

"Not really."

"Then start talking, Sauer. Don't piss me off."

Silence descended.

She'd wait him out. He could stay silent for as long as he wanted, but neither of them would get any sleep until he told her what he knew.

"I met your *friend* Raul today."

She gave him the best glare she could. "So. That's all he is."

"You slept with him."

"He's in my past. Are you gonna hold my past against me, Sauer? I slept with a lot of guys." Arms crossed, she leaned away. "Are you gonna get pissy when you run into every man I slept with?"

His eyes narrowed, not before the pain flickered within

the depths. "I meant, you were just with him not long ago… and now you're with me. Are you still talking to him?"

"You don't trust me?" The sting was swift. More trust issues. She didn't deserve this one.

"I do."

"Doesn't sound like it."

"I do," he said more firmly.

"How did you run into him?"

He sighed, rubbing a hand over his head. "Interesting fact. He works at the strip club that our victim worked at. She was a stripper. Imagine my surprise when I saw him."

"Raul can have a temper, but he'd never hurt anyone."

"He's gotten angry with you before?"

"Sure. I bring it out of everyone." She smirked. Although, Sauer didn't find it amusing as his frown turned fierce. "I stopped talking to him the day I saw you at the cafe. He wasn't happy about it, but he wouldn't hurt me over it. I know I didn't get a good look at my attacker, but I know it wasn't Raul. He doesn't have the tattoo I saw." She primped her hair, then grabbed his hand that rested near her. "Do you think he murdered that woman?"

Pulling her hand to his mouth, he kissed it tenderly. "He was working at the time." Another kiss graced her hand. "I… I'm not your type."

She rolled onto his lap, pressing her lips to his. Soft nibbles to a frenzy, then frantic to slow. He pulled her closer, wrapping his arms tightly around her.

Breaking the kiss, she rested her forehead against his. "You're exactly my type. It just took me forever to figure that out."

SAUER ROLLED HIS HEAD, loosening the muscles and the tension that hadn't receded since last night. Sure, they talked about Raul. Yeah, he did trust her. But it was hard to let the worry go. Especially working with Newman all day, who was surly and grouchy, throwing in a few tidbits about Dee. Maybe it was his jealousy seeping in. He understood he was hurting from what Chrissy had done, but that didn't mean Dee would do the same thing. Didn't mean she was doing it right now. She said she had no contact with Raul since the day at the café. He believed her.

Newman, not so much.

He couldn't have been happier when their shift ended. If Newman kept up his negative vibes, he didn't know what he would do.

"Why is my love bug frowning?"

He shivered with delicious tingles as Dee wrapped her arms around him and pressed her head against his chest.

Love bug? That was new and a little odd coming from her. He kind of liked it.

"Nerves."

Lifting her head, she cocked an eyebrow and tilted her head. "You're the only one who knows how to dance and you're nervous? No way. I'm the one who's nervous."

He cracked a grin. "I hate eyes on me. Being the center of attention. I don't want to be the only one who knows how to dance."

Her hand brushed his cheek, sending more shivers of delight down his body. Shit. He was getting a hard-on.

"Don't do that." It came out as a low growl.

A devious smirk grew as she stroked his other cheek.

"Dee..."

"Wanna leave?"

He wiped the smirk off her face with a kiss. Light and

tender. "And give everyone something to talk about? No, thanks."

She chuckled. "Yeah, they totally would." Clasping his hands, weaving her fingers through his, she pulled him onto the dance floor. They were waiting for the instructor to return from the restroom. The last class ended a few minutes ago.

"Teach me."

He pulled her against his body, still needing to hide the bulge in his pants. The lightest touch from her did things he couldn't control. Having her in his arms wasn't helping.

"You know how to dance."

She crinkled her nose. "Not the fancy dances."

His right hand slid up her back to her shoulder blade. With his left hand, he gently grasped her hand and raised it near shoulder height. "Place your left hand near my shoulder, more so on my bicep."

In position, almost giddy with excitement to be dancing with her like this, he took a step forward with his left foot, then brushed to the side a step, connecting his feet together. Then took a step back, sliding to the side again, creating what his instructor called the 'box step' when he learned as a child. Dee moved with ease, following his low murmurs of instructions as they continued to dance the beginning moves of the waltz.

"Excellent!" A loud clapping of hands. "We have a wonderful dancer among us."

Sauer halted mid-step to look at an older woman with flaming-red hair, almost as gorgeous as Dee's, but not quite, beaming at him with the brightest smile.

"Where did you learn how to dance? Your posture is impeccable. Your movements are fluid." With a sharp glance to Dee, she said, "Keep your posture straight. No slouching.

Keep your head and gaze to his left side." She walked right up to Dee, pushing her shoulders back. "Posture. Posture. Posture. It's all in the posture." She whipped her gaze to him. "How long have you been dancing?"

The nerves jangled forth with ease. His shyness made him want to melt into the floor. It wouldn't be so bad if it were just him, Dee, and the gang, but there were other people in the class he didn't know. He hated eyes on him. With a passion.

Yeah, Dee's posture could've been better, but it was the first time they danced together. He didn't want to ruin the moment. Dancing as they did was like heaven, regardless that she started to slouch a bit.

"Well?"

"Twelve."

She beamed another bright smile, grabbed his hand without warning, and took position. "Let's dance."

Just like that, he was twirling around the room, his face flaming with heat, as all eyes were on him. Exactly what he didn't want. Of course, that didn't mean he didn't dance with grace. The instructor's glittering spark in her eyes and smile said as much. She had to be in her early fifties, if he had to guess, but he felt her strength as they moved as one. She was an excellent dancer. Although, what he wanted was Dee in his arms.

She abruptly stopped, glancing at the class. "By the end, you should be able to dance like that." Side glancing his way, she added, "Well, perhaps not as refined as this handsome man, but close enough."

The floor beneath him opened and swallowed him whole, or at least he wished it would. He knew his face, neck, and perhaps his entire body was red with embarrassment. Especially when he caught Dee's gaze and she smirked at him, licking her lips. Yeah, she liked it when he blushed. The lip licking didn't help the desire swamping his body.

She clapped her hands once again. "Let's dance!"

He quickly shuffled to Dee's side, ignoring the playful grin that he wanted to kiss right off her face. "Stop."

"Whatever do you mean, you handsome, refined dancer you?"

Groaning, he pulled her into his embrace, setting his position to begin the waltz once again.

"Cat got your tongue, snuggly bug?"

"Hand on my arm." He waited patiently as she slid her hand to the correct position, unable to hide the tremble at her soft touch.

She murmured a low moan.

"Really, Dee...must you moan like that." He took a step forward as the instructor started to call commands.

"You know how hot and bothered I get when you turn red as a tomato."

He felt his body tighten in response to her words.

"Hmmm...yes, please."

"You're killing me here." A groan escaped as she wiggled her hips against him, sending him harder than he was before.

"I love dancing with you." Giggling, she moved her hips again. "You definitely should've asked me to dance at Rina's wedding."

"Stop moving like that." He tried to sound stern but knew it fell flat to her ears as she did it once more. "You're asking for it."

"Ooo, a punishment. I likey."

"Focus, people!"

Sauer's gaze snapped to the instructor, who was giving him the evil eye. Or more like, eyeing Dee with unease.

"She's going to whisk you out of my arms if you don't start behaving."

Dee cocked a brow at the woman. "She can sure as hell try. Ain't gonna happen. You're all mine."

"Shit." He mumbled an apology for stepping on her toe.

"My fault. Newbie, remember?"

"I do."

She slapped his shoulder at his honesty. He could only laugh.

"That she-devil can say it all she wants, but you shouldn't."

"She-devil?"

Her eyes bulged. "What, did you forget how she yanked on my shoulders and scolded me?"

A silky grin appeared before he could stop it.

"Ugh! Am I that bad?"

"You just have to work on your posture. It's okay. It's your first lesson."

She leaned closer. "Private lessons?"

Dee jerked back as the instructor pierced a hard glare at her at the same time she molded her body into the correct position. "Posture!" She walked away to Zeke and Zoe. Sauer couldn't stop the laugh at the horror on Zeke's face.

"That was so not funny."

"She reminds me of you."

She gasped. "Excuse me?"

"Red hair and all."

"Of all the—"

"Temperament."

"Things you could—"

"Sternness."

"Say about—"

"Feistiness."

"Me. That just—"

"She doesn't hold a candle to your beauty or sweetness."

Complete silence.

"I'm not sweet."

He broke his impeccable posture and pressed a kiss to her lips. "You are. People just don't see it like I do."

"People! Focus!"

He straightened as Dee chuckled, yet followed his movement with a skill that said she'd have the waltz down in no time. If she managed not to slouch.

"You're slouching."

An evil eye. "I might start hating you."

He knew she was kidding, yet it went straight to his heart. "Please don't." He almost tripped as she stepped on his toe this time.

They stood immobile, staring at each other.

"I was kidding."

"I know."

THE PAIN WAS as clear as a sunny blue sky. She inadvertently hurt him with her teasing. Shit just blurted out of her mouth sometimes. She'd never hate Sauer.

Her body ached to lean in to kiss the pain away, except a quick glance out of her eye had her hesitating. She didn't need that witch to pull her shoulders back again. It's like she hated her. She wasn't slouching that much. Or maybe she was. Sauer even said she was. He was only helping. He'd never be cruel to her on purpose.

"What are you waiting for?"

The pain filtered away as he shyly smiled and continued to move. She tried her hardest to concentrate and move with ease as he glided across the dance floor. He knew how to move so effortlessly. She should've known. He was the same when making love. God, how she wished they were alone, in his home, dancing without eyes on them.

"Forgive me?"

He almost stopped. "For what?"

"My idiotic words. I shouldn't tease you like that."

A sweet grin filtered in as his eyes lit up with love. "Shoulders back."

Laughing at his comeback, she let go, focusing on the dance moves as Sauer twirled her around the dance floor, filling her heart with so much love. Could this happiness really last?

Their hour lesson went fast. Before she knew it, it ended. Zeke and Ben looked exhausted, mentioning a beer sounded nice. Fifteen minutes later, they moved two high-top tables together at Rockster's and ordered drinks.

"Sauer, I don't know how you do it." Zeke chugged his beer. "That woman was a beast."

"She wasn't too bad." Sauer grinned. It slowly died as Dee slid her hand onto his thigh underneath the table.

"That's because you're the only one who can dance like she can." Her fingers slowly inched higher, his arousal within reaching distance.

He coughed, taking a sip of beer.

"She worked us hard, all right. We'll be ready for that ball," Ben said, hugging Rina into his side.

"I can't wait, although, Dee and Sauer are going to show us all up at that ball," Zoe said with a laugh.

"Ha! I suck. Didn't you see that witch yank on my shoulders at least twenty times?"

Sauer squirmed in his seat as her hand finally landed on its prize. "Posture." It came out in a squeak.

"What was that, snookums?" Rubbing up and down, she grinned.

"Nothing." His voice trailed off, as her fingers continued to play and tease.

"Snookums?" Zoe laughed.

"Oh, yeah, I'm trying out pet names. Not sure what one I like best yet." She turned to Sauer as she lightly squeezed. "What do you like best, sugarplum?"

His face turned beet red. "Anything…baby."

Her hand stilled.

His hand landed on her bare skin, just below her skirt. "Call me anything you like…" His hand trailed up underneath her skirt. "Sweetheart."

His boldness. She loved it. So un-Sauer-like.

"Do you two need to get a room down the block?" Zeke asked with a boisterous laugh.

They both snatched their hands away.

"Isn't this where you and Zoe first met?" Dee asked, adding a smirk as Zeke narrowed his eyes.

"Hey, guys. How's it going?"

Everyone turned their heads to Susan, who stood between Sauer and Ben with the same friendly smile she always displayed.

"Just got done with dance lessons. These fine men will be escorting us to the King and Queen's ball in two months," Zoe said.

"Oh, that sounds like so much fun."

Dee liked Susan. And she really wanted to know who she had a crush on. "You should come with us."

"By myself? No, thanks."

"I bet Newman would go with you. It'll be fun." The

smile on Sauer's face was genuine. He might not like attention, but he loved to dance. A man full of so many surprises.

A slight blush ventured from Susan's neck to her cheeks. "Oh, I'm sure Chrissy wouldn't like that."

Sauer started to turn red himself. "Oh, they broke up." He cleared his throat. "You want me to ask him? We'd love if you joined us."

"Definitely, Susan. I can't wait," Rina piped in with enthusiasm.

"No, no, that's okay. I'm sure he wouldn't—it was nice to see you guys." Susan smiled and dashed away.

Odd.

And so very obvious.

Susan had a crush on Newman. Did Sauer pick up on it, too? Plus, he had a secret about Newman. She read between the lines with his nervousness.

Eager to get home, she couldn't wait to interrogate him about what he knew.

Oh, and the delicious things she wanted to do with him.

16

EVERY TIME THEY MADE LOVE, his feelings became stronger. His love grew. How could he hold the words back? He didn't want to. He wanted to say it over and over how much he loved her. Yet, he knew it made her uncomfortable, especially since she never said it back. She wanted to. He hoped so, anyway.

"So? Spill."

His hand stalled as he was caressing her sweet, succulent backside near her ass. Feeling her silky skin made him hungry to take her again. Once was never enough. They barely contained their desire. The minute they stepped inside his house, they were on each other. He'd never look at his kitchen the same again. Clothes were still scattered all over the kitchen floor. The island counter marked with their lovemaking.

Once done there, he had carried her to the bedroom, taking her again with slow ease. Holding her in his arms, stroking her body up and down, he wanted her again. So badly.

"Sauer?"

Oh, right. She was talking to him. Although, he was clueless as hell what he was supposed to confess. Was she talking about the case? He had nothing else to tell her. The case was officially cold.

"What?"

"Something about Newman."

Kissing the top of her head, he chuckled. "What about him?"

"Since when did he break up with Chrissy?"

Dee and intrigue—he should've known she would want all the details. Oh, man, what a predicament. The things Newman told him were something between them. Should he tell her the reason?

"About two weeks ago."

"And?" Her finger doodled on his chest, brushing up and down, teasing him.

"And...what?"

She lifted her head. "They seemed so happy."

"Well...baby—"

A giggle erupted. "Did you just call me baby?"

Grinning, he kissed her. "Just trying out pet names like you. Can't decide if I like baby or not. Do you prefer something else? Sweetheart. Honey. Cupcake."

She slapped his chest playfully, resting her head on him again. "Call me whatever you like." Finger doodling recommenced. "Why did they break up?"

Weaving his fingers with hers, he brought her hand to his mouth for a kiss. "It was something between me and Newman, but..."

"But...what?"

"As my significant other, we should be able to talk and keep it between us, right?"

"Significant other?" She chuckled. "I love how you speak to me." Snuggling closer, she sighed happily. "Yes. We should. You tell me why they broke up and I'll share a secret I shouldn't."

Now he was intrigued. Screw it. He trusted her to keep it between them.

"She cheated on him. He's having a hard time."

Dee tensed. "I imagine so."

He squeezed her hand. "You okay?"

Relaxing just as quickly as she tensed, she nodded. "Susan has a crush on him."

This time he tensed—in shock. "Seriously? How do you know that?"

"Well, she didn't admit it. The phone rang before she could tell me. But by her reaction tonight, I just pieced it together. I'd say we help them get together…"

He heard the unspoken but. "But you don't want to."

"I like Susan." An awkward pause. "Not a fan of Newman."

"In other words, he's a douche."

She kissed his chest. "You know me so well."

He sure did. Loved every little thing about her.

"I love you."

Another sweet kiss to his chest. That was all.

Sooner or later, she'd say it. He couldn't do anything but keep the hope she would.

He slept great, as he always did when Dee was in his bed. While he enjoyed cuddling with her sweet body next to his, she always managed to wiggle out of his embrace, sprawling on her belly or on her side. Of course, he always pulled her back to him, unable to let her sleep without his arm around her. Maybe in time he'd be able to, but he wasn't entirely sure. He dreamed of having her in his arms

for so long, he couldn't help but treasure each moment
with her.

Waking up before her and the alarm, he slipped out of
bed. Using the bathroom first to relieve himself, he then
headed to one of his spare rooms turned workout room and
started lifting weights. Thirty minutes later, the sweat dripping down, his muscles tingling with the aftereffects of a
great workout, he felt her presence immediately. Setting
down the weight, he sat up on the bench. Dee stood in the
doorway looking rumpled from sleep but sexy as hell in
only her black lace panties and a light sheet draped over her
shoulders. His mouth went instantly dry from the beautiful
picture in front of him.

"How long have you been awake?"

He stood up. "Not long." Within two steps, he had her in
his arms. "Wanna take a shower together?"

Scrunching her nose, a soft chuckle shuffled into the air.
"You're all sweaty."

He squeezed her tighter, sinking his head into the crook
of her neck. With a trail of kisses from her neck to her chin,
he ended at her lips. "You're sexy as hell."

"Now I'm dirty with your sweat."

"Hence, the shower. Together."

Her eyes twinkled with delight. "So you did it on
purpose."

"I just love you in my arms."

With a deep sigh, one that concerned him, her head
rested on his chest.

"What's wrong?"

"Nothing. I'm tired." She kissed his chest, then lifted her
beautiful eyes to his. "Race you." She stepped out of his
embrace, dropping the sheet.

A flash of black was all he saw before she disappeared

from his view. He followed her just as quickly, dropping his boxers before hopping into the shower with her. The light and laughter reflected in her eyes, yet her earlier sigh worried him. It wasn't tiredness. Something was bothering her. The word love again. Should he not say the word at all?

The water rained down on them. The magic slowly building, the heat swirling.

Worrying wouldn't help. It never did. He could only live in the moment and hope she didn't give up on them.

SAUER REFILLED his mug with the sludge from the break room, wincing as he took a sip. Anytime Tray made the coffee, it took every ounce in him not to spit it out. They all took turns making the coffee. Whoever found it empty made some more. He really hated when Tray found it empty.

Walking out of the room with Newman next to him, he winced again.

"We should've just made a new pot."

Chuckling at the truth in Newman's words, he took another sip. "And hurt Tray's feelings."

Newman scoffed. "Dude, he knows he makes shitty coffee. Probably does it on purpose."

Sauer took another sip, trying to decide whether he should say something. He wrestled with the decision another few steps before blurting, "Wanna go to the King and Queen's Ball with us?"

Newman's steps halted. "Who would I go with?"

"Susan..."

A frown mixed with the pleasure in his eyes. "No. You

guys have fun. I don't want to go to a ball." His face turned to stone. "And I don't want to go with Susan."

Newman walked away, leaving Sauer standing there very confused—and concerned. He was always a happy guy. Fun-loving, full of jokes. Since he broke up with Chrissy, he'd been nothing but cynical, sour, and full of a bad attitude.

"Don't feel bad."

He jerked, turning around. Susan stood there with a friendly smile on her face. "I'm..." He couldn't say sorry. Well, he could. Because he was. But he didn't want to say those words.

"It's okay, Sauer."

"He's just...well...it's not—"

"I'm okay. Let's pretend I didn't hear and that you didn't ask him." She shifted on her feet. "Vanessa's boyfriend is looking for you. I saw him when I came in. He looks like a mess."

"Thanks." He had no idea what else to say.

Nodding, she turned around to probably head to her office a floor above.

"Susan?"

She swiveled to him, a smile still on her face. He saw behind the happiness to the pain. He always saw it in people. Perfecting a happy front his entire life since child-hood, it always made it easier for him to see.

"He's an idiot. I'd be honored to take you if...if I didn't love Dee."

Joy finally shined in her eyes. "Dee is so lucky. I hope she knows that." Susan turned and walked away.

Damn. He hoped she knew that, too. He couldn't forget the look of unease in her eyes this morning. Oh, they made love in the shower, then once more in the bedroom after breakfast. She never held back. Giving her all. When he dropped her off at work, he saw the worry, an agitation he didn't quite understand. He just wanted to feel at ease with her, to know they were in this relationship together, wanting it to work out. He had doubts that she would stick with it and give them a fair chance.

Walking back to his desk, he tried to shove all the worry to the back of his mind. Thinking about it wouldn't solve anything. Least of all this case. Shawn, Vanessa's boyfriend, sat in a chair next to Newman's desk. His hands were stuck in his hair, his head down, his shoulders shaking. Was he crying?

Sauer slid into his chair, raising a brow and shifting a glance from Newman to Shawn. Newman shrugged and then tapped Shawn on the shoulder. "Talk to us, Mr. Gross. Why are you upset?"

His head lifted slowly, tears still silently rolling down. Wiping them away with the back of his hand, he sniffled a few times. "Don't call me that. Shawn is fine. I feel like my father when you call me Mr. Gross, and he's a real jackass. He'd probably call me a sissy for crying." A tear rolled down. "I just loved Nessy so much. I miss her."

He could appreciate and understand his emotions. If anything ever happened to Dee, whether brutal or not, he'd be a blubbering mess. The tears would never stop. Call him sensitive. He didn't really care.

"We're doing everything we can to try to find who killed her. Unfortunately, we haven't found much yet." Sauer hated to admit that, but he wouldn't give him false hope. If it were him sitting in Shawn's situation, he wouldn't want that. Give him the truth. It might be difficult to swallow, but it was better than lying.

Shawn erased the tears once again. "Start looking at her brother. He did this. I know he did."

He and Newman shared a look. Interesting. And completely out of left field. Vanessa had been estranged from her family. Vince, her brother, had been indifferent to her death. She had been insignificant to him. As if she were nothing more than an acquaintance, not a sister.

"What makes you say that?" Newman asked. "Why wait so long to say something?"

Reaching into his jacket pocket, Shawn pulled out a crumpled piece of paper, tossing it onto Newman's desk. "Because I forgot. I haven't been to work. I barely leave the house for food. I...I just don't care anymore. I need Nessy back."

Newman grabbed the piece of paper, smoothing it out. A look of surprise filtered into his features. "A bank statement. Yours?"

Shawn nodded.

"This is important, why?"

Running a hand under his nose, he stood up and pointed to something on the paper. "See that transaction. Every month, for the past few months, the same amount was deposited into my account. It was always there." He tapped his finger harder. "Every damn month."

Rummaging in his other pocket, he produced another wrinkled piece of paper. Smoothing it out, he laid it down next to the other piece of paper. "I printed this out this morning. As you can clearly see, no deposit."

Newman looked at both pieces of paper and then handed them across the way to him. He looked them over, eyeing Shawn's last month bank statement. Lots of withdrawals for normal mundane things like gas and groceries. On January 5th, a deposit of five thousand dollars was made. Glancing at the statement for February, he saw one withdrawal for gas on the first, a few transactions for bills right after, and then nothing. Absolutely nothing. He didn't lie about not venturing out after Vanessa's death.

"What does this have to do with her brother?" Sauer asked, looking up from the papers to Shawn.

"Because she was blackmailing him." He let that statement sink in for a beat. "She didn't trust her family and..." He shrugged. "Asked if the money could go straight to my account. I didn't mind."

Newman cocked a brow. "Of course not. Five thousand dollars every month is a nice chunk of change."

The fury imploded on Shawn's face. "I never spent a dime of her money. She had access to my account. She spent what was hers, I spent what was mine."

"What was she blackmailing him for? Why didn't you say something right away?" He agreed with Newman's statement. Five thousand dollars was a lot of money.

The fight just as quickly drained from him. "I don't know. She would never tell me. Her brother's an asshole." With a shaky hand, he gestured at the papers. "I forgot about it until my statement came in an email. Then it hit me. He had a reason to kill her."

Sauer thought back to the crime scene. The brutal crime scene. Blood everywhere. Stab wounds covering her body.

The crime scene said it was a crime of passion. It wasn't too far off the mark that her brother killed her in a fit of rage, sick of paying her to keep silent. But on what? What would she blackmail her brother for?

"Can we keep these, Shawn?" Sauer pointed to the papers.

"Definitely. You can have access to my accounts if you want."

"The money was going to your account. What makes you think we won't think you were blackmailing him?" Sauer tossed out, just to see his reaction. He didn't react much other than to shrug with indifference.

"Think what you want. Why would I bring the evidence to you if I was? Why would he suddenly stop sending payments?"

"We'll talk to him. Thanks for coming in," Newman said.

Shawn stood up, looking stronger than when he first appeared. "Nail his ass. He needs to rot in prison for hurting Nessy." An evil look crossed through his eyes. "Actually, he needs to rot six feet under for hurting her." With that, he left.

"I want to say I'm surprised by this development, but I'm not." Newman stood up and started to put his jacket on.

"Yeah, he was cold and unfeeling when we talked to him the first time. I missed the hatred, though." Sauer shivered from the memories of the crime scene. "If he did kill her, he hated her with a passion."

"Definitely."

Sauer followed Newman out of the building. "The question is, why attack Dee?" He paused, the horror washing through him. "Why the hatred for her?"

THE WALLS WERE STARTING to suffocate her. Closing in. Making it difficult to breathe and concentrate. How could she concentrate and be the best damn secretary she could be when her thoughts always rolled to Sauer? The sweet way they made love, whether hard and fast or slow and sensual. The way he whispered tender words in her ear. The things he said that made her heart beat faster and fortified the thought they could make it work.

Would it work? Would he never get sick of her? She was

abrasive. Loud. Outspoken. Why did he love her? Sweet, shy Sauer. Well, not so shy anymore. He was comfortable with her. Open and easy to talk to. She missed his shyness. It still peeked out at moments, and she treasured those moments like the rarity they were. His shyness was what drew her to him. He'd probably never lose it altogether. And she was glad. She wouldn't change a thing about him.

Just like he didn't want to change a thing about her.

Was he too good to be true? He was nothing like the men her mother dated growing up. Nothing even close to those douches. Hell, her mother didn't always pick single men. As long as they bestowed attention on her, she was on them like bees on honey.

Well, at least she wasn't completely like her mother. She never slept with a married man before. She had some decent morals.

She just didn't know what to do about Sauer. Giving into his love should be easy. Giving into his charm even easier. Except it wasn't. The more he showed her what they could have, the more it scared her. It always fell apart. Always.

Damn her insecurities. She shouldn't be waiting for the other shoe to drop. They could make a go of this relationship if she just gave it a real chance.

Let go.

All she had to do was let go of her fear.

"You look like you could use a break."

Dee gazed into Rina's eyes. The questions were there, yet she didn't ask. So typical of Rina.

"I could. Wanna grab a cup of coffee at the café down the street?"

"I'd love to." Then she frowned. "Maybe we shouldn't leave, though."

"It'll be fine."

Dee grabbed her jacket from the coat rack in the corner near Mr. Young's office door and followed Rina to her desk where she grabbed her own jacket. They headed outside to the back parking lot. They always cut across the parking lot to the café that made the best coffee on the block. In the summers, because the weather was obviously nicer, they'd walk around the long way. The coffee was so good it was worth the walk, rain or shine, hot or cold.

"Are you okay, Rina? You seem a little distracted yourself."

Pulling her scarf tighter around her neck to dispel the cold wind, she smiled. "I'm fine. Ben and I had a nice night after we got home from the bar." She blushed. Dee knew it wasn't from the wind. "He always manages to lift my spirits."

Dee figured she was talking about the lack of getting pregnant. If anyone deserved to have a baby, it was Rina. She was the sweetest, nicest person in her life. Even sweeter than Zoe.

"It'll happen. Just keep on having that fun monkey sex."

Rina burst out laughing. "You say the funniest things." Nudging her shoulder, her smile beamed from ear to ear. "Thanks for making me feel better."

They were about halfway through the parking lot, the cold wind almost making her regret their impromptu break.

"Anytime." She pumped her hair a little, wishing she had a hat. "About fun monkey sex...last night I wanted to—"

Rina cried out in pain and crumbled to the ground. Dee turned around, having no time to react before the tire iron hit her in the head.

Instant blackness descended.

17

Mrs. Colton pursed her lips in disapproval. "He's not here."

"Where can we find him?" Newman asked with a silky smile, unaffected by her distaste at their appearance on her doorstep.

"Work." Her brow arched in that refined way people with money who thought they were better than you did. It irked Sauer. A lot.

"That's why we're here. He's not at work." He enjoyed the way her expression went from disdain to panic. Then, just as quickly, she masked her emotions.

"He's at work." Haughtiness back in place. "He probably just doesn't want to be harassed as you're doing to me."

"Why was his sister blackmailing him?" Sauer asked. He didn't like this family. Her eyes displayed the horror at that statement, yet revealed no other emotion. She knew about it.

"He would never allow that woman to do that to him."

"What do you have against Vanessa?"

She pinned a sharp look at Newman. "She was nothing but a nuisance. The only time she came around was to ask for money. He might have slipped her some change here and there, but he'd never let her blackmail him."

"Change?" Sauer asked, slightly confused by that.

"A few hundred, give or take."

"Right." Sauer tried not to shake his head at the ridiculous notion a few hundred was change. To him, some quarters and nickels in his pocket was change. A couple hundred, not so much.

"Look, I have nothing more to say to you. Contact our lawyer for any further questions."

She started to close the door when Sauer asked, "Does your husband have a tattoo? A recent injury to the thigh?"

Her eyes glazed with panic again. "I said to contact our lawyer for any further questions." This time the door closed on them. She didn't slam it, but he still jerked back as if she had.

"Well, that reaction said a lot. I think he's our guy. We could try the secretary again," Newman commented as they walked back to the car. "She said he left for a lunch meeting, but her eyes said she was lying."

"Well, if he is at a lunch meeting, we can make her tell us where. I'm okay interrupting it." Newman was right. Her reaction said a lot. The panic in her eyes. He had to be their perp.

"Me, too." Newman chuckled as he backed out of the driveway and headed back to Vince's office.

"I think she knew about the blackmail. What do you think Vanessa knew?"

"Could be something as simple as him cheating on his wife with his secretary." Newman's hands tightened on the steering wheel. "She blushed anytime we said his name. If he isn't sleeping with his secretary, she at least wants to.

Something like that, he wouldn't want people to know. Image is everything to people like that."

"It's plausible. Enough to kill his sister to keep her quiet?" Sauer couldn't help the flashbacks that pelted him. "She died so brutally."

"As soon as we find him, we'll ask." Newman laughed. "I'll let you interview him. If he's the one who hurt Dee, I'm sure you'll enjoy that."

Yeah, he'd be sorely tempted to beat the living shit out of him. Maybe Newman should interview him.

"All units, be advised..."

The rest trailed off as a loud roaring sound coated his ears. The world shifted, the scenery passing by nothing but a blur as he lost all focus. His breathing became heavy, his chest constricted. Air suddenly became difficult to take in.

He jerked forward, slamming his hands to the dashboard. Jolted out of his sudden panic attack, he looked at Newman.

"Keep it together, Sauer. Breathe!"

The vehicle started moving again. At a high speed.

"I misheard, right?" Sauer fisted his hands as he tried to control the panic. "Tell me I misheard."

Silence.

"You didn't mishear. Dispatch said Dee's workplace address."

"And the part..."

A heavy sigh. "Yeah, man. A request for an ambulance."

Sauer stared out the window the rest of the way, unable to speak. He had nothing to say. Rewinding the last few minutes was about the only thing he wanted to do. Someone was attacked outside Dee's work. No reports of how bad the injury, except an ambulance was requested. He was too afraid to grab the radio and ask. Didn't want to hear how bad it was.

Could it be Dee?

She knew better than to leave the office.

Of course, that didn't mean she wouldn't leave. She had a mind of her own. If she felt like leaving, she would. No matter how many times he asked her to be careful, not to do anything that would put her in danger, she always just cocked her brow in that sexy annoying way and smirked. Every single time he wanted to wipe that smirk off with a kiss.

Ten minutes later, Newman pulled to a screeching stop in the parking lot full of patrol cars and one ambulance. Sauer raced out of the car to the ambulance and halted. Rina sat on the edge, a cloth to her head, crying in Ben's arms.

A comforting hand landed on his shoulder, pushing him forward. Guided by Newman, they met Zeke by the ambulance. The grimace on Zeke's face made him sick to his stomach, bile rising to the back of his throat.

"What happened?" It came out in a croak. He wasn't even sure how he managed to speak.

Ben turned his head, Rina still in his arms. The pain of his wife hurt wasn't what punched Sauer in the gut, making his nerves tingle with dread. It was the look of sorrow mixed in.

"Dee..." He cleared his throat, steeling his spine, pushing all dreadful thoughts out as best as he could. "Where's Dee?"

Rina started to cry harder. Ben turned away, comforting her more than before. Zeke stepped closer to him, blocking his view of the two.

"We don't know." Zeke rubbed his jaw as a heavy breath

fell out. "Rina said they were walking to grab a coffee when she was hit on the head. When she came to, Dee was nowhere in sight. Her purse was lying on the ground."

"He took her."

Sauer slowly looked at Newman, wanting him to take those words back. How could he? They were the truth. The killer had her.

"She knew better than to—"

"Come on, Sauer, we're talking about Dee here. If she wanted to leave for a coffee, nothing was going to stop her." Zeke tossed his head toward Rina. "I know this is hard, but try to be quieter. Rina is not taking it well. Ben wants her to go to the hospital and she's refusing right now. She was damn near hysterical when we got here. She blames herself. She thinks she should've talked Dee out of leaving."

Jaw clenched, he hissed, "She should've."

He was out of line and knew it. Zeke knew he knew it and didn't respond.

"It has to be Vince." Newman looked at him, his hand still on his shoulder. That simple gesture helped him to stay standing because all he wanted to do was drop to the ground in agony.

"Who's that?" Zeke asked.

"Our victim's brother. According to her boyfriend, she was blackmailing her brother, but doesn't know the reason." Sauer started to rub a hand over his head. "How does he know Dee?"

"Didn't he have an alibi?" Zeke asked, his eyes portraying his mind was twirling all the information.

"He did. But I don't trust the wife. She knew about the blackmail, but denied knowing about it. We asked if he had a tattoo and an injury to the leg and I saw the panic in her eyes at the question. But she refused to answer. She would give him an alibi, no doubt about it." Newman let go of his shoulder and crossed his arms. "Maybe they did have a Super Bowl party. Doesn't mean he didn't slip out for an hour or so to go kill his sister."

He turned around, heading for Newman's car. Yanking the door open, he stared at Newman. "Are you coming?"

Newman sprinted to the car, a puzzled look on his face. "Where are we going?"

"Back to talk to his wife. She has to know where he is."

They hustled into the car and left in a hurry. He felt bad for Rina. Truly, he did. But his concern for Dee overrode all those other emotions. She had to be okay. If he lost her, he'd—

Thinking like that had to be stopped immediately.

They had to be right. Because if they weren't, Dee was in so much trouble. If they were wrong, he had no idea where to start looking for her.

Maybe Newman could read his thoughts. Maybe it was written all over his face. Maybe it was pouring out in waves as he sat with his fists clenched, his face hard as granite, his eyes focused ahead.

"She'll fight, Sauer. She'll be fine. If anyone can survive this, it's Dee."

As much as he wanted to hold to that knowledge, knowing it was partly true, he couldn't. What people didn't understand, didn't realize, was Dee was just like everyone else. She wasn't superhuman. She wasn't invisible. She was tough. Strong. Full of spirit. But that didn't make her immune to pain and suffering. To the hands of a killer.

He could hurt her.

Hell, he could've already killed her.

A BLINDING ache throbbed in the back of her head. She reached to rub the spot, just to have her arms jerk in place.

Panic welled inside. Her hands were tied, outstretched above her head. A quick tug of her legs made her realize her feet were tied as well.

Eyes still closed, afraid to see her surroundings, she let her ears do the looking for her.

Silence. Not a peep surrounded her. Not even a sound in the distance. Like cars, or people. Just silence.

What did that mean? Where was she?

Idiot! Just open your eyes and look.

She couldn't. The thought terrified her. Not much scared her. She didn't allow herself to become scared. It was a useless emotion. It didn't solve anything.

That's right. Being scared didn't solve anything. She needed to get out of this predicament. Clenching her eyes shut wouldn't help her find a way out.

A slow, difficult breath eased out as she popped her eyes open. A wooden ceiling hung above her. The frame looked old and worn, almost rotted. Would it fall on her? Break open suddenly and pin her to death to the bed? The soft contours of the mattress filtered into her addled mind— most of it, anyway. She could feel one large lump near her right shoulder.

Turning her head to the left, she saw a dresser, nothing atop it. Ignoring the pounding in her head, she lifted her body up as much as she could. The room was tiny. In the corner near the door, which she assumed was locked even if she managed to get free, sat a wooden chair. It looked stable enough to sit on, but old, like the ceiling.

Goose bumps covered her skin. The fright wanted to sweep back in and claim her, suck her into a reality that would paint a prettier picture than what she faced.

The cold moved over her body—her *naked* body— except for her panties and bra that still, thankfully, covered her.

Shivering from the temperature, slowly getting more and more aware of her situation, she wished for a blanket. She needed something to cover herself. Not just for propriety. The room was freezing. She didn't think the heat was on.

Where was she? Who did this?

That last question really made her wrack her brain as she lay her head back down. She didn't have enough time to process who hit her before she was out cold.

Bolting upright again, she moaned in pain from the sudden movement.

Rina.

Dropping back down, she tried her hardest to keep the tears at bay.

Was Rina okay?

This was her fault. She should've listened when Rina suggested they stay in the office for coffee. Now look what happened. Rina could be dead for all she knew.

"Please...let her be okay." A tear slid down. "I don't care what happens to me, but please let Rina be okay."

"I didn't hit her that hard. I'm sure she's fine." A deadly laugh. "Not like you."

That voice. She recognized it. It was him. The man who attacked her twice. Of course it was him. Who else would kidnap her? Why didn't she hear the door open?

A grimy hand gripped her foot, sliding up her ankle to her thigh, stopping just short of the area that should only be touched by Sauer.

Please, Sauer, find me.

As much as she wanted to know who this man was, she

couldn't look his way. The fear clawed down her throat, stopping a scream from escaping.

His hand brushed over her mound, up her belly, and circled her breast, back and forth between her cleavage. Her eyes glazed over as the fear threatened to consume her.

No! She needed to fight back.

Moving her gaze until it landed on his face, she couldn't hold back the gasp. "I know you." But from where?

Hatred and fury blazed in the black depths of his eyes. His hand cupped a breast and squeezed painfully.

Her lips clamped closed, refusing to scream and give him the satisfaction.

"You're about to know me really well."

Oh, God, no. She couldn't let him do that. Couldn't let him violate her in such a way. Pulling on the ropes wrapped tightly around her hands and ankles, she fought against the restraints as hard as she could.

A chilling laughter coated the room.

"Yes, please. Fight back." He brushed a strand of hair away from the edge of her mouth. "It'll just make it more fun. It's always fun when they fight back."

They? Of course they. He already killed a woman. Sauer, being Sauer, didn't go into details of how she died. Or that she was raped. Obviously, she had been. She also hadn't been his first either. *They.* She wouldn't give him the pleasure of her fear. Because it swarmed every inch of her body, in and out of her veins, threatening to paralyze her. But she wouldn't let it take control. She had to be strong and tough. Like she always was.

His head lowered, his lips a breath away as he whispered, "You brought this on yourself. I'm sorry."

A deep retching pain pierced her arm as a knife sliced straight through.

A POUNDING SO LOUD, so deep, echoed around him. His heart almost synced in perfect rhythm to each bang to the door. Unprofessional? Perhaps. Did he care? Not in the least. Dee's life hung in the balance. They had to be right about this.

The door swung open. His hand fell to his side in a tight fist.

"This is harassment." Mrs. Colton started to slam the door.

Sauer's hand whipped up so fast to halt the movement it wasn't hard to miss the way she flinched back.

Interesting.

"Where is your husband?"

She let go of the door, considering he wasn't going to allow it to close. "At work."

"Quit jerking us around. He's not there. He kidnapped someone." Sauer watched as the color drained from her face. "He killed his sister. He has a tattoo, doesn't he? He has a recent injury to his leg, doesn't he? Start talking!"

Of course, that was all conjecture. They had no actual proof, but by her reaction, the tiny trembles in her hands as she clutched them to her chest, the pasty white tone covering her skin, her wide round eyes in surprise, he was right. Not the kind of surprise he expected. More so, the how-did-you-figure-it-out surprise.

"My husband is a good—"

"A good man, huh? So good he beats you."

She jerked back, almost as if Sauer slapped her.

"If you don't help us, we'll have no choice but to arrest you for obstruction," Newman said quietly next to him. "We don't wish to do that, especially because you're a victim yourself. Isn't it time he stops hurting you?"

A shaky breath escaped. "He doesn't..." She turned her head, trying to control her breathing. Most likely trying to keep the tears at bay. Sauer didn't want to feel sorry for her, or sympathize. He did anyway. Newman was right. She was also a victim. Her husband had years of controlling her, making sure she stayed in line and did nothing to ruin the status quo.

"Where would he go? Somewhere with privacy?" Sauer asked softly. The gesture was a hard one for him, when all he wanted to do was scream and demand she tell him.

With an aching slowness, she looked at him. "I honestly don't know. We have a cabin up north, about three hours away." She blanched. "His father passed away two years ago and left him some property not too far away. It's an old house, in ruins. It needs a ton of work done, yet anytime I mention it, he...he doesn't like to talk about it."

"We'll need both addresses," Sauer said as he nodded at Newman, who already had his notepad at the ready.

She rattled off both, then said softly, "He's cheating on me. With his secretary, with the neighbor down the way, with basically any woman he wants. I have no clue why his sister would blackmail him. But that's a good starting place. He wouldn't want anyone to know he doesn't have a sterling reputation."

The pain finally poured from her eyes. Not stoic indifference. Not haughtiness. Just plain sad pain. She was giving up the fight. How long had she been fighting? Sauer imagined for a very long time.

"He'll never hurt you again."

A quick nod. "That's what you think. He hurts me every time I close my eyes. He has a tattoo on his right forearm and on his left bicep." Her breath hitched. "He's been limping lately, but I don't know why." The door closed gently.

Sauer didn't have time to make her feel better, but when this was all over, he'd make sure she got the help she needed. Lots of counseling.

They dashed for the car. Newman peeled out of the driveway heading for the location not far from Rockville. Sauer made a call to the department up north, asking for assistance, for someone to check out the property and have someone sit there in case he showed up. If he did take Dee there, he wouldn't arrive for another two hours, at least.

The throbbing beat of his heart still hadn't subsided. It never would until Dee was safe in his arms. He finally had their perp, and it didn't matter. Because he had Dee.

The entire drive was silent. There wasn't much to say, and Sauer was grateful Newman didn't try to give him false platitudes. He didn't want any of that. The only thing he wanted was Dee. In his arms. Safe. That's all he wanted.

It's as if time stilled. His heart hammering in one beat, then stopping, dead silence in the next.

"He's here."

A twitch of his head indicated he heard Newman, then nothing. He needed his focus. They slipped out of the car, leaving the doors open a crack to avoid any unnecessary noise. Crouching low, they darted along the tree line passing Vince's car that told them he was here. What it didn't tell them was Dee's fate.

She had to be alive.

Twenty feet from the house that looked ready to fall to pieces, a loud scream perforated the air.

He didn't think, didn't stop to question procedure. He bolted up the stairs and busted through the front door.

18

A CRAZY LAUGH split the air. She couldn't help it. Just as she couldn't help but scream when he stabbed her in the arm above the other wound that bled steadily. Earlier, he had pierced her skin with ease, twisting the knife like the bastard he was, then left. Walked out of the room with evil in his eyes.

She had stared at the ceiling the entire time he was gone, trying to control her breathing from the pain and the panic threatening to paralyze her. It took every ounce of strength she had to keep her demeanor calm and cool.

It royally pissed him off.

Which made her happy as could be.

"Do it again, asshole. I like the pain."

His eyes raged. His lips thinned with fury.

Maybe it was dumb and stupid of her to make him even madder, but she couldn't help it. Call her crazy. Oh, wait, people already did. She laughed, enjoying the way his nostrils flared. He looked like a bull ready to plow down a cowboy.

This asshole seriously underestimated her if he thought

she'd fall prey to his madness. If anything, the more he hurt her, the more the crazy came out. She couldn't stop laughing.

Whack!

Her cheek stung from the slap.

"Quit laughing." His eyes blazed as black as death, his words resonating within her.

She finally remembered. She knew him. None of it made sense.

"Why are you doing this? You're as sick as your father."

The laughter finally appeared in his eyes. "Ah, so you remember. It's about damn time." His hand grazed down her chest. "I remember the exact moment when I recognized you at the mall. So beautiful. Just like when you were a teenager." He slapped her again. "And you passed by me without acknowledging me. Nobody ignores me like that. Let's have some real fun."

The blade swung above his head. Preparing for the pain was difficult. She knew she wouldn't be able to hold in her scream, even as she wanted to with a passion. Every time she screamed, he reveled in it.

The door slammed against the wall.

"Police. Drop it or I will shoot."

She laughed. More so in happy delight that Sauer found her, not to aggravate him. Of course, she should've known it would piss him off. Holding it in was impossible. Hearing Sauer's voice sent her into a tailspin of peace, thankfulness, and laughter. So much laughter because not once did she doubt Sauer. She knew he'd find her. How? She had no clue. But she had clung to that hope, something she never did for any man. Sauer was just different. She believed in him as he believed in her.

Vince's hand stood poised in the air, rigid, the intent

clear in his eyes. He wanted to impale her over and over. She saw it. His eyes looked so black. So cold. So filled with death.

Her mother had an affair with his father when she was fifteen or sixteen. She couldn't recall the exact age since her mother dated way too many men. The affair ended when Vince found out and attacked her mother, as if it were her fault. Her mother, being the type of woman she was, refused to call the police. "He didn't mean it. He was just upset." So dumb. Of course, it didn't surprise her. Vince's father had also hit her mother a few times. Like father, like son.

Fifteen years later, here Vince wanted to terrorize her, kill her. And why? Because he saw her in the mall and she didn't say anything to him. She didn't even know what he was talking about. She couldn't recall seeing him anywhere. But she could see his face clear as day as the man who attacked her in her home.

"I said drop it. I won't say it again."

Dee focused on Sauer's voice. Although he spoke calmly, she heard the rage behind each word.

A flash of silver sparkled in her eyes as the knife came down. A loud shot echoed, ringing in her ears. A slash of pain cut across her stomach. No scream fell from her lips. This time, hot tears left.

"Shit, Dee." Rough, jerky movements touched her wrist as Sauer tried to untie her. "Shit, baby, are you okay?" He groaned. "Dumb question. Ignore me. You're not okay. You're bleeding...badly."

Pain stretched up and down her arm as he helped lower it to her side. Then, he reached across the bed, getting the other hand. He worked fast and efficiently. Gentle tugging at her feet had her looking down to see Newman quietly working. He offered a small smile, yet said nothing.

What could he say? Sauer was occupying the space with his trembling, mumbling words. He was speaking, but it didn't make much sense. His typical way of stringing words together. She loved it when he did that.

Yeah, she loved it. Loved him.

"I'm...kill him...damn! He's already dead. Kill him again...that bastard..."

Every time she moved her arm, it stung, throbbing everywhere. But, while she loved his mumbling, she didn't enjoy hearing the agony in his voice. She touched his cheek, stalling any more words. He bent his head, resting it against her forehead.

"Dee..."

"I'm okay."

"Baby, you're bleeding." He jerked upright. "Shit, you're bleeding." He tugged off his coat, throwing it to the ground. Then ripped off his suit jacket, wrapping it around her arm as gently as possible. "He sliced your stomach, but it's not bleeding as badly as your arm. The bed is..."

She knew what he couldn't finish. The bed was soaked in her blood. That's probably why she was starting to feel woozy, disoriented. All she wanted to do was focus on Sauer and his handsome face, yet everything was starting to blur a little.

"Marry me?"

"What?"

He leaned closer, whispering against her lips, "Marry me?"

Maybe she was losing it. More delusional than she thought. He couldn't have said what she thought he said.

"No."

He shifted away, his hands still holding tight pressure against her arm, the confusion written all over. "No?"

He was so damn adorable. She smiled as a small laugh drifted out, her eyes blurring some more. "I don't even know your first name. How can I marry someone and I don't know his first name?"

The confusion ebbed away as a small grin punctured the corner of his mouth. "It's—"

The world went black.

OPENING HER EYES, she groaned. A soft hand squeezed her hand, offering comfort. She appreciated the concern and thoughtfulness, but she didn't want his comfort.

"Why is it your ugly face I see when I open my eyes?"

Zeke chuckled, squeezing her hand one more time before letting go. "You know you love me. I'm like your annoying older brother. Admit it."

Cracking a small smile and nothing else, she glanced around the room. She was in the hospital. The room was empty besides Zeke.

"Where is..." Never mind asking that question. He probably hated her. "Where is Zoe and Rina?" There. That question made more sense.

Zeke gave her a look that said he knew what she really wanted to ask. "Rina's down the hallway in her own room." He held up a hand before she could make any sound. "She's fine. She just suffered a small concussion and the doctors want to monitor her for a little bit." He sighed. "Ben made her come. She didn't take it so well when she woke up and found you gone. She knows you're okay now and is getting better. Zoe's been walking back and forth between your rooms. She's with Rina right now."

"You swear she's okay?"

He nodded. "She's going to be fine. Just a nasty bump to the head." Gesturing at her arm, he said, "You lost a lot of blood. Thankfully, not enough to be too alarming. They stitched you up pretty quickly. The knife didn't hit anything vital. You have a small cut on your stomach, but not deep enough to require stitches. You should be out of here today." He let out a deep breath. "I'm so glad, too, because I hate the hospital."

That was no lie. Zoe had been hurt one too many times over a year ago. She didn't like venturing to the hospital to see her friend in pain and lying in bed. She might give him a hard time, but she did like him. He was good for Zoe. As much as she wanted to see Sauer standing by her bedside, she was oddly okay with Zeke being the first person she saw.

"He's on the phone."

She blinked a few times. "Who?"

Zeke smirked. "You know who. Sauer." Another small squeeze to her hand. "He hasn't left your side...until now, that is. His mother has been calling him off the hook."

"Why?"

Chuckling, he pointed at her. "Because of you."

"But he hates me."

That threw Zeke off, his face falling into a frown. "Sauer doesn't hate you. Why would you say that?"

The memory assaulted her. She couldn't recall everything he said. But she remembered what she said. No.

"He asked me to marry him."

"I know."

"I said no, Zeke."

He grinned. "I don't think Sauer took you seriously. His mom called, for whatever reason, and he let it slip he couldn't talk because his fiancée was injured. She's been blowing up his phone since, wondering if you woke up yet.

His parents are in Florida on vacation, but they're trying to get a flight home as soon as possible."

"But they don't even know me."

Shrugging, he sat down in a chair near the window. "I think they're just excited he's getting married."

"He doesn't hate me?"

"I'd never hate you."

Her head twisted to the doorway. Sauer's handsome face filled the space. His joy and relief shined all the way to her heart. He hesitated once, then made the walk to her bed with confidence.

"That's my cue to leave." Zeke smiled at them and walked out, closing the door behind him.

"How are you feeling?" His fingers wove into her hand. She clung to it, to him, happier than she ever thought possible.

"I'm okay."

"Really?" He looked at her arm that had a large white bandage wrapped around it. Then his eyes slid down her body. "Did he...did he..."

Shaking her head, she pulled on his hand gently. He sat down on the edge of her bed. "He didn't touch me. Not much." She smiled to ease the torture on his face.

"He can't hurt you anymore. Or anyone else."

"I knew him. From a long time ago. His father had an affair with my mother." She glanced down at their hands locked together. "He hit my mother when he found out about the affair, but she did nothing about it." She kept her gaze to their hands. "He said he saw me in the mall and I ignored him. That upset him so much he wanted to hurt me. It just doesn't make sense."

"He was a sick bastard. He can't hurt you anymore. That's what matters."

"Who did he kill?"

Sauer remained silent.

Cocking an eyebrow with a silky grin to go with it, she waited patiently. For about five seconds. "You're not going to tell me? It's over. What does it matter?"

"You just have to know everything, don't you?"

"It'll never change."

He lowered his mouth, careful not to move her arm much as he kissed the back of her hand. "I don't want you to change. I love every little part of you."

"I love you, too. Now quit changing the subject and tell me."

HIS HEART WAS BEATING DOUBLE-TIME at seeing her beautiful eyes staring into his. He worried the entire time from the moment she passed out to the moment they wheeled her into this room and she didn't wake up. Less than three hours had passed since they arrived, but long enough for him to go out of his mind.

Now, she blew his mind again. *I love you, too.*

He'd been dying to hear those words since the first time he said it. He wanted to hear it over and over and over. He sensed she didn't want him to make a big deal about it. Reaching for control he didn't think he possessed, he smiled in response to her sweet words.

"His sister."

"Why?"

A simple shrug. "She was blackmailing him with something. We have no idea why, but I'm starting to get a good picture. He beat his wife. Image was important. Could've been something simple as that. Or it could've..."

"Could've what?"

He didn't want to tell her. He didn't even want to think about it.

"Sauer, just talk to me."

"Newman's still at the house. There's evidence that suggests his sister wasn't the first person he killed. Maybe she found out he was hurting other women and blackmailed him to keep quiet."

Dee glanced out the window, exerting some pressure on his hand. "He said I'm sorry right before he stabbed me the first time. Obviously, he wasn't sorry, but he said it in a way like he was. His tattoo..." She met his eyes again. "The initials. I. S. It could stand for I'm sorry. It's a strange thing to have tattooed, but he's clearly deranged. Stitch must not have found anything out. He would've heard something by now. I hate mysteries."

"Don't let him win. Don't think about him anymore. Let it go."

Sauer didn't know how to help her, but he'd do everything in his power to help her through this. She was tough, yes, but she wasn't immune to everything.

"I love you. I was scared. I'm not anymore. Love. Love. Love. See, I can say it now."

"You can say it any time you want." He smiled as he leaned down and kissed her. "I love you. I'm not letting you get away. We'll get married next week."

Backing away, he almost felt bad for shocking her like that. She coughed and sputtered. "Excuse me? I thought I said no."

"I panicked for about half a second before I realized it didn't matter. You scared the living daylights out of me. We're getting married."

A silky smile graced her face. "Ah, yes, you and getting

scared. The first time you kissed me as if you were dying. The second time I scared you, you said you loved me. Now, this time, you say we're getting married." Love sparkled in her eyes. "Who am I to argue?"

"You love to argue with me."

"Not this time." She wiggled her fingers. "Where's my ring?"

He laughed. It felt so good to laugh and see her smile. To see her happy. To see her safe. "It's coming. I'm not prepared to leave your side yet."

"Please don't." Her voice held a hint of insecurity. Then she frowned. "I can't marry you."

He tried not to let his heart pitter-patter into chaos at her words. He had to stay strong and confident.

"I still don't know your first name."

The chaos instantly settled as he grinned. "I told you."

She squeezed his fingers in a way that said she was trying to hurt him because of his teasing. "I passed out before I heard it."

That reminder dimmed his smile easily. Bending forward, he brushed his lips to hers. "Brent."

Her good arm snaked around his neck, her hand venturing to the back of his head. Her lips met his more firmly, her tongue sweeping in, devouring him. Oh, how he wanted to take her home, right then and there. He planned to do so many delicious things to her. He would show her how deeply he loved her and erase any bad memories that lingered. Or try to, at least. That would take time. She might say she was okay, but he knew she was just suppressing it. He'd coax it out of her and eventually erase every bad memory.

Pausing for air, she whispered, "You don't look like a Brent."

"You can call me whatever you want, sweetheart."

She traced his mouth with her tongue, followed by small, tender kisses. "You'll always be Sauer to me." Another soft kiss. "Or honey buns." One more kiss. "Sweet cheeks."

Chuckling, he stopped her from saying any more silly pet names with a deep kiss that had her moaning for more than he could give her right now. "Let's get you home."

"Yes, please," she whispered breathlessly.

God, he loved this woman. He couldn't wait to show her every piece of his love at home.

Home. Their home. She was moving in, whether she wanted to or not.

Yeah. He could get used to this assertiveness.

"So what's this about your mother knowing all about me?"

Just like that, his nerves hit him like a ton of bricks.

"Uh?"

19

DEE SNUGGLED into Sauer's embrace as best as she could as he guided her down the hallway to Rina's room. She lit a fire in the nurse to get her discharged. She had enough of this place. Plus, she wanted to go home and just let Sauer hold her. She needed that so badly it wasn't funny. Thinking of why she needed it wasn't smart either.

Her arm tightened around him.

This was right. He was right. He wasn't like any other man. How many times did she tell herself that? Tons. Lots. All the time.

It was finally sinking in. That's why she needed his arms around her so much it hurt to breathe. He'd soothe the aches roaming her body from head to toe. His touch would wipe away the grimy feeling of *his* hands on her. Never had she felt so violated—

No. She wouldn't think about that asshole.

"You okay?" His warm breath slid down her neck in soothing waves as his soft voice comforted her.

"I'm perfect."

They continued down the long hallway.

She had insisted on seeing Rina before she left. It was all her fault Rina got hurt. Forgiving herself would take a long time. If ever. Not that Rina would hold her responsible.

They paused outside a door. Her feet stalled, the simple movement of putting one foot in front of the other gone. Sauer could probably sense her hesitation and nerves, because he rubbed his hand up and down her arm a few times before kissing the side of her head.

"It's okay."

It was okay. He was right. She knew this, but it was hard to put into words how horrible she felt. If only she would've played it safe. Listened for once. If she never would've suggested coffee at the café, Rina wouldn't be lying in the hospital with a concussion.

"It's my fault."

His grip intensified, his strength seeping into her. "It's not. Don't ever think that again."

"But—"

A finger touched her lips. "He chose to hurt Rina. He chose to attack you and take you. He chose his fate. Not you. Got it?"

Opening her mouth, his finger fell in. She lightly nibbled, then sucked on it until he pulled it out. "Got it."

His breathing became heavy. "The things you do…"

"You okay, Sauer?"

"I'm perfect."

She laughed at his words and entered the room after he pushed the door open for her. Rina sat up in bed, her hand clasped with Ben's, who sat as close to the bed as he possibly could.

"Dee, I'm so glad to see you. They said you were okay, but…it's good to see you with my own eyes."

She bent down and hugged her. "I know the feeling.

Rina, forgive me?" She couldn't let go, or stop the tears from leaving.

Rina's soft cries melded with hers. "I don't blame you for anything."

They sat hugging for what seemed like ages, which probably only lasted seconds, before she stepped back, turning her head away to wipe the evidence of her tears. She didn't need Ben to see her so weak.

"Glad to see you're okay, Dee."

She slowly faced Ben, who had nothing but compassion in his eyes. Apparently, he didn't blame her either. He should. They all should.

No matter how hard she tried, she couldn't hold it in. The tears came full force, dripping like a water faucet on full blast. Sauer's arms went around her immediately. She buried her head in his chest. So damn weak. How could she fall apart like this? What did they think of her now? Pathetic. Nothing but pathetic and weak.

"No one thinks that."

Shit. Did she say that out loud?

His arms wrapped her up in a safe cocoon as he bent his head close to her ear. "You are not weak or pathetic. It's okay to cry. No one blames you. Please believe that."

She wanted to believe that. Maybe in time, but not yet. She couldn't. Especially knowing that she was going home and Rina had to stay for observation.

Perhaps minutes passed. Seconds. She had no idea. The tears eventually stopped. Lifting her head brought a wave of fear. She had to look terrible. Now what did everyone think?

Deciding it couldn't be any worse than what they thought before, she pulled away from Sauer and wiped her face once again of the tear stains. Taking a fortifying breath, she turned toward Ben and Rina.

Rina had a sweet, calm look on her face. No blame whatsoever. Ben looked just as comfortable and calm as Rina. They were so sickeningly perfect for each other.

Would her and Sauer eventually look alike in their mannerisms?

"I should be able to go home soon. This was just a precaution. It's not as bad as it looks." Rina's reassurance made her feel a little better. Not by much, but it was something.

"I'm so glad to hear that."

"Hey. Don't think this gets you out of dancing. We have a ball to prepare for."

Of all the things she thought Ben would say that wasn't one of them. It started to sink in they didn't blame her. A corner of her mouth lifted in amusement.

"Yeah, and don't forget that Brent and I are going to be the best on the dance floor."

"Brent?" Rina and Ben asked at the same time.

Dee gently wrapped her arms around Sauer's waist and chuckled. "That's Sauer's first name. I thought I'd try it out a little." Gazing up at him, she smiled tentatively. "I think I still like Sauer better."

A kiss touched the tip of her nose. "Call me whatever you like."

"Brent. Wow. I can't believe I never knew your first name." Ben shook his head with surprise. "It's kinda weird."

"My name?" Sauer asked, tensing in her arms.

"No, dude," Ben said immediately. "That I never knew your first name."

"Oh, right. Of course."

Time to go. She wanted to crash in bed with Sauer's arms locked around her. Maybe even talk some. She and Sauer didn't touch the topic of their childhood much. His reaction to Ben said they should. If they wanted to make it in any capacity, marriage especially, they needed no secrets between them. What a difficult talk ahead. But, oh so necessary.

"I'm ready." She wasn't. But there'd be no better time than right now to get the hard crummy stuff over with.

"Then let's go." There was a quiet promise in his words. Maybe he knew what was going to happen. Either way, she suddenly wasn't afraid to face any of it.

SAUER HAD NEVER SEEN Dee cry so much in his life. Sure, the one time in the bathroom. Besides that, never. Why would he? She was strong and tough. Something people said and associated with her all the time. He knew better. Nothing but a mask to her fragility. Inside, she was a big old softie. No one saw it but him. And maybe Stitch, too, but he didn't want to think about him.

When they got home, they took a shower together, then settled into his bed with nothing between them but skin. Without warning, she started talking in a low, quiet voice where he had to bend his head as close to her mouth as he could to hear the trembling words. The longer she talked, the stronger they came out. The tears mingled with each word.

Her childhood hadn't been happy or full of the love and carefree bliss that a child should have. No. She lived with a mother who had more concern for herself and what new man would walk into her life than she had for her own daughter. When there wasn't a man to cling to, she still ignored her daughter by searching heavily for the perfect man. Her mother had died hoping, praying that her Prince Charming would pop into her life. She died alone.

When she stopped talking, the silence swirling around them, he didn't respond with the typical words. I'm sorry to hear that. That's terrible. What a horrible way to grow up. I can't believe your mother would do that.

None of that left his mouth, even though they punctured his thoughts.

Instead, he started softly speaking about his childhood, almost as low as she had when she first started. The teasing, the bullies that made his life hell. The lack of friends and people he could share his worries, some laughs, some good times with. His awkwardness with girls, then with women. His insecurities that still to this day he struggled with.

When he finished speaking, she answered his words with a kiss. Light and tender to his lips. The kiss turned from sweet to erotic in seconds. Their hands stroked from place to place, exploring, as if it were the first time.

With one whispered kiss, he asked if he could take her without a condom. Her response was a gentle smile and one nod.

He entered her with a desperate ache that only her touch could ease. They moved slow, then fast, then back to slow. The air around them became thick with heat, their bodies slick with sweat as they took their time to savor the love developing between them. Sure, he said he loved her before. She also said the words at the hospital. But this. This moment. The love shined through it all. Through the pain. Through the anger. Through the embarrassment.

True love. He believed in it. He always had. He just never thought he'd find it. Never thought he'd meet a woman who would love him for him. Shyness and all.

Dee embraced him as a man who could turn red as a

tomato at the drop of a dime, who could wrap his words into a garbled message, yet understand exactly what he meant. She didn't mock or tease or look at him with scorn. She looked at him with love and understanding.

Was he surprised? Not anymore. He believed they were more alike than anyone ever realized. He would never utter a word she said to another person to explain either. It wasn't anyone's business.

He made sure to be gentle as possible as he slid in and out. Hurting her was the last thing he ever wanted. Avoiding her arm wrapped in a bandage was almost impossible as she clung to him, as if she never wanted to let go. The energy sparking between them was more profound than ever before.

He couldn't explain it. Didn't even want to think about it. He just wanted to absorb it all. Trap it into one of the sweetest memories he ever had.

She tensed beneath him, moaning a delightful moan. The sound sent him into instant bliss, tensing as well. Unable to hold himself up, he sank into her body. She made no protest. If anything, she wrapped her arms tighter around him, telling him not to move an inch.

"I love you so much, Dee. So damn much."

"You better."

That was his Dee. Always saying something he never expected. God, if he didn't love her even more for that wonderful trait. He'd never be bored with her, that's for sure.

He rolled to his back, not wanting to suffocate her with his heavy weight. Pulling her gently into his arms, he stroked her back as her head lay on his chest, her arm tight against him.

"I love you, Sauer."

"I know."

And he did. Even if she never said it again. He knew. She said it every time she touched him.

"When do I get my ring?"

She still surprised him with her outrageous words. A laugh fell out as he kissed the top of her head. "Whenever you want. Tomorrow. The biggest diamond you want."

Her fingers brushed up and down his chest, tickling, teasing, enticing him to take her again.

"Can I get a ruby instead of a diamond?"

"Anything you want. Why a ruby?"

"Because it's beautiful and it's my birthstone. I'm a fan of red."

Threading his fingers through her hair, he sighed happily. "So am I."

"Did you mean it?"

"What?"

"About getting married next week."

He hesitated. How did he answer that properly? Because he meant it. Of course he meant it, especially since they didn't use a condom. Sure, she was on the pill, but he'd love nothing more than for her to get pregnant. He wanted to marry her as soon as possible and start a family. If he wasn't mistaken, he thought Dee would want to get married just as quickly. She didn't seem like the type to want a bunch of hoopla. He sure didn't. The center of attention? No, thanks.

But he could be wrong. Maybe she did want all the bells and whistles when it came to a wedding. A big white dress. A large audience in a beautiful chapel. A reception that spoke of elegance and warmth.

Definitely, no, thank you. Find a judge, sign the papers, and be a married man.

"Sauer?" Her hand froze as she waited for his answer. Whatever that was. He still wasn't sure.

"If I could make you my wife right now, I would."

Best damn answer he could think of without saying either way.

Swift, soft strokes recommenced.

"I need to have the perfect dress."

So she did want all the big to-do when it came to a wedding. That's okay. He'd survive. For her. He'd do anything.

"Of course."

"A week seems plenty of time for me."

"Wait, what?" He met her gaze as she lifted her head. "You do wanna get married next week?"

"Yeah. I don't want a big thing. We can go to the courthouse. But I'm wearing a dress that's going to have you speechless the entire time." A silky smile spread across her face. "A dress that'll have you wishing you could have me to yourself. Sneak me away to a closet and have your dirty way with me."

He moved like lightning, rolling her to her back, and entered her with one smooth stroke. The feeling of skin-to-skin, no barrier, sent him spiraling into a bliss that could almost be described as painful. "I can't wait to have my dirty way with you. How does now sound?"

Murmuring her pleasure, she moved with him.

Once again, the heat built. The love swirled. The magic soared to newer heights.

He loved her until she couldn't speak. Until her moans were incoherent. Until the day faded into night.

She fell asleep in his arms. He stayed awake just watching her sleep. Thankful that everything turned out okay. That he didn't lose her to a madman.

In a week's time, she'd be his wife. Life couldn't get any better than that.

20

Sᴀᴜᴇʀ sᴡɪᴘᴇᴅ at the hand tugging on his tie. "It's fine."

"Dude, it's not straight."

"It's fine."

Newman arched a brow, then shrugged. "Just trying to help."

"Me, too." He paused, then decided to go for it. "Did you change your mind yet about asking Susan to the ball? It'll be fun. You guys can just go as friends."

"Friends? No way." Newman leaned against the wall outside the judge's chambers.

Dee, Rina, and Zoe were in the bathroom putting some final touches on Dee. Or so Zoe told him. He hadn't seen Dee yet. All day, in fact. It was only noon, but it was killing him. She didn't even stay at his house last night, having a girls' night at her own house.

The past week had been one of the longest weeks of his life. He was back on duty, after a few days of administrative leave—the normal protocol when there was a police-involved shooting. He understood the reason for it, even welcomed it. He had never fired his weapon before. Those days were spent thinking things through. Going over everything in his head. Did he have to shoot him? Yes, he did. He would've hurt Dee even more. The department agreed.

Some nights he wished he could kill him again for the pain he put Dee through. Nightmares plagued her. The things she said in her sleep—well, he didn't like to think about it. But it never woke her up, only him. He always whispered sweet words into her ear until she quieted down and continued to sleep in peace. In the mornings, he ached to ask her about them, but fear held him back. Fear she'd spiral to a place he couldn't help her. Fear he couldn't handle to hear her pain. Just so much fear. They needed to address it soon. He needed to address it. Now wasn't the time to be acting like a chickenshit.

For some insane reason, he started to press Newman every day about Susan. Something he never did. It bugged him that Newman didn't want to take her to the dance. Even as friends. He wasn't an idiot. He could read between the lines. Newman didn't want to be just friends with Susan. He wanted more. Or maybe he was reading him wrong. Newman did just break up with Chrissy. What the hell did he know? He was no expert at relationships. Look how many times he screwed up with Dee.

"So you want more than friends?"

"Why do you keep bugging me about Susan every day?"

Sauer shrugged. He couldn't say because he was still trying to figure that out himself.

"Look, I like Susan. She's great to work with, but we're co-workers. Not friends. That's it."

In other words, Newman had a thing for her and didn't want to ruin the great working relationship they had. Sauer, in the beginning, would've taken friends only with Dee. Now that he thought about it, he would've never survived it.

Newman had the right idea. Being friends would just tear a guy apart. He should quit bugging him about it.

"Okay."

Newman nodded, then stood up straighter as Zeke and Ben approached. Zeke grinned as he opened a clear plastic container in his hands. He took out the white boutonniere and pinned it to his suit jacket.

"My mom made it. She insisted you wear it, so you can't argue."

Sauer touched it lightly, then smiled. "It's great. Tell her thanks."

"You can tell her yourself. She's with my dad. We can go into his office if you want. You sure you want my dad doing the ceremony?" Zeke glanced around. "Where are your parents?"

Sauer wanted nothing more than Judge Chance to perform the quick ceremony. Out of the judges he interacted with, he was his favorite. Always nice and fair when they needed a warrant signed. Plus, being friends with Zeke, it just seemed appropriate.

"I think my mom's with Dee. They took to each other really well. My mom loves Dee, which I knew she would. They've been inseparable, shopping every day for the perfect dress, as Dee liked to tell me." Sauer leaned closer, whispering in case his mom suddenly appeared. "My dad went for a quick smoke. She thinks he quit, but he's struggling."

"I have no idea what you're talking about. I did quit." His dad, Bob, wrapped a big arm around his shoulder and winked at everyone.

"Of course you did, Dad." Sauer didn't even bother to tell his dad he caught a whiff of a faint lingering smell of smoke on him. His mom probably knew his dad was struggling and wouldn't give him a hard time about it. At least, not too much.

Laughter followed as Zeke opened the door to his dad's office and they piled in after him. Judge Chance sat behind his desk, pen in hand, concentration on his face. His hand swiftly flew across the paper. Deborah, Zeke's mom, sat on a couch to the right of the room, her attention on her phone. Of course, the minute they both saw everyone enter the office, Judge Chance shoved the paper in front of him into a folder and closed it, then stood with a beaming smile. Deborah stood up as well.

"Is it time?"

"Almost." Sauer walked slowly to the desk and shook hands with him. "Thank you for doing this on such short notice."

Judge Chance squeezed his hand warmly, slapping a hand to his shoulder. "Anytime. Dee's a firecracker. I've always liked her. Plus, she'd rip me a new one if I would've said no."

"Ain't that the truth," Zeke muttered under his breath as he shook his head with a tiny smirk.

Sauer then turned to Deborah and gave her a small hug. "Thank you for the boutonniere. I'm glad you could be here."

"You're welcome. You look very handsome." She smiled a sweet smile. "I even peeked in on Dee, and she's looking gorgeous."

"You're all going to your house for a small reception, correct? I took the rest of the day off. I don't want to miss any fun," Judge Chance said as he wrapped an arm around his wife. The gesture was adorable. He could already picture himself at that age wrapping a tender arm around Dee and holding her close.

"Yep. My mom set it all up. Food's waiting for us. My dad offered to be our DJ. Newman helped me set up the bar area. We're ready for the party."

"And I bought the cigars," Ben piped in with a mischievous smile to Bob, who winked again.

"Well, should I go knock on the bathroom door and hurry them up? I'm ready to party." Zeke started toward the door.

Judge Chance cleared his throat. "Have you learned nothing from me? You don't rush women while they're trying to beautify themselves. Especially for a wedding."

"My wife is beautiful no matter what she does." Zeke walked back to the original spot he was standing.

"Good answer." Bob stood next to Sauer, but leaned closer to Ben. "So, what kind of cigars did you buy? Just curious."

Sauer couldn't hold in his laugh. "Dad, Mom is not going to let you have a cigar."

"Of course not. I can still hear what kind he bought." Although, his eyes told a different story. He'd be sneaking a cigar at some point. Nothing would stop him, not even his wife.

Sauer just smiled as Ben went into detail on the type of cigars he picked for the special occasion. He wasn't a smoker. Neither was anyone else, besides his dad. But at Ben and Zeke's wedding, cigars were smoked at the reception. He figured it was a small tradition they wanted to do at his wedding. He liked the idea of being included in a tradition, even if he didn't care for cigars much. He smoked one at their weddings, so he was smoking one at his own. That was that.

He glanced at his watch continuously, wondering what was taking so long. He knew, and agreed with Judge Chance, that women liked to take their time getting ready, especially Dee. She always needed an extra half hour in the mornings to use the bathroom. He never knew what she did in there for so long, but she always came out looking gorgeous and sexy. There was no stopping him. He loved to mess up the look by taking her back to the bedroom and having his way with her. She never argued with him, but for the sake of it, gave him a smirk of disapproval for messing her hair up.

Since she started staying with him, she hadn't been back to her house, except to grab more clothes. And by more clothes, he meant her entire closet. His closet was so full of her clothes he was thinking they needed to buy another dresser. He was okay with that.

They hadn't talked about what they were going to do with her house yet, but it was just automatically assumed they'd be living in his house. Besides her clothes, she hadn't transferred anything else to his house. Only a matter of time before they did. Not many opportunities arose in the past week. They had been too busy enjoying each other's company, and the fact his mom had been at his house every day talking wedding plans with Dee. Oddly enough, Dee enjoyed it.

What was taking so long?

If he had to wait much longer, he might start sweating that she was changing her mind. Maybe she finally realized she couldn't handle his shyness and awkwardness at times. Maybe they just weren't compatible enough for each other. Maybe she pretended all week she liked his mother when she really didn't. Maybe—

The door to the chambers opened.

"Get that look of fright off your face, sweetie. Deena wanted to look perfect." His mom, Francine, or Franny to friends and family, walked up to him and kissed his cheek, instantly soothing his rattled nerves. His mom always had that affect on him.

"She's always perfect to me."

"I know." She patted his cheek affectionately, then clapped her hands excitedly. "Places, people. My son is getting married."

Like that, his mother took charge. As a child, it always made him look at her with awe at how confident and sure of herself she was in every little thing she did and said. As an adult, he still appreciated the poise in which she conducted herself. She arranged him right next to Judge Chance, Newman next to him as his best man, then Zeke and Ben after him. On the other side of Judge Chance, she positioned Zoe, then Rina. Deborah stood to the side, a few steps away from them. When she appeared satisfied everyone stood in the correct spot, she poked her head out of the door, then took a spot next to his dad, who stood not too far away from Ben.

He glanced around the room, happiness filling his heart at who stood with him. Sadness filtered in a tiny bit. He even told Dee to ask Stitch to come, trying not to let the jealousy consume him, but Dee declined, insisting Stitch wouldn't feel comfortable being here. She added she wanted it small, no fuss. So he didn't argue with her about it.

The door slowly opened.

He lost his breath. His knees went weak. No words could describe how he felt. Hell, words were impossible to form. She left him utterly speechless.

He loved many things about Dee. Her fiery attitude. Her loyalty. Her protectiveness of the people she cared about. Her beauty. Her hair, so crazy and curly and always full of character. Perhaps she knew that. Because what he loved most about her as she took gradual steps toward him, her eyes locked with his, was her gorgeous red hair. Not coiled to perfection into an up-do that he thought she might do, but hanging loose, wild, and carefree. Just like the Dee he loved.

And the dress.

Whew!

What could he say? Words were stuck in his throat.

He knew she loved her clothes tight, short, and revealing in all the right places. Hell, just two nights ago he had her perform a fashion show for him so he could see all her dresses. He never had so much fun in his life, watching her dress and undress in front of him, then parade the skimpy dress around the room. She tried on four dresses before he couldn't take it anymore and tossed her onto the bed for a different kind of fun. The closet definitely held more than four dresses.

Her wedding dress, which she painstakingly shopped for, was white. Bright white with sparkling glitter from top to bottom. She shimmered like the most prized jewel in the world. It came just above her knees, a little longer than he expected, but fit the picture in front of him. It had no straps, scooping around her shoulders, emphasizing her cleavage in all its beautiful glory. In true Dee fashion, it clung to her body, molding to every delicious curve. He absolutely loved it. Every part.

She stopped right next to him, a devilish smirk shining. "Well?"

"Exquisite." He linked hands with her, leaning in. "And mine."

Her wily smirk melted into a tender smile. "You always know the best thing to say."

A few minutes later, Judge Chance announced them husband and wife. The kiss was short and sweet, because any longer would've had him doing inappropriate things in front of their friends and family. He wasn't sure how much longer he could contain his excitement. She was officially his wife.

Deena Sauer. It sounded perfect to him.

"Brent." Tilting her head, she let his name roll off her tongue a few more times. "Brent. Brent. Brent."

"You might want to speak up. Not sure he'll hear you when he's in the house and you're outside."

Dee looked to her right, keeping eye contact with Sauer's dad as he took a seat next to her on the back porch swing. Feeling a little claustrophobic, although having a good time, she didn't hesitate to step outside in the blistering cold for a moment to herself. She just needed a breather from everyone. Clear her mind. Settle her nerves.

"I was just..." How did she explain how she was feeling? She never lost her way with words. Most of the time words came out without her thinking. Offending people as if she intended to when she didn't. She just spoke with honesty. Here she sat, thinking away for the longest time and words still wouldn't come.

Bob lifted his gaze to the sky, a gentle smile on his face. "Brent used to come outside at night and just sit under the stars when he was having a frustrating day. He loved to listen to the quiet. He liked the solitude."

"That sounds like Sauer—Brent."

Bob looked at her, his eyes assessing, judging almost. She wanted to say it unnerved her, but she couldn't. There was an underlying tenderness to the look. Fatherly, even.

"What's troubling you, Deena? Everything went fast. No

harm if you think you made a mistake. Brent would understand."

She still couldn't get used to hearing his first name. Brent. It just didn't fit him. He'd always be Sauer to her. Now, she was Deena Sauer. It was just...weird.

"I love him. I didn't make a mistake." Maybe he'd come to realize he made the mistake. Maybe he'd see how hard she was to live with. Maybe he'd get annoyed with her within a week. A month. A year. When would they divorce?

"Franny, bless her heart, puts up with my crazy ways. Marriage isn't easy. Anyone who says different doesn't have a real marriage. It takes time, understanding, patience. Forgiveness at times."

It's as if Bob could hear her thoughts. Answering her with words she needed to hear. Even Sauer's mother said all the right things this past week. She bonded with her more in one week than she ever had with her own mother. It made her feel guilty as hell.

A strong pair of arms wrapped her in a warm hug. The love she felt almost made her cry. This man, whom she barely knew, understood her pain without her having to tell him. Was this what it felt like to have a father? He just knew your pain without having to ask.

"Welcome to the family, Deena. Franny and I already love you."

Damn this man. He was going to make her cry. Sucking in a deep breath to keep the tears at bay, she snuggled more into his embrace. It felt like a hug from a father. She loved every second of it.

"You just let us know if you ever need anything. We'll be here."

Words still wouldn't come. Her throat was clogged. If

one little word slipped out, she knew the tears would come as well. So she said nothing.

A soft kiss touched her head. Then, as quickly as he appeared, he let her go and walked away. The conversation, if one could call it that, was short and sweet, yet powerful. He managed to make her feel more grounded, accepted. He didn't say much either. But what he said made all the difference. Like father, like son. Sauer was like his dad in so many ways.

She closed her eyes as a tear slid down her cheek. How did she ever manage to snag a good man like Sauer? Did she even deserve a good man like him? A good family?

Another warm, strong pair of arms circled her, pulling her into his embrace. She inhaled the musky scent of Sauer, wondering if his dad told him where she was. Not that she disappeared completely, because she didn't. Normally the life of the party, she sat in her own little corner while everyone else had fun. What was wrong with her?

A few more tears escaped as Sauer said nothing, but held her in his arms, softly running a hand up and down her arm. The quietness, the peace surrounding them soothed her more than any words could have done.

"I'm so—forgive me?" She still couldn't open her eyes.

"For what?"

"I have no idea." Lifting her head from his chest, she slowly met his gaze that was filled with love and concern. "Everything. I've made so many things difficult for you. I'll probably continue to do so. I should've recognized him. I knew him when I was younger. I should've been able to identify him, and because I didn't, Rina got hurt."

"You're sitting outside thinking about Vince? I was worried you were having second thoughts about us." He cracked a smile, probably trying to elicit a smile out of her.

When she didn't, he continued. "It's not your fault. I'll keep repeating that until you believe it. He was sick."

She looked away, back at the dark night sky. "I wasn't really thinking of just him, but everything. My life. The way your family accepted me so quickly. I keep wondering when it'll all fall apart and you'll leave. It always happened with my mother."

He tensed slightly, then relaxed just as quickly. "I'm not going to leave you. Not without fighting for you. We'll probably fight. I have no doubt about that." He squeezed her tighter, a soft chuckle renting the air. "Love survives it all. Fights. Mistakes. Hard times. How do I know? My parents. I saw a doozy of a fight when I was seven. My dad went drinking and drove home drunk. My mom was so pissed at him. He said he didn't want to wake her up, then have to wake me up so we could go get him. I thought for sure with the words they said to each other they were done. I never heard them yell like that. The next morning I woke up prepared for the worst. Do you know what I saw?"

A kiss touched her forehead. She wanted to look at him. Instead, she shook her head for him to continue.

"My mom making breakfast with a smile and my dad sitting at the table with a cup of coffee as if nothing happened. It confused the hell out of me. I didn't say anything, but my mom just knows things. She came to my room later and explained what happened last night was a part of life. A part of marriage. You have arguments and disagreements and you let it out. Then you make up and move on. It's when you lose the love the relationship falls apart. I don't ever see myself losing my love for you. I can't say it any plainer than that."

He sighed softly. "I know you don't have the best example from your mom, but I'm not like all those guys. If I was going to leave so quickly, don't you think I already would've? You haven't exactly made things easy on me, as you so clearly pointed out."

Since sitting outside, letting her thoughts take her away, she smiled. A bright smile. "That's a good point. I can't explain my insecurities right now." A laugh bubbled out, even though nothing was funny. He laughed with her. The sound soothed her rattled nerves.

"Remember that the next time you get the crazy thought I'm going to leave. Because I'm not. Hell, I have the same fear. What can shy, quiet Sauer possibly offer crazy, beautiful Dee?"

"Hey!" She nudged him, not very gracefully, as his arms were still locked around her. "I'm not crazy." His brow rose. "Not that crazy, anyway. Just a touch."

"Give me a sprinkle of crazy, a dose of loudness, with a shower of beauty, and I have all I want."

"We make such a perfect pair, uh? Shy and quiet with a mixture of loud and crazy."

"I wouldn't have it any other way." He kissed her lightly. "Let me know when you're worried. About anything."

"What bad timing to get all emotional. It's our wedding night and I'm ruining it."

Framing her face with his hands, he got nose to nose with her. "Who said it's ruined? It's the best day of my life. It'll get even better when we kick everyone out."

"What are you waiting for?"

His tongue swooped in, making her heart soar to the beautiful night sky. His kisses always had a way of calming her down. Before the kiss turned into a territory that would be indecent, he pulled away, breathing heavily.

"I want you."

"You have me."

A silky smile graced his face. "I do." A low chuckle escaped. "Care to let the crazy out?"

"Meaning?"

"Go tell everyone to get the hell out so I can make sweet love to my wife."

Cocking a brow, a slow smile built into a beaming one that had him tilting his head in confusion. "As you wish." She slid out of his embrace and stood up.

"Well, not in those exact words..."

With a little pump to her hair, she placed a hand to her hip. "You asked for crazy. You married crazy. Crazy is what you're gonna get."

She started to walk away when Sauer's hand grasped hers.

"Coming along for the ride, are you?"

"I don't wanna miss any of their expressions when you say that. It's one of the things I love about you. The things that come out of your mouth."

Right then, she knew. It slapped her squarely in the face. All her doubts melted away. How could she still worry that he'd leave her? He loved her—every outrageous part of her. He embraced who she was. For that, she loved him even more.

She laughed.

"What's so funny?"

"My little bit of crazy is rubbing off on you."

He let go of her hand and looped an arm around her. "I could say something dirty to that."

She laughed even harder. "In less than a minute, you can do all the dirty things you want to me."

His eyes lit up with desire, his arm tightening, then relaxing as he opened the sliding door. They stepped inside, took their coats off, and made their way to the living room where everyone was. He positioned himself behind her, wrapping his arms around her, resting his chin on her shoulder as she cleared her throat. The words almost stalled as she felt his hardness pressed delightfully against her ass. He wanted her. She wanted him just as badly.

"It's time to get the hell out so Sauer can make sweet love to me."

She almost let embarrassment wash over her that she said something so rude-like in front of Sauer's parents and Zeke's parents. Instead of horror or disdain hitting their features, everyone laughed.

"I was wondering when we'd get kicked out." Richard winked at her, as he helped Deborah up from a chair.

"The things you say." Zeke chuckled, yet set his drink down.

Franny walked up to them as everyone else started to leave. "You two have fun. I would love to have lunch one day next week, Deena."

"What about me?"

She almost laughed at the way the words left his mouth, as if he were wounded. "I'd love that, Franny."

"Perfect." She touched her cheek in a motherly way that made her feel the love, then kissed Sauer's cheek. "Don't keep your wife waiting. We'll lock the door."

"Thanks, Mom, but I got it."

It wasn't quite under a minute like she told him, but within ten minutes, everyone was gone. She waited in the threshold of the living room as Sauer closed the front door, set the alarm, then turned toward her.

"So, about that sweet lovemaking?"

"I'd thought you'd never ask." He grinned, a blissful twinkle in his eyes as he scooped her into his arms. "Notice how no one seemed affected by your words?"

"Yeah, they're used to my wild ways." She started to press tiny kisses on his neck. "Next time I'll do it while we're in a public restaurant or something."

He stumbled in his footsteps, almost dropping her before reaching the bed. "You wouldn't?" Then he chuckled. "Of course you would. Let's work up to that."

She couldn't help but laugh. "Of course."

Everyone needed to work up to that level of crazy. She knew Sauer was just the man for the job.

EPILOGUE

Dee plucked two glasses of champagne from a passing waiter, then handed one to Rina. Zoe already had one in her hand, slowly sipping as if it were the grossest thing she ever tasted. They paid good money for these tickets, the dresses, the lessons. Dee planned to live it up and enjoy every single minute of this night.

And whew! Her husband and a tux. Say no more. The man knew how to fill out a tux. Hands down, he was the handsomest man in the room.

"No, thanks."

Cocking a brow, she shoved the glass a little closer to Rina. "Drink it. You haven't had one glass tonight. The night is only half over. One little glass isn't going to kill you."

"Unless you're pregnant. I mean, it won't kill you, but it's not good—" Zoe stopped talking when Rina turned red. "Holy shit! Are you seriously pregnant?"

Rina's eyes bulged as Dee chuckled at how loud Zoe said that. "I...we...don't talk so loud."

Zoe had the grace to look bashful, then stepped closer and lowered her voice. "Were you guys keeping it a secret for a bit?"

"I never said I was."

"Rina, sweetie, you can't get anything by us. You didn't admit it, but you did." Dee smiled, then took a sip of champagne. A large one, since she had to drink two glasses now.

"I'm not that far along...it took awhile to get pregnant. I don't want to jinx it."

"We won't say anything. I have faith it'll all be okay." Zoe gave Rina a hug.

"Congrats. You're going to make a wonderful mother." She gave her another smile, truly meaning her words. If anyone would make a good mother, it would be Rina. She was one of the nicest, sweetest people. So caring and friendly. Always helping others.

They didn't use condoms anymore, but she was still on the pill. She hadn't gotten pregnant yet, and she wasn't sure she was ready. What kind of mother would she be? A crazy one. Sauer would even their child out with his quiet and calmness.

Boy, did she need that trait of his so much in the past two months. About a week after their wedding, she finally spoke up about her nightmares that tended to plague her during the day as well. She could never get shit-face, or in a kinder word, Vince, out of her mind. From there, they talked. Sauer was the best listener. Sometimes, she would talk and talk and talk, wondering if he fell asleep on her. But no. He was listening intently, his face one of serious concentration. The wonderful thing about Sauer was he never said anything back. She didn't need him to say anything. She just needed him to listen. Now, the nightmares weren't as frequent.

"Thanks, Dee. You will, too."

She almost spit out her champagne at those words. Would she make a good mother? Maybe she'd stop taking the pill soon and find out. Just maybe.

"Susan's having fun with Stitch. I can't believe you hid that hunk of a man from us for as long as you did," Zoe said with a laugh.

Dee laughed with her, not disputing how gorgeous Stitch was. Sauer had told her what happened with Newman. That Susan overheard he didn't want to go with her. Dee knew Susan wanted to go to this ball, so she didn't hesitate to ask Stitch to step in and help her with what he would consider a huge favor. Stitch didn't date nice, normal women like Susan. But for Dee, he'd do just about anything. By the smiles and laughter coming from them, they were having a great time together. It was a good thing. She still didn't like Newman.

Although, Stitch and Susan were an odd pair. He was over six feet. She was maybe 5'5". Susan was sweet and gentle. Stitch, more rough and dangerous. In appearances, maybe. In reality, he was sweet and gentle. She liked them as a couple. Who knew what would happen after tonight? Stitch was only helping her out, but she could see he was enjoying himself. They hadn't left each other's side the entire night.

"He's a great guy. What can I say? I got busy with my life, and so did he."

"They're sort of cute together." Rina smiled as they all glanced at Susan and Stitch dancing away.

"It was good thinking on your part, Dee. I like Susan. Maybe we should ask her to start joining us for drinks on Fridays," Zoe said.

They all liked that idea, agreeing that Dee would make

the offer to Susan. Soon after, they scattered to the dance floor with their husbands.

"So, what did you men talk about?"

"Baseball." Dee giggled, tucking her head into his chest. Immediately, Sauer corrected her stance and winked. "Posture, remember."

"If I didn't love you so much, I'd step on your toes just because."

He swooped in and kissed her, breaking his perfect posture, lingering longer than she expected. Every time they kissed, it felt like heaven. The heat would ignite into a flaming inferno. The desire swift and aching. She wanted him so badly.

He ended the kiss, sweeping her across the dance floor as elegantly as he always did. She loved dancing with him. So many times at home, he'd sweep her into his arms and dance away down the hallway, to the living room, to the bedroom. Just everywhere. Anytime he had a chance, he'd wrap his arms around her. It cemented her love for him a little more every time.

"Would I make a good mother?"

HIS STEPS FALTERED, almost stepping on her toes, which would've hurt her like hell since she was wearing open-toed heels. Just as quickly, he corrected his stance and kept twirling her around the ballroom.

"Of course. You're going to make a beautiful mother. Why would you ask such a silly question? You're nothing like your mother."

"Do you want kids?"

"As many as you want."

"Five."

He almost tripped in his steps again, but stopped himself before he looked like a complete fool. She could still manage to surprise him with her words. He figured by now, although they hadn't been married that long, she wouldn't catch him off guard anymore. So untrue. She normally said something daily that had him pausing in whatever he was doing.

"Five it is, then."

"Seriously?" She laughed. "You'll have five kids if that's what I want?"

"Five rambunctious, beautiful kids like you? Why wouldn't I want that? It sounds perfect."

She playfully slapped his shoulder. "You always say the right thing. Stop it."

Her dress swirled and twirled as they danced the waltz. As much as Ben and Zeke griped about taking dance lessons, they were having a great time. Even Stitch looked like he was having a good time. He agreed right away when Dee mentioned asking him to take Susan. He still felt guilty and horrible that Susan overheard what Newman said. While he didn't see Stitch too often, the guy was starting to grow on him. He was making Susan happy. That's what mattered at the moment.

This night, with this woman, was one of the best nights he ever had. He never made it to prom, or any other dance function his high school had. Admitting that to Dee had been difficult. Once he did, he felt lighter. More free. She said right away, "This'll be our night. The prom you never had." And damn if it wasn't. He loved every minute of the night so far. Even the strange talk about kids, something they had never done before, even with using no condoms. The talk about having kids was always ignored.

"Did I tell you I love you yet today?"

Smirking in that delicious way she smirked, she leaned closer, ruining her posture and planted a kiss on his lips. "Tell me again."

Slowing down, he pressed her closer. "I love you."

"I'd like two kids."

"What happened to five?"

"If you insist."

Laughing, they started up again. Sauer didn't miss the way Zeke and Ben kept glancing at them and grinning like idiots. He talked such big talk about how he was going to dominate them on the dance floor, and here he was, continually stopping and starting as if he didn't know what he was doing. Kissing his wife superseded anything else.

"I'm not supposed to say anything."

His brow rose. She never could keep anything to herself when it came to what others said. He knew with certainty she never divulged anything that was said between them. But everyone else was fair game. She always got this little delicious gleam in her eye. Excitement bubbling from her lips to share her juicy news. Hell, he'd come home sometimes, she'd be in his face to talk some cases with him, wanting to help him solve it. He hated that part. He didn't want her involved in another case of his ever again.

At least her nightmares were getting better. Slowly, she was moving on from what that bastard had done to her. Some days, he wanted to kill him all over again. Especially with all the evidence they uncovered in that rundown house. They found five bodies buried in the backyard, evidence in the house as well, where he most likely raped then killed the women. He hated thinking how they would've never caught him if he hadn't killed his sister, then attacked Dee. His madness had started to unravel. Thank goodness for that because he couldn't hurt another woman again. While they still didn't know why his sister black-mailed him, they figured it had something to do with kidnapping, raping, and murdering five women. What else could've it been?

He needed to stop thinking about that bastard. Some-times, it was hard not to let it take over his thoughts, espe-cially when he saw Dee struggle with what happened. She wasn't struggling now. The delicious glimmer in her eyes to share her exciting news was turning him on. He loved seeing her excited about anything and everything.

"Do you wanna know what it is?" Her eyes sparkled brighter with mischief, the anticipation to tell him. He loved the moment right before she told him whatever it was she wanted to tell him. He just loved the way her eyes glittered with eagerness.

"Do tell."

"Rina's pregnant. Not far along and she's a little nervous because it took awhile, but she's excited."

That explained the conversation about kids. "That's great news."

"It is. But you don't know yet, so act surprised if Ben tells you. They're keeping it a secret for right now."

"How come you know?"

Her brow cocked in the delectable way he loved. "Because it's my job to know everything about my best friends. Plus, Rina let it slip a little, and we just put two and two together."

To his surprise, her smile dipped, her brows creasing with what looked like sadness.

"What's wrong?" He stopped dancing, pulling her off the dance floor to a quiet corner.

"Do you really think I'll make a good mother?"

He pulled her snug against his body, his arms tightening around her. "The best. Never doubt it. Please."

"Can we start tonight?"

At the thought of making love with her, especially to create a child together, he perked up. A slow smile grew on her lips, indicating she could feel how excited that thought made him.

"I'll take that as a yes."

"I'm ready to leave whenever you are."

"The night's only half over."

Bending his head, pressing light kisses onto her neck up to her ear, he nibbled before whispering, "The night hasn't even started."

"You're officially crazy."

His kisses made their way down, across her chest and up the other side of her neck to her other ear where he nibbled some more.

"We're in a room full of people, Sauer. You're devouring me as if we're alone."

Not stopping his torrent of kisses, he made a path to her lips, delivering one light and tender kiss that said it all. "I'm embracing the crazy. You're my everything, and I'm not afraid to show it."

"Mmm...yes. Crazy. I like this side of you."

He devoured her mouth once again, his hands roaming to places they shouldn't in a room full of people.

Yeah, he was crazy.

Crazy in love.

DON'T MISS THE NEXT BOOK IN THIS EXCITING ROMANTIC SUSPENSE SERIES! EVIDENCE OF SIN

FOR ZEKE AND ZOE'S STORY
WON'T LET YOU GO
A SLAYING LOVE NOVEL, #1

A determined detective. A woman refusing to bend. A killer who will make sure there are no second chances.

One night of passion became Zoe Sullivan's worst nightmare when Detective Zeke Chance mistook her for a prostitute. Now she wants nothing more than to forget the humiliation —and the man who caused it. But when her boss is brutally murdered, fate throws them together again as Zeke becomes the lead detective on the case.

Zeke knows he screwed up royally, and he's determined to make amends while keeping Zoe safe. But as the investigation deepens, it becomes clear that someone wants Zoe silenced permanently. With a killer closing in and their undeniable attraction reigniting, Zeke must overcome Zoe's distrust before they both become the next victims.

As danger escalates and passion burns hotter than ever, they'll discover that some mistakes are worth making twice —if they survive long enough to get their second chance.

Get ready for steamy romance, heart-pounding suspense, and a detective who'll risk everything to earn back the woman he wronged.

FOR BEN & RINA'S STORY
DOOMED LOVE
A SLAYING LOVE NOVEL, #2

A protective detective. A woman with dangerous secrets. A killer who will stop at nothing to have his way.

Detective Ben Stoyer has wanted Rina Chastain for far too long, but she keeps turning him down with sweet excuses he's tired of hearing. When the victim in his latest murder case looks exactly like her, Ben's protective instincts kick into overdrive—and this time, he won't take no for an answer.

Rina wants to give in to Ben's relentless charm, but her controlling father has destroyed every relationship she's ever tried to have. Now, with a serial killer targeting women who look like her, she's caught between the detective who's determined to protect her and the man who's determined to control her.

As the body count rises and Ben's investigation intensifies, they'll discover that some dangers come from within, and the deadliest enemy might be the one you trust most.

Get ready for pulse-pounding suspense, sizzling chemistry, and a detective who'll defy everyone—including the woman he loves— to keep her safe.

FOR STITCH & SUSAN'S STORY
EVIDENCE OF SIN
A SLAYING LOVE NOVEL, #4

A tattooed bad boy with a record. A police department analyst who should know better. A killer who's making it personal.

One night of scorching passion with straight-laced Susan left tattoo artist Stitch running scared—straight out of her life. But now he's back, and everything about the woman he can't forget terrifies him in the best possible way. She's law enforcement, he's got a record—they'll never work, but when she's in his arms, none of it matters.

Susan knew getting involved with Stitch wouldn't end well, but she can't resist the way he makes her feel alive with just one heated look. She should be focusing on the latest string of brutal murders—no evidence, no leads, no time to waste —but Stitch keeps dragging her into dangerous territory, and she has no idea how close the killer is to making her his final victim.

As the killer's obsession with Susan escalates, Stitch realizes his criminal past might be exactly what she needs to survive. Because sometimes the only way to protect what you love is to embrace the darkness inside.

Get ready for sizzling chemistry, heart-stopping suspense, and a bad boy who'll risk everything—including his freedom—to save the woman who owns his soul.

For Newman & Amelia's Story
Finding Redemption
A Slaying Love Novel, #5

A disgraced ex-detective. A woman who won't give up. A case that could save them both.

Ex-Detective Newman wants to be left alone to wallow in the wreckage of his ruined career and shattered life. When a gorgeous woman with vibrant pink hair and a stubborn streak shows up at his door, he wants nothing to do with her case—or the way she makes him feel like he might be worth saving.

Amelia Benedict doesn't take no for an answer, especially when her younger brother's life hangs in the balance. The police think he ran away, but she knows something terrible has happened. A disgraced ex-cop with nothing left to lose and everything to prove, Newman definitely isn't the right guy for the case—but he's her last hope. But as they dig deeper into her brother's disappearance, they uncover a web of danger that threatens to destroy what's left of Newman's soul and put Amelia in the crosshairs of a killer.

In a race against time to save an innocent boy, Newman must decide if redemption is worth the risk—because this time, failure doesn't just mean losing his last chance at salvation. It means losing the woman who believed in him when no one else would.

Get ready for second-chance redemption, heart-stopping suspense, & a broken hero who'll risk everything to prove he's worth loving.

For Rory & Brooke's story
OBSESSED HOPE
A SLAYING LOVE NOVEL, #6

A detective with lethal instincts. A woman who attracts danger. An obsession that could destroy them both.

Detective Rory Walker's latest murder case should be simple —kinky sex gone wrong. Until he meets his prime suspect. Sweet, adorable Brooke Duncan with her terrifying cat and hidden depths is everything he never knew he needed. One look, one touch, and he's a goner. But as he digs deeper into the case, he realizes the dead man had enemies everywhere, and Brooke might be next on someone's list.

Brooke knows she should stay away from the intense detective who looks at her like she's both his salvation and his downfall. But when the investigation takes a deadly turn, Rory becomes her only protection against a killer who's growing more obsessed by the day. Now she must decide whether to trust the man whose obsession matches the killer's intensity...or face a predator alone.

As the case spirals out of control and the killer closes in, Rory will discover that sometimes love and obsession are separated by the thinnest of lines—and crossing it might be the only way to keep them both alive.

Get ready for possessive passion, heart-stopping suspense, and a detective whose protective instincts know no boundaries when the woman he loves is threatened.

ABOUT THE AUTHOR

I'm a *USA Today* Bestselling Author that loves to write contemporary romance and romantic suspense novels, although I am partial to romantic suspense. I even dabble in paranormal. Honestly, I love anything that has to do with romance. As long as there's a happy ending, I'm a happy camper. And insta-love...yes, please! I love baseball (Go Twins!) and creating awesome crafts. I graduated with a Bachelor's Degree in Criminal Justice, working in that field for several years before I became a stay-at-home mom. I have a few more amazing stories in the works. If you would like to learn more about me and my books, head to my website by scanning the QR code. Thanks for reading!

Scan me